THE LAIRD'S LADLE

LOSERS CLUB BOOK TWO

YVONNE VINCENT

Copyright © 2022 Yvonne Vincent
All rights reserved.

By Yvonne Vincent:

The Big Blue Jobbie
The Big Blue Jobbie #2
The Wee Hairy Anthology

Frock In Hell

Losers Club (Losers Club Book 1)
The Laird's Ladle (Losers Club Book 2)
The Angels' Share (Losers Club Book 3)
Sleighed! (Losers Club Book 4)
The Juniper Key (Losers Club Book 5)
Beacon Brodie (Losers Club Book 6)

To my sister

Who else could I trust to help me find the best method of poisoning people?

A FEW WORDS BEFORE WE BEGIN

This is not a historical mystery, but it is inspired by the Jacobite rising and the legend of treasure hidden at Loch Arkaig. If you want the context, here's a wee potted history. Otherwise, feel free to skip this bit.

1688 was a busy year for the Catholic King James II or VII, (depending on whether you were English or Scottish), who had succeeded his brother, Charles II, as King of England, Scotland and Ireland three years earlier. Not only did he have a new-born son, James Frances Edward Stuart, later known as the Old Pretender, but he was deposed in a relatively bloodless coup dubbed The Glorious Revolution and replaced by his Protestant daughter, Mary, who was then succeeded by the last Stuart monarch, her sister Anne.

Neither Mary nor Anne had children, which left things in a bit of a pickle succession-wise, and there was rather a fuss about the need for a Protestant heir. James Frances Edward Stuart, who I'll call the Old Pretender from now on because I'm too lazy to type all those names, would have very much liked to be the big cheese, but Parliament had passed laws which said "no Catholics on ye olde throne, thank ye very much" or words to that effect. In 1714, Anne's Hanoverian cousin, George I, succeeded to the throne. Not to be outdone, the Old Pretender asked the Pope for help with a Jacobite rising.

We often think of the Jacobites as a "Scottish thing", yet they weren't. The House of Stuart may have derived from Scottish kings and queens, but they had ruled in England and Ireland (and later Great Britain) since the death of Elizabeth I in 1603. There were English, Welsh and Irish Jacobites too. Jacobitism was a political movement based on the belief that monarchs were appointed by God and could not be removed.

The first Jacobite rising took place in 1689, but we will fast-forward to 27th August 1715, when supporters of the Old Pretender's claim to the throne raised the Jacobite standard in Braemar, Aberdeenshire. Parliament responded by confiscating the rebels' land. The Scottish Jacobites quickly took Scotland north of Edinburgh and, joined by English Jacobites, marched into England where, on 14th November, they surrendered at Preston. By the time the Old Pretender arrived at Peterhead, Aberdeenshire, on 22nd December, things were in a sorry state, and on 5th February 1716 he gave up and sailed off. However, this was not the end of the story.

The Old Pretender came back for a second go in 1719 but was again defeated. Then, in 1745, his son, Charles Edward (lots of other names) Stuart, came back for round three, only to meet disastrous defeat at Culloden in 1746. The story of Bonnie Prince Charlie is well known, yet I'll provide a recap:

In 1743, the Old Pretender named his son Prince Regent, which meant that Charlie could act in his father's name. Happy 23rd birthday, son, now go raise an army and get me my throne. After a false start with the Spanish in 1744, Charlie duly got the French on board and set sail for Scotland to raise said army. He and seven buddies landed at Eriskay on 23rd July 1745. The French fleet supporting him was damaged by the good old British weather and limped back home, so it was all down to Charlie and his mates to rile up the Highland clans, who took one look at him and expressed their doubts.

Nevertheless, loyalty among the Scots was not in short supply. Before long, men were recruited, Edinburgh had surrendered, and Charlie's army had defeated the Government forces at Prestonpans. His army got as far south as Derbyshire whereupon, fearing they'd be cut off by Government forces and discovering that Charles had told a few untruths about the level of English and French support, they turned back to Scotland. Once back in the motherland, poor leadership on the part of Charles and his officers, combined with lack of supplies and exhausted troops, led to that final defeat by the Duke of Cumberland's troops at the Battle of Culloden on 16th April 1746.

For the men and women of Scotland there was cruel retribution. The wounded were killed, and those prisoners not executed were transported to indentured slavery in the British colonies. Towns and villages across Scotland were brutally raided by the Government army in their hunt for sympathisers.

Following the defeat at Culloden, the French refused to fund any further uprisings and eventually the cause fizzled out. However, rumours abound of a lost Jacobite treasure, hidden at Loch Arkaig in Lochaber. Spain, France and the Pope had pledged financial support for the cause, but it arrived too late. Seven caskets of Spanish gold were delivered by ship. One was stolen and the remaining six were taken to Loch Arkaig, where they were entrusted to a series of secret keepers. Over the years, the secret died with its keepers, yet the legend remains.

It is believed that some of the treasure did eventually make its way to Charles on the Continent. In 2018, a silver cup gifted by Charles Stuart was sold to a British buyer who commissioned research into its provenance. Newspaper reports from the summer of 2020 claim that the cup was given as a reward to an Englishman who smuggled most of the treasure to Charles Stuart in France, with the remainder having been stolen or given away. Nevertheless, later in 2020, a hoard of musket balls, coins and gilt buttons, believed to have been part of the shipment, was found at a ruined croft which once belonged to Charles' Gaelic tutor. What really happened to the treasure may never be known for sure.

The tale of a lost treasure and the fact that many of the ships destined to aid Bonnie Prince Charlie never made it that far intrigued me. In researching the Jacobites, I found links to my homeland of Aberdeenshire that I hadn't known existed and which they really should be ramming down the throat of every tourist who braves the Granite City and its surrounds. So, what does all of this mean for my imaginary little Isle of Vik, stuck out there in the North Sea? Let's follow the money and find out.

PROLOGUE

12th April 1746

Far out at sea, the ship was a dark shadow; a void where the men on the beach would expect to see stars or the reflection of faint moonlight on the water, through the persistent light drizzle that was seeping into their kilts, causing the material to become heavy and stick to the backs of their legs.

Despite the cold and the damp, the men had lit a signal fire and were in good spirits as they watched two small, wooden boats approach the beach. The boats sat low in the water, their precious cargo weighing far more than the few men struggling to row against the tide. The rowers had urged the ship's captain to wait for the tide to turn, but he was anxious to deliver the caskets and head back to France before they were caught in the impending storm or by the British Navy, whose ships prowled the Scottish coast and had already intercepted Le Mars and La Bellone. The captain was under strict instructions from Louis XV to deliver the gold to Monsieur James Alexander Macrae, and after the losses sustained thus far, the French king would brook no failure. Thus, with a rising sense that any delay was tempting fate, the captain had ordered La Reine be steered as close as possible to the Isle of Vik and the boats loaded. Grumbling, the men had complied and, back muscles straining against the pull of the waves, had set off towards the distant beach and the small knot of waiting Scotsmen.

On the shore, there was similar grumbling, this time about the chances of successfully delivering the gold to Charles Stuart on the mainland.

'Look at the sea. We all know there's a storm coming. Ah canna see how we're going to get it to the mainland before we get cut off, James-Alec.'

James-Alec, a man used to towering over others, looked up at his even larger friend.

'Och, stop being such an old woman, Bruce,' he snapped. 'It's just a wee bit of rain and wind. We'll split it among the fishing boats. That way, if one is lost, hopefully the others will make it through. They've only got to get as far as Peterhead.'

'Aye, that's fine for you to say. You're not the one risking life and limb for the cause,' Bruce muttered.

'Speak for yourself. If anyone is caught, it'll be my head on a spike ootside the Tower of London, so either stop your moaning or get yourself home to Mhairi and a fine tattie scone by your safe, warm fireplace.'

Bruce shot James-Alec a defiant glare, but the other man had already turned away and was signalling to the rest of the group to wade out with him and help pull the boats ashore.

Some minutes later, a small cheer went up as the French sailors heaved themselves, exhausted, onto the sand. The group of Scotsmen, kilts tucked up and bare bottoms flashing pale in the moonlight, were hauling the boats the last few yards. With the ice-cold North Sea lapping at his knees, James-Alec looked back at the solitary figure silhouetted against the dying light of the fire.

'C'moan, Bruce,' James-Alec called. 'Help us get the boats

unloaded. It's that cold in here ma balls are trying to escape through ma mouth.'

Bruce stood, unmoving, so James-Alec tried again.

'I'm sorry. I shouldn't have said what I said. You know me and ma big mouth.'

'Aye, well, your wee balls would be rattling around in there.' Bruce held up his hands, made two tiny circles with his thumbs and forefingers and shouted, 'My balls are huge. Ah could put my balls in your mouth. That would fill it up.'

The men at the boats stopped moving and, as one, turned towards Bruce who, realising what he had just said, stiffened and attempted to backtrack.

'Eh, no. Ah didn't mean…ah wasn't offering to…well…ye ken me and my own big mouth.' He took a deep breath and ploughed on. 'Ah'm sorry too. Aye, ah'll help ye unload.'

He looked at the faces of the men, who were still staring at him, and clarified, 'Unload the boats, ye heathens.'

The peals of laughter rang across the beach as Bruce tucked up his kilt and joined his companions in the freezing water, ignoring the good-natured cries of "keep your lips sealed, men."

A short while later, fortified by some good whisky, the Frenchmen returned to the boats and made their way back to the ship. Surveying the collection of chests before him, James-Alec reminded his men of the plan.

'We'll take this lot up to the cart at the top of the cliff path and I'll hide it overnight. If anything happens to me, Bruce is the secret keeper. He'll know where it's hidden and appoint a second secret keeper in case anything happens to him, and so on and so forth.

'We shouldn't need to do any of that because the plan is to load it onto the fishing boats tomorrow. You'll go to Peterhead with the boats and meet up with carts sent by the Mackenzies to take the load the rest of the way. There's enough gold in here to keep the army going for a good while. Any questions?'

A man at the back of the group raised his hand and James-Alec sighed, knowing that nothing sensible was coming. 'Aye, Ian. What is it?'

'Can I go with Brucie? If the boat's in trouble, I can think of a couple of things that would make good ballast.'

Laughing, the group broke up, hoisted the chests onto shoulders and began to make their way up the cliff path.

Trudging upwards through the darkness, trying to keep their footing on the uneven ground, none of the men felt the wind change or noticed the faint moon disappearing as it was blanketed by a thicker layer of cloud.

By the next morning, the fishing boats in the bay were ragged things, straining at their moorings, battered by the unrelenting wind and waves. There would be no sailing to Peterhead that day. In fact, thanks to the ferocity of the storm, there would be no sailing anywhere for a week.

Shortly after daybreak, the men began to arrive at Bruce's cottage, a small stone building huddled against the wind on the side of a bleak, rocky hill. One by one they made their way up the muddy track, leaning into the wind as it whipped through gaps in the drystane dykes either side of them, swearing as feet slipped on stones and mud splashed the backs of their kilts.

Eventually, the group stood in front of Bruce's fireplace, backsides gently steaming, grumbling good-naturedly as Mhairi nudged them aside so she could turn the bannocks on the girdle suspended over the fire. Declaring it too early for the whisky, she bustled off to find some ale and the men got down to business.

'It's clear we'll not be in Peterhead today. What's the plan?' asked Ian.

Bruce spread his arms wide and shrugged. 'Ah dinna ken, lads. Did ye see James-Alec on yer way here? He left an hour ago to check on the—,' Bruce looked around to check whether Mhairi was in earshot, 'you-ken-what,' he whispered.

A voice shouted through from the back of the house.

'I know fine what you mean. I do have ears, Bruce Duguid. You and James-Alec are not as discreet as you think when you're in your cups. Blood oath of secrecy my—'

'Thanks, Mhairi,' Bruce called back, rolling his eyes at the men. 'Noo, if you've any idea where James-Alec is, maybe you could share that with the rest of us.'

Mhairi came through and stood, hands on hips, frowning at the men. 'Sounds to me like you should be out there looking for him instead of standing around here, ruining my bannocks with the steam off your arses.'

Reluctantly, the men agreed to venture back outside and brave the foul weather in search of their leader. After all, he couldn't have gone far. They agreed to split up and meet back at the cottage in an hour.

Bruce was the first one back. He stumbled through the door, bringing with him a blast of wind that scattered the straw on the floor. His dark hair was matted and drops of rain and sweat mingled to form a salty sheen on his flushed cheeks. In his arms was a large bundle, covered by a long woollen cloak.

'Mhairi,' he gasped. 'Ah found him. Oh, God save us, ah found him.'

As Mhairi came running through to the front room, Bruce laid the bundle gently on the floor and peeled the cloak back to reveal the body of James Alexander Macrae, his childhood friend who, through sheer determination and loose family connections, had raised himself up from shepherd to friend of the Mackenzies and confidant of the prince himself. James-Alec Macrae had been wild and confident and, at times, breathtakingly reckless. Quick to laugh and slow to anger, he was trusted and loved by all who met him. And now he was no more. Now, he was a cold and bloody corpse, a spark forever extinguished.

Mhairi ran to her husband's side as he sat hunched over the body. She put her arms around him, murmuring words of comfort, but he felt stiff and unyielding. They sat there on the floor, by the fire and the still figure of their friend, as the other men slowly returned to the cottage.

Biting back his tears, Bruce growled, 'He was in a ditch over at Hillside farm. He's been stabbed in the chest, more than once ah think. Whoever did this must have been after the gold, which means it was one of us. Nobody else kent about the gold.'

He looked up at the group and they shifted uncomfortably, casting their eyes downwards to avoid his furious glare.

Eventually, Ian cleared his throat and asked, 'Eh, I don't mean to be indelicate, but is the gold still there?'

Bruce turned on him, wild-eyed.

'Why would you ask that, Ian? Is the gold more important than the man? Do you have something you'd like to confess to the rest of us?'

Ian looked away and said, 'No. We've known each other since we were bairns, Bruce. You surely think better of me than that.'

Bruce relented and sighed. 'Aye, ah do, and ah would not think it of you if it was not the case that someone here must have done this terrible deed.'

Ian raised his hands in supplication. 'I was thinking of how he'd want us to finish this task.'

'You're right. Whatever happened out there at the farm, he didn't tell where he'd stashed the gold. It's still there, but it will soon be moved to somewhere more secure. You have my word on that. The man who did this will not profit by his misdeeds. You may all go now, said Bruce stiffly. 'Ah have to arrange the burial of my friend.'

Silently, the men slipped out of the cottage, drew their cloaks around them and, the wind at their backs, made their way home.

In the years that followed, rumours ran throughout the

island, becoming ever more fanciful in the telling. Some blamed Bruce Duguid, saying the two had fallen out over treasure, although nobody was quite sure how the sons of a shepherd and a crofter would possess such a thing. Some said that James-Alec had stolen from the prince himself and had been killed as an act of revenge. However, the murderer was never caught, and devastated by the loss of his childhood friend, Bruce shut himself away and took to the whisky.

As for the location of the treasure, that remained a mystery. Bruce never spoke of it. Shortly after the storm abated, word reached the island of the defeat at Culloden. Messages were sent from the prince to arrange for the gold to be delivered to the mainland, but even among the tight-knit group of men who had carried it up from the beach, there was uncertainty as to who was now the secret keeper and whether the gold ever made it off the island.

Over the centuries, the legend grew of French gold buried somewhere on the Isle of Vik and the murder of James-Alec Macrae was all but forgotten. Only a small cross in the undergrowth, behind a stone cottage at the foot of a bleak hill, marked his passing.

CHAPTER 1

Vik Herald

12th April

RISING STARS BEGIN FILMING ON VIK

Filming has begun on the Isle of Vik for Hollywood blockbuster, The Rising. The cast and crew arrived last week, among them legendary actor Johnny Munroe, who plays the lead, and Alex Moon, ex-husband of Vik's own Penny Moon.

They are supported by a horde of local people who have volunteered as extras. With their sword fighting prowess, battle re-enactment group the Warrior Islanders were recruited to play minor roles as loyal followers of Johnny Munroe's character, Alastair MacDonell of Glengarry, also known as Pickle the Spy.

"Johnny's a lovely man. He'll do anything for a jube jube. He gobbles them up and leaves empty bags wherever he goes," said Mary Hopper, Alex Moon's former mother-in-law and a leading light in the Warrior Islanders.

The making of the movie on Vik has reignited interest in the Vik Treasure. It has long been believed that a French ship bearing French and Spanish gold destined for Bonnie Prince Charlie sank off the island during a storm in 1745. There are no contemporaneous records of the ship, but legend has it that at least some of the gold made it ashore and is buried somewhere on the island. The story is lent some credence by the discovery of a ring bearing the seal of Mary Queen of Scots at Hillside farm last year.

As a result of this and the filming, the islanders are looking forward to a higher than usual number of visitors this year. VisitScotland has advised that already, hotels and bed and breakfasts are fully booked until October. Captain Kev, co-owner of the local ferry, recommends that day trippers book their tickets early.

Vik has also been in the news recently following the arrest of Araminta Hubbard for a mass poisoning. Click here for more on the Chiller Killer.

. . .

```
Update


13th April


The Vik Herald offers its sincere apologies
to Johnny Munroe for any offence caused by
yesterday's article. We have since been
informed that, as well as being an
Aberdeenshire term for a fruity sweet, jube
jube is urban slang for a small penis.
```

Penny clicked off the article and scrolled down her contacts until she came to D. Dragon, Annoying Old. She listened to the ringing at the other end and imagined Mary Hopper rummaging through the handbag of doom, pulling her phone out from under a pile of tissues, an interesting rock, cat toothpaste and a battered copy of The Big Blue Jobbie.

'Hello, Chunky,' said Mary. 'Have you freed Mrs Hubbard yet? I bought the loveliest scarf in Marks and Spencer today. It's blue with red flowers. I was going to buy it for you, but I liked it so much that I bought it for me instead. Will you finish in time for lunch?'

'Jube jubes, Mum?' Penny tutted. 'You did that on purpose.'

'I have no idea what you're talking about.'

'You know exactly what I'm talking about. I distinctly remember you snickering like a teenager when Edith told Hector he'd never get another boyfriend with a jube jube like his.'

'Oh, alright. But that vile man deserves everything he gets. When the nice boy from the paper called asking for a quote, well, I couldn't help myself. Only, don't tell your father. He's still annoyed with me for accidentally sexting Rabbi Hoffman. Honestly, it was such an easy mistake to make. Len Hopper and Leo Hoffman.'

'Which reminds me, Mum. Did you pick up your new glasses from the opticians?'

'Yes, but I do think you're all making quite a fuss about nothing.'

Penny heard a rustle and some clicks, then her phone pinged. She opened the text to find a photograph of her mother wearing a pair of lurid pink horn-rimmed spectacles. In the background she could see Sandra Next Door, glaring furiously at a young woman behind a counter.

'Where are you?' Penny asked her mum.

'We're in the fabric shop. Sandra Next Door is making me a kilt. The one they made for the film is very unflattering and really, if I'm starring in this thing, I want to look my best.'

'You only have one line!' said Penny, exasperated.

'It's a very important line!' Mary replied. 'They can hardly go off to war without their porridge. And how will we ever know if anyone wants porridge unless I ask, "Would you like some porridge?" They could lose the entire battle for want of a bowl of porridge.'

Penny silently cursed her ex-husband for getting Mary a speaking part. She had been insufferable ever since. Her father was at home, ill in bed and in no fit state to curb Mary's worst excesses. His own excesses, i.e., his love of Mrs Hubbard's ice cream, had been his undoing.

'Newsflash,' Penny told her mother. 'We lost at Culloden. Listen, I'll call you as soon as we know what's happening with Mrs Hubbard. Just enjoy your day out at the Aberdeen shops.'

Penny disconnected the call and returned to the bank of plastic seats where Elsie sat huddled in an oversized beige cardigan, as if trying to blend in with the dismal café au lait theme that some deluded designer had thought fitting for the modern police station. She assumed it was supposed to feel calming and neutral; something to soothe the nerves of anxious people trapped in this waiting area, unsure of what was going to happen to them or their loved ones. Instead, the magnolia walls with their light brown painted circles sucked the light out of the place, leaving the room cast in a sickly glow reminiscent of the pictures Penny had seen of old public buildings from the 1970s. The effect was only amplified by the dark green utilitarian linoleum and the glass wall, behind which three women acted as gatekeepers of the large grey door leading to the custody suite. Somewhere beyond those doors sat Mrs Hubbard, frightened and alone. Penny fervently hoped that someone had told her that she and Elsie were here.

'Is Mary okay?' asked Elsie.

'Yes. It was a good idea to ask Sandra Next Door to babysit her. Poor Dad's not fit to argue if she comes home with five pairs of tap shoes and declares she's turning his shed into a dance studio.'

Elsie paled. 'She wouldn't do that, would she? Where would we put the…er…you-know-what.' She glanced around, checking for cameras, and added, 'Shh! They've probably got the place bugged so they can catch people incriminating themselves.'

Penny laughed. 'You've been working in the library for too long. Too many spy novels. Don't worry, the you-know-what will be fine, and mum's notions fade as quickly as they start. Last week she was all for creating a donkey sanctuary called Ass Lovers. Dad had to have a word with Captain Rab and Captain Kev to stop her bringing ten of them over on the ferry.'

Elsie gave her a tight smile. She disapproved of Mary and her notions. Len was a far steadier character. Dependable and always ready to lend a hand. Whether it was fixing something or growing you-know-what to ease the aches and pains of the local pensioners, you could count on Len Hopper. Elsie felt that she and Len were kindred spirits, both quiet types with a steel core. Like her, he was happy to stay in the background but would fight his corner if necessary. She supposed that was why Len and Mary Hopper had stayed the course; someone had to rein the woman in, yet Mary's unpredictability probably kept Len on his toes. Elsie wondered if her life was perhaps too quiet. Since her Archie died, she hadn't really done anything but go to work at the library, do her rounds in the van and go to Losers Club for some company once a week. Sometimes she'd take a sherry at the pub with Minty Hubbard, but the place was full of bright young things, and she was very conscious that she looked out of place, this dreary old woman with her perm and her beige mac. Elsie thought she would like to be a little more exciting, except she didn't know where to begin. Perhaps she wasn't so much disapproving of Mary's notions, as a little jealous.

'Are you thinking about poor Mrs Hubbard?' Penny asked.

'Yes,' Elsie lied. 'How much longer do you think they'll hold her?

'Mrs Taylor died,' said Detective Inspector Mitchell, 'and you still deny any knowledge. So far, forty-six islanders who ate your ice cream have become seriously ill. Including our own Sergeant Wilson. And we don't take kindly to our own people being poisoned. Isn't that right, DC Khan?

The Detective Constable, who thus far had been relegated to note-taking and daydreaming while the Inspector enjoyed a good rant, started at the sound of her own name.

'That's right, sir. We don't take kindly to poisoning police officers.'

'It's my retirement do tonight and this "woe is me" act is getting very old. Very old indeed. Isn't that right, DC Khan?'

'That's right, sir. You're very old indeed,' said the DC

who, believing her role in proceedings was over, had momentarily slipped back into trying to recall what time her supermarket delivery was arriving that evening. All this talk of ice cream was making her hungry.

DI Mitchell shot her a malevolent look and continued. 'The lab has confirmed salmonella. Either you're negligent or you deliberately set out to poison your friends and neighbours. Which is it, Mrs Hubbard?'

Mrs Hubbard buried her face in her hands and, through her sobs, wailed, 'I don't know. I don't know how it happened. I make all my ice cream with…with…strict hygiene. The certificate is on the wall of the shop. My Douglas will show you.'

'Well, I'm sure he would if he wasn't in Vik Hospital after eating three cones of strawberry choc chip while watching reruns of Strictly Come Dancing.' Inspector Mitchell hissed. 'The lab results show that the salmonella came from your ice cream.'

Mrs Hubbard sobbed even harder and, seeing the Detective Inspector puff himself up to new heights of outrage, her solicitor interrupted with a sharp, 'DI Mitchell, my client is clearly distressed. Now might be a good time for a break?'

DI Mitchell deflated slightly and nodded. 'Aye. Interview suspended. The time is 12:46.'

He reached over to switch the recorder off, and as he did so, there was a rap on the door. The DI barked, 'What?' and a young, uniformed PC appeared.

'Sorry to interrupt, sir,' he said nervously. 'There's a fresh report in from the lab that you'll want to see.'

With a sigh, the DI scraped back the chair and drew himself up to his full height. At 6'2" and carrying his fair share of middle-aged spread, he dominated the space. Looming menacingly over his elderly suspect, he growled, 'I'll be there in a minute. Take this one back to her cell.'

With DC Khan scuttling behind him, the DI ducked

through the doorway, leaving behind him only the sound of a sobbing woman.

As the PC hovered uncertainly, the solicitor gave his client a kindly pat on the arm.

'Now there, Mrs Hubbard. Let's just see what this new lab report says.'

He helped her to her feet and as she wobbled slightly, the PC reached out to steady her.

'If you come with me,' the constable told her, 'I'll get you a nice cup of tea. Well, it won't be nice because it comes from the machine. It'll be quite horrible, actually. But I know where there's a packet of Jammy Dodgers, so at least you'll have a biscuit to go with it. Only, don't tell DC Khan. They're her Jammy Dodgers.'

He smiled encouragingly at Mrs Hubbard and gently guided her out of the interview room, towards the custody suite.

She looked back at her solicitor, her cheeks still wet with tears, and said, 'Will you tell Penny and Elsie not to wait any longer for me?'

Her solicitor nodded. 'For all the good it will do.'

Back in the waiting area, Penny and Elsie were pacing to and fro under the watchful eye of the woman behind the front desk. Elsie had declared that the plastic chairs were cutting off the circulation to her legs and had begun hobbling around the room, wincing and muttering about pins and needles in her corns. After a futile attempt to get the front desk lady to provide more information on what was happening to Mrs Hubbard, Penny had joined her.

Both came to a sudden halt when the doors leading to the inner sanctum of the police station swung open and Mrs Hubbard's solicitor strode out.

'Any news?' asked Penny.

'We're taking a break,' the solicitor told her. 'She's asked me to tell you not to wait for her.'

'Not wait!' exclaimed Elsie. 'I've been her friend for fifty years. If she thinks I can't spare a few more hours, well, tell the silly woman I'll be here as long as it takes. You can go if you want to, Penny.'

'I'm staying too. I've been her friend for…a while. Anyway, I'm staying. How long do you think it will take?'

The solicitor looked at the pair over the top of his spectacles and rubbed a hand over his thinning, dark hair.

'I'll be honest. They know the salmonella came from her ice cream and she's admitted to making it. There's a good chance they'll charge her, in which case she'll remain in custody until she appears in court tomorrow morning.'

'But Mrs Hubbard wouldn't deliberately poison anyone,' Penny protested.

'Even if it's not deliberate, they'll say she was negligent. Mrs Taylor died, so they're not going to let her off with a slap on the wrist. We're still waiting for the full post-mortem, but there was half a tub of strawberry whirl and a dead dog with its muzzle covered in ice cream next to her.' The solicitor pushed his glasses back up his nose. 'I doubt she'll be out today. You may as well go home.'

Penny was starting to think he was right. She was just about to say so when she saw Elsie stiffen beside her.

'We're staying,' said Elsie, crossing her arms and glaring defiantly at the solicitor. 'It's your job to make sure Minty is *not* charged and, just so we're clear, that's what we're paying you for. We'll take our lunch at the pub across the road, then we'll be back. Please keep us informed of any developments. Penny, give him your mobile cell thing number.'

Penny knew that it was pointless to argue with Elsie. The woman was kind and quiet, but she was made of strong stuff. Meekly, she scribbled her mobile number on the flyleaf of her book, tore it off and handed it over. With an indignant sniff, Elsie tucked her arm into Penny's, spun them around and marched towards the front door of the police station. Goodness, thought Penny, for a woman with poor circulation and terrible corns, she's surprisingly nippy.

The Gavel and Gallows was a shabby, old-fashioned relic; the patina of decades of cigarette smoke still clinging to what was once white anaglypta wallpaper. Over the years, thousands of feet had worn a scarred path in the linoleum, between a piece of yellow tape on the floor and the darts board. The bare wood of the round tables, which had long lost their varnish, was polished smooth by thousands of elbows. At the back of the room was a small bar, behind which a barman stood, idly scratching his crotch.

As they got their drinks, Penny asked the barman if the pub served lunch. He smiled, revealing a mouth full of what could only be described as nicotine-stained stubs, and handed her two burgundy, faux-leather covered menus. Back at the table, Penny opened hers and regarded with dismay the dog-eared piece of card in its plastic pocket.

'Scampi and chips, chicken and chips, fish and chips or steak and chips. Which culinary delight with chips shall we have?' she asked.

Elsie thought for a moment then flashed her a wicked grin. 'I'm having the pizza and chips, but you should probably ask them to hold the chips. Mary's right. You're looking a bit broad around the beam again.'

Penny wasn't quite sure what to say to this. On the one hand, as leader of her very own weight loss group, she should set an example. On the other hand, Elsie was a cheeky cow. If Jim was here, he'd laugh like a drain and spend the next week making jokes at her expense. He'd find every opportunity to point out a beam and ask her opinion as to its breadth. Just as well that he was currently at Hillside farm helping Night, a cranky, headstrong mare, give birth to her first foal. Between this and lambing, she'd hardly seen him since February. He had, however, kept up a steady stream of vet jokes by text.

A ewe urinated on me this morning. It was quite embarrassing. Guess how I felt…
…
Sheepish.

Graham Christie's dog ate his desk lamp this morning…
…
Graham's de-lighted.

Graham Christie's dog ate a snake this morning…
…
I've prescribed antihisstamines.

Tina Shaw has run up a huge bill for her cat's operation and doesn't know how to pay…
…
I told her Spaypal would be fine…

Penny smiled to herself and decided to have the chicken and chips. At least half the meal would be vaguely healthy. As she took the menus to the bar to place their orders, she briefly considered asking the barman if they did veg, but looking at the pallor of him, she suspected he hadn't eaten anything green since 1982. Around the same time as he last had a shower. In fact, you could probably fry the chips in his hair. The thought made Penny feel slightly ill and she crossed her fingers, hoping that someone else – someone clean – was doing the cooking. Maybe she wouldn't order the chips after all. Maybe *this* was how people stayed slim. Sod the healthy diet and exercise. Chuck the degree in nutrition out the window. All she had to do was imagine every meal cooked by a pasty-looking, greasy fella in a manky Aberdeen football top, and the pounds would drop off. She decided not to pass this top tip onto her Losers Club members. After all, she needed the income and folk would hardly pay their subscriptions if she rocked up with the barman in tow and said, 'Right, imagine this guy picking his nose while he makes you a nice fry-up.' Come to think of it, she wasn't sure she even wanted the chicken now.

Half an hour later, Elsie was happily devouring her pizza while Penny pushed the culinary equivalent of shoe leather round her plate. In the end, she had eschewed chips and made a tentative enquiry as to the availability of vegetables. The result? Breaded Doc Marten in a sea of baked beans.

Elsie eyed the plate. 'Do you want those beans? Because there's no point in them going to waste.'

Penny pushed the plate towards her and said, 'For such a little person, you sure can put it away. I suppose we should count ourselves lucky. Poor Mrs Hubbard is probably getting slops and gruel.'

'Mince and tatties, actually,' said a voice at the door.

Both women whipped round and instantly chairs were scraped back as they stood to greet the new arrival.

Elsie scuttled over and, eyes brimming with tears, embraced her friend. 'Oh, Minty. I thought that next time we saw you, you'd be–' she glanced around the room to check that they were alone, lowered her voice and whispered, 'a lesbian.'

Over her head, Mrs Hubbard looked at Penny quizzically. Penny bit her lip, frowned and shrugged. 'Mum suggested she watch Orange is the New Black to prepare her for visiting you in…erm…you know, prison. Sorry.'

The awkward silence which followed was eventually broken by Mrs Hubbard, who put her head on Elsie's shoulder and began to wheeze. Her back heaved spasmodically, and at first Penny thought she was crying. It soon became clear, however, that she was laughing. Standing there, in the doorway of the crappiest pub in Aberdeen, having been interrogated for hours by what must surely be the world's grumpiest policeman, Mrs Hubbard howled with mirth.

'Oh goodness,' she said, wiping her streaming eyes and leaning on Elsie for support, 'I needed that. I know it's very serious, everything that's happened, but can you imagine my Douglas if, at the grand old age of seventy-something, I emerged from the cupboard? I don't know what you were thinking, Elsie.'

Penny could see that the thought of her husband's reaction was about to set Mrs Hubbard off again, so she gently unpeeled Elsie who, still clinging to her friend, looked rather baffled by the sudden bout of hilarity, and steered them both towards the table.

'What would you like to drink?' she asked, once they were seated.

Mrs Hubbard looked around the pub and grimaced. 'I don't suppose they do cocktails in here.'

'Well, I'd pay good money to watch you ask the barman for a Screaming Orgasm,' Penny commented wryly.

Elsie tutted disapprovingly and said, 'For once in your life, just get a lemonade like a sensible person.'

'Maybe I'll ask for a Porn Star Martini,' said Mrs Hubbard defiantly.

The barman appeared and gave Mrs Hubbard the full benefit of his rocky relationship with dentistry. Beaming widely at her, he winked and said, 'Nobody warned me an angel would come into my life today. What heavenly nectar can I get you?'

Somewhat discomfited, Mrs Hubbard looked away, patted her silver curls and muttered, 'Just a lemonade, please.'

Once they were settled with their drinks, both Penny and

Elsie expressed their surprise at Mrs Hubbard's sudden appearance.

'From what your solicitor said, we weren't sure you'd be released at all,' Penny explained.

'I was quite surprised myself, dearie,' said Mrs Hubbard. 'They said the post-mortem came back on Mrs Taylor and they'd had another report in from the lab which they wanted to follow up. To be honest, it would almost have been a relief to be charged and have this over and done with.'

'You can't say that,' Elsie told her firmly. 'You haven't done anything wrong.'

'It's clear my ice cream poisoned half the island. I must have done something wrong. I've agonised about it, but I can't think how it happened. I really didn't do anything differently. And poor Mrs Taylor. To think that I'm responsible. I can hardly live with myself.'

This time, the tears were borne of deep misery. Elsie produced a neatly folded white handkerchief from her bag and passed it to her friend.

'There's no point in torturing yourself,' she said then, turning to Penny, she asked, 'Will you call Mary and Sandra Next Door to let them know we can meet them?'

Penny nodded and, pulling her phone from her pocket, went to sit at another table to make the call. She reckoned that Mrs Hubbard and Elsie would appreciate a few minutes alone together. Once more, she dialled Dragon, Annoying Old and heard the strident voice of a woman in full flow.

'Not the flowery one, you silly woman,' said Mary Hopper. 'The leopard skin next to it. Sorry, Chunky, we're looking at new wallpaper for the living room and Sandra Next Door has dreadful taste. Have you any news about Mrs Hubbard?'

'That's why I'm calling. She's been released. They're still investigating and she's not off the hook, so please be sensitive when you see her.'

'As you well know, I'm the soul of discretion. Let's meet

in…hang on…' Penny held the phone away from her ear as her mother bellowed, 'Sandra Next Door – are we still going to the shoe shop to get some high heels for your Geoff?' Penny could hear a faint voice in the background then her mother returned, sounding quite miffed. 'Well, I don't know what's got her knickers in a twist. Never mind. We'll meet you in the Marks and Sparks café in an hour.'

Penny made another call then returned to her friends. 'I've ordered a taxi,' she told them. 'It'll be here in five minutes. Do you want to wait in here or outside?'

'Outside, if you don't mind,' said Mrs Hubbard. 'The fresh air will do me good.'

As they rose to leave, the barman shuffled over, his eyes fixed on Mrs Hubbard. 'Leaving so soon? I was going to ask for your number. I am, as they say, a man of substance. A businessman and proprietor.' He said the latter in a French accent with a strong hint of Paisley, "pro-pree-eteur." He looked around and gestured at the bar. 'Quite the catch for a lady of your years. And, added bonus, I know somewhere we could go for a quiet drink.'

Mrs Hubbard paused for a moment, her eyes travelling from his stained football shirt to the suspicious bulge in the front of his filthy jeans, before making their way back up and coming to rest on a face of which a mother rat would be proud. Then she drew herself up to her full height and haughtily declared, 'I am a lesbian,' before stalking out of the pub.

Elsie grinned and practically skipped out the door, calling over her shoulder, 'And I'm her wife!'

Penny smiled weakly at the barman and shrugged. 'Me too?' Then she beat her own hasty retreat.

That evening, Detective Inspector Mitchell leaned back in his chair and regarded the packed Social Club. He wondered who was doing any actual policing tonight, as every officer in

Aberdeen seemed to be here, at his retirement do. Mind you, they'd done him proud. An excellent meal, rounded off by a toast from the Chief Constable of Police Scotland, who was enjoying the excuse to extract herself from the clutches of Tulliallan HQ and come home to see family, old friends and, of course, old colleagues. He'd trained her himself and was proud to see her rise from nervous probationer, cocking up her first arrest, through to assured politician, who somehow managed to stay on the right side of the press, the public and the people who worked for her. DI Mitchell caught her eye and raised his glass, letting her know that he appreciated her speech.

Finally, before the drinking began in earnest, DI Mitchell stood to make his own speech. He clinked a teaspoon on a glass, calling for silence. The hubbub died down a little, but many continued their conversations. He clinked again. Nothing. The Chief Constable stood up and roared, 'Quiet!' Instantly, silence fell, and DI Mitchell cleared his throat.

'Thank you, ma'am. And thank you all for coming tonight.'

The DI spoke about memorable cases he had worked over the decades and the memorable colleagues with whom he had had the honour to serve. There was laughter at his account of sledging on riot shields in Duthie Park and the time that the whole unit turned up for shift a little the worse for wear. The very disgruntled Sergeant had sent them all outside for ten minutes to get some fresh air, so they duly commandeered a police van and went in search of strong black coffee and a burger. An hour later, the same Sergeant got a call to ask if someone could please come and get them because nobody could remember where they'd parked the van.

Overall, DI Mitchell later reflected, the speech went down well. As did the copious amount of whisky afterwards. The £200 he had put behind the bar was gone within the first half hour, and by the end of the second half hour, an air of relaxed bonhomie filled the room. By the end of the third hour, Aberdeen's finest were doing a drunken conga to DJ Ötzi's Hey Baby, stopping only to thrust their hips at the "ooh aah" parts; the problem being that some people were oohing when they should have been aahing, resulting in several members being forcefully ejected from the conga by their colleagues'… erm…members. There will be a few harsh words come tomorrow, thought DI Mitchell, but I won't be there to hear them.

Now, with the lights up and last orders called, only a few stragglers remained. The DI went in search of the manager to settle his tab and thank him for a memorable night. He popped his head around the door of the office but saw only a woman who he recognised as a member of the catering staff.

'Sorry,' he said, 'I was looking for Charlie.'

'He's just popped out for a smoke. He'll be back in a minute. You can come in and wait for him, if you like,' the woman offered.

DI Mitchell sidled into the small room, trying to squeeze his bulk past an aspidistra in a tall pot without knocking it over. He took a seat in one of the low, leather visitors chairs and smiled at the woman.

'I'm John Mitchell. It was my retirement do tonight.'

'Congratulations,' she said and held out a hand. 'Kerry Price, catering manager and Charlie's partner. I hope you enjoyed the food.'

'Oh, aye,' said DI Mitchell, shaking her hand and nodding enthusiastically. 'It was a good spread. I liked that you sourced everything locally.'

'Thanks. You can't beat a bit of Angus beef.'

'Aye, and the cake was delicious.'

'That's my favourite. I get it from a place out towards Huntly. It pairs really well with the strawberry ice cream.'

'Where do you get the ice cream?'

No sooner had the words left his lips, than DI Mitchell felt something inside his stomach shift, and it wasn't just a growing sense of dread.

'I'll let you in on a secret,' Kerry said, leaning towards him. 'There's this little old lady out on Vik who makes her own.'

She went on to rhapsodise about the various flavours, but DI Mitchell had stopped listening. He was too busy contemplating the fact that he'd inadvertently poisoned himself, the entire police force of Aberdeen and the Chief Constable. Oh, bugger.

CHAPTER 2

'Get off ma damn boat,' Captain Rab's voice growled over the intercom.

There was a general shuffling of shopping bags and swollen feet as the day-trippers from Vik prepared to disembark the evening ferry. Every now and again, the natives would jump back and shout "Whoa!" as a backpack-wearing tourist turned around too quickly and nearly took them out like a line of skittles. Ironically, only a regular commuter on the London Underground would truly understand the reflexes of an islander, thought Penny, as she neatly ducked under a swinging rucksack without dropping a single bag. And there were many bags. Her mother had bought half of Marks and Spencer before declaring herself far too important to be carrying everything. Then she'd hitched up her handbag and swanned off like the movie star she believed herself to be, leaving Penny to struggle down the fifty million steps to the Union Square shopping centre after her. Penny was clearly the overburdened lackey in this scenario.

Thank goodness Jim had offered to pick them up. His car, fondly known as Phil, had a huge boot in which they could lock Mum. The shopping would go on the back seat with Penny and Elsie. Sadly, Mrs Hubbard had called shotgun.

Quite literally. She'd shouted it so loudly that several people looked around in alarm and there had been an uncomfortable exchange of words with the security guard in Hollister. Nevertheless, at least there was one advantage to having a shameless mother. Penny, now too embarrassed to be in the shop, had sent Mary back with instructions to buy t-shirts for the twins, while she'd crammed Mary's bags under the table of a nearby café and collapsed gratefully into a chair.

During the journey home, she'd spilled an entire latte down the front of her top and had been about to fish one of the kids' t-shirts out of the bag, when Mary stopped her.

'No need. It'll just spoil the surprise for Hector and Edith. Wait there because I have the perfect solution.'

Mary disappeared, leaving Penny trying to hold the rapidly cooling material away from her skin. When her mother returned ten minutes and one trip to the ferry gift shop later, Penny wondered whether she wouldn't have been better off simply trying to rinse her top in the loos. Never mind that the hand dryers weren't working.

'Oh, I'm not wearing that,' she said.

'Of course you are. It's only a little bit of fun for the tourists, and I got it cheap,' her mother insisted.

Penny snorted. 'Because nobody in their right mind would buy it!'

'Look,' said Mary, as if throwing in her finest bargaining chip, 'I even got it in a bigger size. They don't always do them in your size. You're being very ungrateful.'

'And they wonder why I have low self-esteem,' Penny muttered. 'Okay, give it here.'

She reluctantly took the proffered sweatshirt and went to the ladies to change. A few minutes later, ignoring the titters around her, Penny returned to her seat and, like a petulant teenager, flumped down, arms crossed over her chest.

'It isn't that bad, dearie,' Mrs Hubbard reassured her.

'You look delightful!' her mother exclaimed.

'You look fine,' said Elsie.

'You look like a bit of a twat,' said Sandra, not bothering to disguise a malicious grin.

Sulkily, Penny had donned her coat and refused to take it off for the rest of the journey, no matter that the passenger lounge was hotter than the devil's armpits.

Now, shuffling forwards, Penny felt a cool breeze on her face and realised that she must be near the ferry door. Confident that, in the press of people, nobody would notice the offending sweatshirt, she unzipped her coat and, whilst trying to surreptitiously waft some cool air down her top, looked around for her companions. After the stresses of today, she thought, the last thing I need is for one of them to go missing.

To her relief, her eye caught a flash of blue ahead and, recognising it as Elsie's cardigan, she pressed through the crowd just in time to see poor Elsie being accidentally floored by a large man with an oversized rucksack. The man glowered at Elsie, as if it was her fault, and Penny watched as the small, elderly woman staggered to her feet, clinging to the rucksack for support. The man muttered something, which Penny assumed was unkind, given the shocked look on Elsie's face. Mrs Hubbard appeared beside her and looked like she was going to intervene, but Elsie waved her off. As they reached the door, Penny was momentarily distracted when the man stumbled forwards and fell face-first onto the metal gangway. Those who had witnessed the altercation did nothing to help the man and simply walked around him, with the other passengers following in their wake. She dragged her attention away from the flailing figure, pinned down by the weight of his backpack, and looked around for Elsie. Who, strangely, seemed to have melted away into the crowd.

Penny had never been so pleased to see Jim before. There he was, standing behind the Land Rover known as Phil, stoically loading shopping bags into the boot as three pensioners roared, 'No, don't put that one underneath. It goes on top!'

As she approached him, Jim's eyes fell on Penny's chest. He grinned at her, winked and said, 'Aye. Beep, beep.'

Penny glared at him but, with her hands full of shopping bags, could do little to cover up the fact that emblazoned across her bosom, above an image of a horned Viking helmet, were the words "HONK IF YOU'RE HORNY".

She was about to launch into a rant about the fifty shades of idiot at the tourist office who'd commissioned the design, when she was interrupted by Mrs Hubbard and Elsie, who appeared to have discovered even more shopping bags and were bickering about how they'd fit them all in.

Jim sighed, resigned to playing a round of car boot Tetris.

'I suppose this is why they call the evening ferry the Buckaroo Boat,' he said, squashing a bag into a tiny space in the corner.

With an apologetic look, Penny handed him her mother's bags.

'Sorry. If you think this is bad, try going shopping with them. I'll be glad to get home for some peace and quiet… scratch that…Mum will be there, so I'm probably setting the bar too high. I'll settle for pyjamas and a nice cup of tea.'

Jim grimaced. 'It's me who should be saying sorry. Can we drop this lot off then will you come with me?'

Penny opened her mouth to ask why, but he held up a hand to stall her.

'I'll tell you later. Have you seen Sandra Next Door? Geoff's over there waiting for her.'

'She probably jumped overboard after spending the day with Mum. Don't worry. She was definitely on the ferry. She spent half the journey moaning about the quality of the coffee and the other half bitching about some woman who was dressed to the nines in designer gear.'

'What? Like fancy sportswear?'

Penny snorted. 'No, it was all posh stuff and a handbag that probably cost more than Geoff earns in a year. Look there she is now.'

Jim turned, expecting to see a supermodel type sashaying down the gangway, but it was only Sandra Next Door, stomping her way towards the jetty, complaining loudly about "some fool who thinks this is a good place for a lie down." In fact, she was stomping so hard that Penny could see the rucksack on the back of the fallen tourist bobbing up and down with every step. Behind her, picking her way elegantly around the man, was a tall, slim woman wearing a cashmere shawl and sunglasses. Penny could practically smell the Chanel No. 5 from where she was standing. The woman flicked back a lock of impossibly glossy dark hair and scanned the waiting cars, her gaze alighting on one further down the harbour road. Holding her small case aloft to avoid the supine man, she waved then turned back to the ferry doorway to speak to someone inside. Penny gasped as she recognised the short, pigeon-chested, older man who appeared, hefting a large suitcase.

'Goodness, that's Captain Rab. And he's being…helpful!'

'Well bugger me with a box of toy soldiers. That's not like him,' said Jim.

'Why?' asked Penny.

'Well, he's usually very rude and unfriendly.'

'No. Why a box of toy soldiers? How does shoving a battalion of small painted men up there help express your surprise?'

'Erm,' said Jim, pausing for a moment to think. 'They're unexpected and a bit spiky, what with the little guns and all. And if they're from more than a hundred years ago, they probably have bayonets as well.'

'Fair enough.'

Jim regarded her for a moment then smiled. 'I've missed our little chats.'

Penny had too, although she wasn't going to tell him that, even though he was looking at her like he wanted her to say something. There was no point in letting his head get any bigger than it already was. Instead, she squeezed into the back seat beside her mother and Elsie.

Elsie was now wearing her mac, which at least explained how she'd melted into the crowd, and was telling Mary, 'I've no idea how it happened. One minute he was instructing me to take my effing hands off his rucksack, and the next he was on the floor, poor man.'

'Are you sure that one of your feet didn't accidentally get in the way?' asked Mary.

'Really, Mary, what a thing to say,' sniffed Elsie, then she lapsed into silence for the rest of the journey.

They dropped Mrs Hubbard and Elsie off first. As Mrs Hubbard left the car, she briefly clasped Penny's arm.

'Thank you, dearie. It's been an awful day, and I truly appreciate you all being there for me.'

Penny saw tears glistening in her eyes. Capturing Mrs Hubbard's hand in hers, she rubbed the smooth skin, feeling the soft ridges of the veins as they slid under her fingers.

'We're a team, Mrs Hubbard. We've got your back. You have Elsie for company until Douglas gets home from the hospital and you can call any of us any time. It'll all be okay, I promise.'

'That's a promise you can't keep, dear, but I thank you for making it anyway. And thank you for the lift, Jim. No, no, I don't need any help.' Mrs Hubbard nodded politely at the other figure in the back seat. 'Mary.'

The only response was a grunting snore, as Mary stirred vaguely at the sound of her own name. She had been using her Moschino handbag as a pillow, and as she turned her head, a line of drool slid down the large M imprinted on her cheek.

As Mrs Hubbard scuttled off after Elsie, weighed down with shopping bags, Jim eyed Mary and gave a wry smile. 'That's what I always admired about your mother, Penny, her dignity. Hang on, I've just remembered something. Stay there, I'll be back in a minute.'

He quickly got out of the car, leaving his door open, and did some scuttling of his own, calling out to Mrs Hubbard, 'Hold up there, Mrs H.' When he caught up to the older woman, Penny was sure she heard him saying, 'Do you sell shower caps?' Very strange. What was he up to?

Mrs Hubbard, who had been about to head for the house behind the village shop, pivoted and led Jim and Elsie towards the store front. In the doorway below the "Mrs Hubbard's Cupboard" sign, a security light blinked into life, and Penny could see Mrs Hubbard fiddling with the lock. Jim bent to help her, and a few moments later the trio disappeared inside. Penny smiled to herself and wondered if she should ask Jim whether he enjoyed a fumble in the shop doorway with Mrs Hubbard. That would be a good joke.

A few minutes later, Jim got back into the driver's seat and tossed a bag onto Penny's lap. She opened it to inspect the contents then turned to him, baffled.

'Six shower caps, four pairs of rubber gloves, four aprons and a box of face masks?'

'Trust me, we'll need them. Come on, let's get Sleeping Beauty home then I'll tell you what's going on. By the way,' he grinned at her, 'I quite enjoyed a quick fumble with Mrs Hubbard in the shop doorway.'

Penny looked at him blankly for a moment, then sniffed and said, 'That's very disrespectful of Mrs Hubbard. Poor woman, after everything she's been through today.'

They arrived at Penny's parents' house, Valhalla, to be greeted by Edith and Hector, who were far more interested in the prospect of presents than their mother's sojourn or the fate of Mrs Hubbard.

Edith caught sight of Penny's sweatshirt and commented,

'Grandad must be gagging for it, then. He's been honking his guts up all day.'

'Serves him right for raiding the freezer in the middle of the night,' said a voice from the back seat. 'Hello my wee chickens. Do you want to see what Granny bought you?'

Mary opened the door and gestured with a thumb to the boot.

'Come and give an old lady a hand. Honestly, I've been lugging things around all day. Your mother was no help at all!'

As Mary stumbled out of her seat, still slightly befuddled with sleep, the twins hurried to unload the shopping. Hector paused for a moment, noting that his mother was making no move to leave the vehicle.

'Are you coming?' he asked.

'I just have to run an errand with Jim,' she said. 'I'll be back to tuck you in.'

'For goodness' sake, mother. I'm not a child anymore.'

'Maybe not to the rest of the world,' said Penny wistfully, 'but you'll always be my child, so you just have to put up with being loved.'

'Dad came round today,' said Hector, suddenly very interested in the gravel beneath his feet.

On the inside, Penny was rolling her eyes. However, she managed to refrain from asking "and how was the chief wankpuffin?" Instead, she smiled fondly at Hector and said, 'How lovely that you're able to see so much of him.'

Jim cleared his throat and she told Hector that they had to go. She blew him a kiss and, as Jim turned Phil around in the wide drive, she looked over her shoulder to watch him, laden with bags, trudging into the bungalow.

'I suppose it's a good thing that he's able to see a bit more of Alex,' she told Jim. 'He seems to be over the divorce now, but he still idolises his dad.'

Jim, who was slightly less keen on the reappearance of Alex in Penny's life, merely grunted in response. Alex was the reason he'd taken on all the extra work recently. His father, who was the island vet before him and still hadn't entirely retired, had offered to help with the lambing, but Jim had turned him down. As her friend, he had no claim on Penny's affections, yet he had always felt that there was more going on than friendship. With Alex back in the picture, Jim didn't stand a chance, so he'd done the only reasonable thing; stepped aside. It was better that he never meet Alex because, what with him being an expert in shoving his hands up arses and what with Alex being a total arse for the way he'd treated Penny, Jim reckoned he might be tempted to treat the man to a tonsillectomy from the wrong end. Therefore, as far as Penny was concerned, he was simply very busy doing important vet stuff. Except tonight. Tonight, there was other important stuff to do.

'I said I'd tell you what this is about. I've been commandeered by Doc Harris as the only other medical professional on the island,' he told her.

Penny was confused. 'Eh?'

'I'VE BEEN COMMANDEERED BY—'

'No, I heard you. Just, what are you talking about?'

Jim took a moment to regroup and tried again.

'Doc Harris is down with the salmonella, same as half the island, and asked for my help with something. You see he got a call from—'

'Whoa. Watch out!' Penny cried, as a deer ran across the road, its eyes glinting bright in the headlights. 'You always drive so fast. Why do you have to drive like a boy racer?'

'Why do you have to drive like a granny?' Jim retorted.

'If you mean my mother, I don't drive anything like her. She's an absolute maniac behind the wheel. You know, Kenny has had to fix her horn three times because she wore it out. Have you ever heard of anyone wearing out a horn before?'

'At least she's the only person on the island who can't respond to your sweatshirt,' Jim assured her.

Penny wasn't sure whether to agree or be annoyed, so

confined herself to dark mutterings about people who think they belong on a racetrack. The tone set, she and Jim bickered all the way back into Port Vik. It was only as he barrelled up Low Street and pulled to a stop outside a row of terraced houses that he remembered he still had to explain their mysterious errand.

'For fuck's sake. We got here in one piece, didn't we?' he huffed. 'Anyway, if you'd just shut your big gob for one minute, I'll tell you why we're here.'

With a great effort of will, Penny refrained from telling him off for swearing. She was actually quite curious about the reason for the trip back to town.

'Okay, shoot,' she said.

'Gladly,' muttered Jim, then clocked her glare and decided that it was perhaps best to move on. Mostly. 'As I was saying, before I was so rudely interrupted.'

'Because you nearly ran over a deer.'

Jim took a deep breath and counted to three. 'As I was saying, Doc Harris is down with the salmonella and all the nursing staff are either sick themselves or looking after the sick folk, so he asked me to stand in for him for a couple of days. Just the urgent but easy stuff. That's why we're here.'

'Has one of his patients got fleas?'

'No. One of his patients is having a baby.'

'A baby!' Penny exclaimed.

'Marie Knox. The woman who runs the ice cream van down at the beach. You know her – tall, speccy wifie, always stinks of onions.'

'Is she tall, though? Maybe a whisker above average.'

'Definitely tall,' said Jim, nodding sagely. 'Has a permanent stoop from bending over in the van, so she looks shorter than she actually is.'

'You'd think she'd get a different job, somewhere with higher ceilings. Like the church or the big supermarket. Which reminds me, they're having a sale on Saturday. Would you like to come?'

'What? Why would I want to go there for a sale?'

'For the injured dolphins.'

'Eh? Do they have them on the shelf alongside the battered sausages and the minced meat?'

It took Penny a moment to realise. 'The church sale, you idiot. Not the supermarket.'

'Oh. Aye. Fine. Is Mrs Hay doing peppermint slices for the teas? If she wasn't eighty-five with a husband still on the go, I'd marry that woman for her peppermint slices alone. I can't get enough of them.' Jim stopped talking to ruminate for a moment about the wonder of Mrs Hay's peppermint slices. Then he gave himself a little shake and said, 'Anyway, shall we go in or would you prefer to talk some more about Mrs Hay's baking?'

'Hold on a sec, why am I here? And, if it's a baby on the way, why did you bugger about with picking us up from the ferry?'

'Fair questions,' said Jim. 'The baby's not due yet. Marie has…uh…constipation. I'll probably have to give her a suppository and I just needed someone to hold my hand.'

'What? While you're sticking it up there?'

'No. I mean, I need a woman there. I'm used to doing this on animals, not people. What if I get the wrong hole or something? I can't be fumbling about down there unaccompanied, like some pervert.'

Penny was trying very hard not to laugh. Poor Jim looked so uncomfortable.

'You have seen a bum before, haven't you?'

Jim shifted in his seat. 'Aye, but…look, will you just come in with me so it's all above board and I can't be accused of anything. Fuck's sake. You don't get this much trouble with dogs.'

'Why? What are you doing with dogs?'

The sheer horror on Jim's face as he squeaked, 'Nothing!' was too much for Penny. The dam broke and she hooted with laughter.

Jim undid his seatbelt and got out of the car, slamming the door behind him. Walking round to her side, he wrenched her door open, grabbed the bag of what she presumed was supposed to be protective equipment, and marched up to Marie's front door. Penny quickly got out of the car and caught up with him as he knocked for a second time.

'Sorry,' she mumbled, taking pity on him.

Jim said nothing, just shot her a black look as the door opened to reveal a heavily pregnant woman in a pink dressing gown and slippers, with a pained look upon her face.

'Hiya, Jim. Thanks for doing this. I'm so glad you're here. I don't think I can stand it much longer. Nice to see you too, Penny. Didn't know you were coming,' she said, giving them a weak smile.

'I'm just here to chaperone Jim,' said Penny, deciding to leave out the bit about the wrong hole.

'Ah, you're okay. I'm sure Jim will do fine, and I don't really need an audience. I just want to get this out of me. Honestly, it's like someone shoved golf balls up there. I'm that glad to see you. If James Dyson himself turned up to trial his latest vacuum cleaner on me, I couldn't be happier.'

She guided them inside and pointed Penny towards the kitchen. 'Why don't you make us all a nice cup of tea while Jim sorts me out.'

Trying not to think about what was going on upstairs, Penny clattered around the cheerful little room, opening a yellow cupboard door to find mugs, then fishing around the cluttered dresser to locate the tea bags.

The kettle had boiled, and she was filling the mugs, when she heard footsteps on the stairs. She popped her head round the kitchen door to see Jim coming towards her, a stunned look on his unusually pale face.

'Are you okay?' she asked, taking his arm and gently steering him towards a small table and chairs in the corner of the kitchen.

'Well, I got a hole in one, if that's what you're asking. But it turns out that what takes a while to work on dogs, works pretty much straight away on humans.'

'She didn't…'

'Aye, she did.'

'Was it bad?'

'Have you ever seen one of them tennis ball machines?'

'Holy shit.'

'God was definitely not involved.'

'Were you wearing your apron?'

'The one that says "Don't mess with the chef".'

'You'll need that cup of tea.'

'Aye, I will.'

Penny slid a mug towards him and took a sip of her own. They sat together in companionable silence for a long while, until their individual reveries were broken by the sound of a flushing toilet, followed by Marie's footsteps on the stairs. A moment later, the woman came bustling into the kitchen, looking far more cheerful than when Penny had last seen her.

Penny quickly stood up. 'Would you like a seat, Marie?'

'Oh, no. I'm not sure I could sit down quite yet, but I feel much better. How about we celebrate with an ice cream? I can't fit behind the wheel of the van at the moment, what with this wee bundle of joy.' Marie patted her stomach and gave a mock grimace. 'I've put what's left of the ice cream in here.'

For a moment, Penny thought she meant her belly, but to her relief, Marie reached into the freezer and began to root around.

'It's not Mrs Hubbard's ice cream, is it?' Penny asked, a note of concern in her voice.

'No. I buy the cheap stuff for the van. I feel a bit guilty for not buying local, but people are just looking for a treat that doesn't matter if it gets dropped in the sand. Ah! Here we are.'

Marie held up a tub of ice cream and waddled over to the

kitchen counter. She found a scoop in a drawer and expertly filled three cones, before turning to Penny and Jim and asking, 'Now, how about a flake?'

Jim eyed the three chocolate balls and looked as though he might throw up.

CHAPTER 3

Penny had never been so relieved to see her bed. By the time she had arrived home, the house was in darkness, its occupants having opted for (or, more likely, her mother having declared) an early night. She'd bypassed tucking Hector in, even though she suspected that, despite his protestations about being far too grown up, he secretly liked that she still came into his room to kiss his forehead, and had headed straight for her own bedroom, with its comfy bed where she could nestle her bottom into the dip in the mattress and say goodnight to Chesney Hawkes.

Chesney, or Chezza to those who liked to converse with posters on bedroom walls, was a relic of Penny's youth; a teenage popstar who loudly declared himself to be "The One and Only". Since moving back into her parents' house following her split with Alex, for whom, as it turned out, she was *not* the one and only, she'd had many productive chats with the Chezster. He'd turned out to be an excellent listener, gazing mutely down at her, his paper eyes silently promising not to tell a single soul as she poured out her innermost to him.

Feeling slightly sorry for young Chezza, Penny had decided to give him a bit of company. This was a spur of the moment decision taken at the last church sale, when she'd come across an old poster of Sharleen Spiteri; she of Texas fame, who had told the world that she didn't need a lover, she just needed a friend. It had been pretty much how Penny had felt at that moment, still licking her wounds from the divorce. There was a spark between herself and Jim, she knew, but she wasn't ready to make that commitment again. She was, however, ready to move on with a strong imaginary friend above her bed, so Sharleen had taken pride of place on the wall next to Chezza and was there for Penny whenever she needed to give herself a good talking to. She had no idea what the Sharlster was like in real life but as a no-nonsense, straight-talking poster, she gave Penny a much needed kick up the backside to get her life in order.

That morning, Penny stretched lazily and groaned, 'Hello, my lovelies,' to the posters.

'What shall we do to avoid Alex today?' she asked them. 'The bastard only suggested filming here to annoy me. And possibly to see his children. But mostly to annoy me, I'm sure.'

Sharleen stared down at her and Penny could have sworn she spotted a look of disapproval in the woman's eyes.

'Oh, alright. I'm being a cow. It's just that Mum's being so nice to him because he got her that line in the film, and everyone is fawning on him wherever he goes. I feel...I dunno...I wish someone would dislike him with me.'

Sharleen said nothing, but Penny could see that she was silently trying to communicate an excellent idea.

'Ooh, excellent idea, Sharleen. I'll go round to Eileen's for a good moan. Best friends always stick up for you. She'll bitch about him with me, then I'll feel better and be able to be nice to him when Mum does something stupid like invite him over for dinner.'

She winced at herself. All those years in fancy London had brainwashed her into calling it dinner. In London, you had lunch then dinner. On Vik, you had dinner then tea. Due to

Penny's numerous trips to "pick up a bottle of something for dinner", the checkout lady in the supermarket was convinced she was some sort of day-drinking reprobate.

Feeling the warmth of the sun on her arm, Penny realised that she must have forgotten to close the curtains the night before. She rolled over to face the window, eyes blinking in the sunlight, and almost screamed at the contorted face pressed up against the glass. Almost screamed, but not quite. Instead, she gave a short squeal, roared, 'Jim!' and leapt out of bed to hurriedly sweep the curtains together.

A muffled voice came from beyond the curtains.

'Were you talking to the posters?'

'Go away,' she shouted.

'I saw you. You were talking to the posters.'

She hastily pulled back the curtains and opened a window.

'Go away. It's too early for an argument,' she hissed at Jim.

He'd pulled back from the window, leaving a face mark on the glass. His own face, she could see, had dark blotches where the dirt had adhered to his skin. With his unbrushed brown hair and old clothes, he looked like a leering scarecrow.

'It's after seven,' he told her. 'I've been up at Hillside farm since the early hours. Some of the lambs aren't doing too well. Randy Mair was quite worried, but I told him it wasn't too baaaaad. Can I come in?'

Sighing, Penny closed the window, put on her slippers and shuffled across the wooden floor of the hall to open the front door to a grinning Jim. He looked down at her chest and said, 'I never believed the rumours until now,' before pushing past her and seeing himself to the kitchen.

Penny looked down at her chest, where her nightdress declared "I sleep around." She pulled at the front, where the material had rucked up beneath her breasts, and the words "the clock" appeared. Lordy, that man was irritating, she thought, as she followed him through to the kitchen.

Already, Jim was filling the kettle and rummaging in the bread bin for something suitable to toast. With a satisfied grunt, he produced a bagel.

'I see your mum's diversifying,' he said, popping it in the toaster.

'No, she's going through an American phase. Some of these film people are from the States, so she's taken to watching West Side Story on repeat and eating food that she thinks is, I quote, "Americany". I think she's stealing the bagels from the catering van on set.'

'Has she pinched any cream cheese?'

'Fridge, top shelf.'

Jim checked the fridge and held up a small tub. 'Philadelphia. Does she know it's made in England?'

'No, and for goodness' sake don't tell the old bag.'

'Don't tell me what, dear?' said a voice from the kitchen door. Mary stood there in a lurid yellow nightgown, green socks and a violet dressing gown, looking for all the world like a six-foot pansy. Her short hair was sticking out at odd angles, made worse by the fact that her cat, Mojo, had crawled up her shoulder and was having a rummage through the blonde nest for lord knows what. Bats, knowing Mum, thought Penny.

Penny was about to tell her mum to mind her own business when Jim said, 'Nothing. We're off on a mission today and it's all very hush hush. Come on, Penny. Pop some clothes on. Can't wait around for you all day.'

Penny looked at him curiously, but he put a finger to his lips and jerked his head in the direction of her bedroom.

As her mother headed for the back door to dispose of the cat, Penny scooted behind her, waving her arms and mouthing, 'What? What?' at Jim.

He simply shook his head and made a shooing motion with his hands, so she rolled her eyes, threw her own hands in the air and left.

As she passed her parents' bedroom, she decided to look

in on her father. She lightly tapped on the door and heard her father's faint voice. Assuming he'd invited her to come in, she slipped inside the darkened room and was about to speak when the lump on the bed said, 'Please, please go away, Mary. I told you, I don't want pastrami on rye. I don't even know what a pastrami is, but I feel sick at the very thought of it.'

Penny gave the lump a gentle poke and said, 'It's me, Dad. How are you feeling?'

The lump moved and, after some mild swearing, untangled itself from the sheets until, finally, Len's head emerged, shiny and sweaty, with something suspiciously vomity attached to his moustache.

'Hello, Penny-farthing. Much better, thanks. You know, I can keep water down now.'

He said this like a small child who had just been awarded a best handwriting in class certificate and was going to be allowed to write with, drum roll please, a pen.

Penny smiled. 'That's great, Dad. You're on the mend at last.'

'Was that Jim I heard?' Len asked.

'Yes. He's told me to get dressed. Apparently, we're off on a mission.'

'Well, you better do as he says then,' said Len. 'Probably best, anyway. Your mum's invited Alex over for dinner.'

'Dinner lunch or dinner tea?'

'Lunch. He's taking the twins to visit the set afterwards, assuming they're up, of course.'

'I'm sure Mum can stretch lunch out until four o' clock to give them time to wake up.'

'Can we stop talking about lunch please? It's making me feel ill. In fact, I'll be far too ill to get out of bed until after he's gone. Never could stand the man.'

Penny looked at her dad in surprise.

'I thought you liked him. You're always so nice to him.'

'For your sake. And the twins'. But I could tell from the moment I met him that he's shallow. All front. He was never good enough for you. Now, give your old Dad a hug, then away and tell that Jim he's not to do my crossword.'

Penny gave her father's shoulder a gentle squeeze, grateful for the unexpected ally. 'Sorry, Dad. I can't give you a hug.' She reached over to the dressing table then handed him a packet of Mary's make-up wipes. 'Vomity tache.'

She left him, sitting up in bed, vigorously attacking his moustache with a small white rectangle and muttering something about it being a cold day in hell before *he* ate a pastrami.

It was only as they sped up the High Street and pulled to a stop outside the Vik History Museum that Jim remembered he still had to explain their mysterious errand.

'For fuck's sake. We got here in one piece, didn't we?' he huffed. 'Anyway, if you'd just shut your gob for one minute, I'll tell you why we're here.'

Struck by a sense of déjà vu, Penny contented herself with a good old-fashioned hard stare.

'Okay, hit me with it,' she said.

'Gladly,' muttered Jim. 'As I was saying, before I was so rudely interrupted.'

'Because you nearly ran over Mrs Hay, thus depriving yourself and the poor dolphins.'

Jim took a deep breath and counted to three. 'As. I. Was. Saying. Doc Harris is down with the salmonella and with me being the only available medical professional–'

'Except for your dad.'

'Who didn't do two years of human medicine before switching to veterinary medicine.'

'And old Doc Glennie.'

'Who is currently unavailable due to him having a wee rest in Vik cemetery.'

'And…no, I've run out. Carry on with you being the only medical professional yada, yada, yada.'

'He's asked me to examine one of his patients.'

'Wait,' said Penny. 'Does this have anything to do with bums? Because you should have told him you're no good with bums.'

'No, this one is dead.'

'Dead! Who?'

Jim gestured to the building beside them. 'Colin Dogood. The museum curator. You know him – small, spotty, Australian, terrible breath.'

'Is he small, though? Maybe a whisker below average.'

'Cowboy boots,' said Jim, nodding sagely. 'I can't wear the things. I'm too tall. Tried them once on a school trip to Fyvie Castle and nearly gave myself a concussion on a lintel.'

'I was on that trip. So was Eileen. She went looking for the secret room and we found her three hours later, locked in a wardrobe in the staff lounge. She was okay, though. She'd discovered a packet of crisps and a bottle of apple juice in somebody's coat pocket.'

'Was she not bursting for a pee?' asked Jim.

'Let's just say that a while later, one of the stewards took a swig of his apple juice and made a formal complaint to the school. Anyway, what about Colin?'

'Aye, Colin. He was discovered dead in the museum when the cleaner went in this morning. What with the doc being laid up and Sergeant Wilson being in hospital, there's nobody to…eh…deal with it. The police were going to send someone, but half the force has come down with food poisoning after some eejit's retirement do and the other half is only just about coping. Apparently, there's been a break in at Balmoral and the family are in residence, so they'll be over on the evening ferry at the earliest.'

'I don't think the Queen will take kindly to Captain Rab telling her to get off his damn boat. Mind you, Princess Anne would look right bonny in a Honk if You're Horny sweatshirt.'

It was Jim's turn to glare at Penny. She grinned back, perfectly aware that she was being obtuse.

'Police people,' he growled. 'Pathologist, whatever. Anyway, the doc has asked me to check the temperature and photograph the body for him.'

'Hang on. Why am I here?' asked Penny.

'Company.'

'Company! You're dragging me along to see a corpse because you want company! I thought you were taking me somewhere nice! I wore my good cashmere jumper for this!' Penny exclaimed.

'Okay. Not exactly company. It's because I'm terrified of doing this on my own,' Jim confessed.

In an instant, Penny's outrage turned to pity. No, not pity, she thought. Exasperation. That was it. Healthy exasperation.

She considered having a good swear of her own but opted for, 'Well then, for goodness' sake, stop your havering and let's go.'

She left the car and strode to the museum door, muttering loudly about people who stop to eat bagels instead of sticking thermometers into dead people. She was just about to turn the door handle when Jim caught up to her, slightly out of breath. He had a plastic bag in one hand and his vet bag in the other.

'We'll do this together,' he said. 'Are you ready? On my count. One–'

Penny pushed the door open and went in, leaving him saying, '–Two, Three, Go,' behind her.

Then silence. The sort of oppressive silence you get when there are so many old things in one place. It briefly flitted through her mind that she should save that one for when they next visited Eileen's granny in the nursing home. Ooh, that was wildly inappropriate, but truth be told, she was slightly freaking out right now. It wasn't just the silence; it was the gloom. Almost as if the windows were sucking the light *out* of the place. Dreading what was to come, she felt around for the light switch and flicked it on. Then slowly released the breath that she hadn't realised she'd been holding. She looked around. Nothing. She'd been braced for a corpse but could see nothing.

'Where's the dead guy?' she asked, mildly outraged that the man had had the cheek to drop down dead somewhere out of sight.

'Round by the Vikings in Vik video. God, you wouldn't want to say that after a few. Here,' said Jim, pulling items from the plastic bag. 'Put these shower caps over your shoes to protect them in case there's…fluids. You don't seem bothered. Why are you not bothered about seeing a dead guy?'

Penny thought about this for a moment while she slipped on the shower caps and rummaged in the bag for an apron. You couldn't be too careful with body fluids and cashmere.

'I blame television,' she eventually said, nodding wisely. 'Also, we had loads of dead guys last summer, when Old Archie was murdered.'

'Just the two,' said Jim.

'And then there was all the people who ended up in hospital.'

'Just the two.'

'All I'm saying is, Vik's a small island riddled with big city crime.'

'Just the one crime.'

'I think I might be immune to it now,' Penny declared, as they picked their way carefully through the museum, trying not to let their shower cap feet slip on the polished wooden floor. Nevertheless, when they turned the corner by the video display, she skidded to a halt, gasping, 'Or maybe not.'

Jim skidded to a halt behind her. There, in front of the benches where visitors would normally sit to watch a video of the Viking history of Vik, lay Colin Dogood; naked, sightless eyes fixed on Jim and Penny, a pool of blood congealing around his head.

Jim could feel his heart begin to race. Keep it together, he told himself. Deep breaths. In through the nose, out through the mouth. Be brave for Penny, because who needs a six-foot cowardy custard passing out on them. Too late, he thought, as his vision wavered. He sat down heavily on one of the benches and felt it creak as Penny joined him.

'You're hyperventilating,' she told him, putting a comforting arm around his shoulders. 'Slow it down. That's it. Nice and steady. Feeling better?'

Jim nodded and Penny looked relieved. Her own face was pale, he saw, and he felt a distinct tremor in the hand that had now slid downwards and was rhythmically rubbing his back.

Jim slowly shifted his gaze to the figure on the floor and noted that the man's head was turned slightly to one side. His face was a ruined mess, the features obliterated to the point that Jim would have been hard pressed to even say it was definitely Colin. Yet something glinted amid the gore. What was that? Despite every fibre of his being urging him to leave, leave now, Jim bent over to take a closer look, then quickly straightened up. Something shiny was sticking out of Colin's mouth.

'What exactly did Doc Harris tell you when he phoned?' Penny asked, stifling the urge to vomit all over what was clearly a crime scene.

Still in shock, Jim rubbed a hand across his forehead and took a moment to think.

'Only that Colin had died. The cleaner phoned the police, who phoned the doc. Everyone assumed it was a heart attack or something. Fuck. Actually, where is the cleaner? She's sodded off and left the doors open. Anyone could have walked in on this.'

'Just as well they're all too busy gawking at the film stars or hunting for lost treasure. Listen, are you okay to do what you need to do? Whatever happens, they'll still want time of death and photos. I'll phone Sergeant Wilson. She may be in hospital, but she can at least tell me who we need to contact.'

. . .

Half an hour later, Penny laid her phone down on the bench. The bench at the back, not the front. She was hardly going to sit next to what was left of Colin Dogood, saying things like "Hiya, you know that man on Vik you thought had a heart attack? Well, he's lying here in a pool of blood with a vet in shower cap shoes and Marigolds shoving a thermometer where the sun no longer shines." That would be disrespectful, Penny felt.

'I spoke to Superintendent Ferguson. She says she can't get a team to us until the day after tomorrow. Anyone who isn't off with food poisoning has been roped into the Balmoral thing or a firearms incident in Union Square.'

Penny stopped and wondered whether the Union Square thing…no, it couldn't possibly be. Could it? She shrugged off the thought and continued.

'She's going to get someone up from Edinburgh and has asked us to secure the scene for now. Obviously, we can't leave the body here, so I said we'd video everything then put it in cold storage until the police get here.'

Jim looked concerned. 'And by cold storage you mean?'

'I phoned Doc Harris. The morgue at the hospital is full. Mrs Taylor, as you know.' Penny began to tick people off on her fingers. 'Then there's the line dancers who do-si-doed the wrong way and electrocuted themselves on an amplifier, then there's Mr Fisher (hill-walking accident) and Geordie Mantiss.'

'Man Tits the English teacher? He was ancient when we were at school. Surprised he's still around. Well, obviously he's not still around because he just died. He must have been a fair age, though,' said Jim.

'A hundred and three, apparently. Mum told me about it. He fell asleep while reading a book and simply never woke up. They found him in his armchair, a smile on his face, still holding the book. What a peaceful way to go.' Penny glanced at the bloody cadaver on the floor and sighed. 'Poor Colin. What are we going to do with him?'

'There will be loads of stuff for wrapping things in the back. I'll go and have a look,' Jim offered.

He returned ten minutes later with what looked like a giant roll of cling film and a white, cotton sheet.

'Pallet wrap,' he told her. 'By the way, I had a look for spare keys back there and couldn't find any. Right, you take an end of this stuff and we'll lay strips of it out on the floor. We'll put the sheet on top, then pop him on and seal him up. That way, everything that's on him will stay within the sheet.'

'Okay,' said Penny, 'but before we do that, can we have a peek at what's in his mouth?'

Jim shuddered. 'Ugh. Isn't this creepy enough for you? The man's lying there with his skull caved in and you want to go poking around?'

'For once in your life, Mr Space, you're right. There's no point in contaminating the crime scene any more than is necessary. I'll take a look once he's on the sheet.'

Jim shook his head but said nothing. He simply handed her the loose end of the pallet wrap and walked backwards, carefully unfurling a length onto the floor.

They worked in silence, and soon the makeshift body bag was ready for its occupant.

Jim took his phone from his pocket, walking around to carefully record the scene from every angle, then asked, 'Heads or tails?'

'Tails,' said Penny, pulling on a pair of gloves. 'Less messy and a bit lighter. Also, you can probably reach to pick him up without standing in the blood.'

She could scarcely believe those words had come out of her mouth. Two hours ago, she'd been about to Google pastrami, so she could put her father's mind at rest. Now, here she was, about to cling film a corpse. Goodness, he was stiff as a board. Freaky, but a lot easier to move.

As Jim lifted the shoulders, Penny lifted the legs and, carefully, they laid Colin onto the sheet in the same position as they'd found him.

'Do you know how long he's been dead?' she asked.

'Not precisely, but the body temperature and rigor mortis suggest he was killed about six or seven last night.'

'What on earth would he be doing in the museum at that time?'

'Who knows. Let's get him wrapped up and the police can worry about the rest.'

'Hang on a sec. I want to see his mouth.'

Penny bent over the corpse and peered at the shiny object protruding from between its shattered teeth. She could just make out some engraving on what appeared to be a silver handle. She took out her phone and shone the torch onto the man's battered face. The opening of his jaw was unnaturally wide, and despite the blood and tissue, she could see that whatever was on the other end of the handle must be a large object which had been rammed down his throat with some force. She said a silent prayer that it had been done post-mortem because, if he'd been alive, it didn't bear thinking about. This was going to stay with her for a long time and she didn't want to imagine it any worse than it already was.

She stood up and cleared her throat.

'Have you any idea what it is?' asked Jim.

'Not yet,' she said quietly. 'Let's do what you said. Wrap him up and the police can worry about it.'

Together, they gently folded the sheet around Colin's body then lifted the ends of the pallet wrap to secure it in place. That done, they rolled a few more layers of pallet wrap until what lay before them was unrecognisable as a human being.

'We need to put him somewhere. Like a fridge or a freezer. Good job he's only a little one.,' said Jim.

'We can hardly ask Mrs Hubbard to keep him in her freezer when that's a crime scene on its own,' said Penny.

'I have an idea,' said Jim, removing his rubber gloves and pulling his phone from his pocket. 'Wait there. I'll be back in half an hour.'

. . .

Sitting in the silence of the museum, next to a pool of blood and a murdered man, was definitely the creepiest thing ever, Penny decided. As soon as Jim had left, she'd made a few phone calls. That done, she suddenly felt very vulnerable in this giant mausoleum for the possessions of the long departed, where not so long ago a man had suffered a violent death. With the adrenaline of discovering the body and wrapping it wearing off, she felt quite shaky, and her mind began to play events in a loop. She had tried to distract herself by watching the Vikings video, but it was soon over, and she was once again alone with her racing thoughts.

Well, when life gives you lemons and all that jazz, she thought, may as well put it to some use. She allowed her mind to focus on the shiny handle, closing her eyes as she recalled the engraving on the surface. Some sort of lettering and a pattern. She pictured the thing, trying to make out the lettering, but it wasn't clear. All she got was an overall impression of perhaps a crest. Yet it felt like she should know what it was. There was something familiar about it, but every time she sensed that the answer was in reach, it danced away again. She had begun to feel quite frustrated with her own miscreant brain when a sound called her back to the present.

Penny opened her eyes and strained to listen to the distant, slightly off-key, rendition of Greensleeves. Slowly, the tune got closer and louder until, with a short, disappointed wail, it was cut off.

Grinning, she shuffled back through the museum and threw open the front door in time to see Jim pull up in Marie Knox's pink and white ice cream van.

He wound down the window and shouted, 'Marie isn't using it, so she said we could borrow it. We just need to keep charging the freezer overnight. We can park it at my place.'

'I never thought I'd say this, but you're a bloody genius, Jim.'

Jim got out of the vehicle and sauntered towards her, looking like the very cleverest of clogs.

'I can't believe it's taken you this long to notice. Anyway, we can't move him until we find someone to mind the shop. No keys, open door and missing cleaner, remember?'

'Don't worry,' said Penny, her own face reflecting a certain self-esteem in the clog department, 'it's all taken care of. Losers Club is on its way.'

CHAPTER 4

Mrs Hubbard and Elsie were first to arrive, trundling up the High Street at a stately pace in Elsie's library van. There was a soft squeal as the vehicle shuddered to a halt behind the ice cream van, followed by a rattle and two thunks as its occupants disembarked.

There had clearly been some words had on the way, with Mrs Hubbard grumbling loudly that it was like driving around in a mobile crack den.

'I don't know why you would say that,' said Elsie, buttoning up her second favourite raincoat and tightening her headscarf against the morning chill. 'I sell special medicine to arthritic pensioners and those in need. It has nothing to do with cracks or dens.'

'I've heard about you gangstas. I watch TV. The next thing you know, you'll be riding your pimp,' declared Mrs Hubbard.

Elsie looked horrified and Penny suppressed a smile as she intervened between the bickering pair. 'I think you mean pimping your ride, Mrs H, and I doubt that will be necessary. It's not as if Dad and Elsie are hanging around the school gates. It's more like a…a…gardening hobby they share. In Dad's shed. With UV lights and temperature controls.'

'Well, I heard Eileen's granny is one of her best customers, and I don't think Mrs Campbell would look too kindly on Elsie for selling her mother cannabis,' said Mrs Hubbard.

Elsie, usually preferring quiet revenge over direct confrontation, surprised Penny by telling Mrs Hubbard firmly, 'Jeanie Campbell is also one of my best customers.'

She tugged at her pocket, eventually withdrawing a battered notebook and a pair of spectacles. She perched the spectacles on the end of her nose, licked a finger and began flicking through the pages. 'Here, look, page twelve. Campbell, Jeanie – Friday rounds – Contemporary Romance and seven grams.'

Jim shuffled awkwardly. His dad had been seeing Eileen's mum for a while now. What exactly had they been getting up to?

He cleared his throat and asked, 'What about Space, Ivor? Is he in your book there, Elsie?'

Elsie tapped the side of her nose. 'Client confidentiality and data protection. I'm forbidden by the library authorities from disclosing details of my library van rounds.'

'But you just said that Jeanie–'

'That was different. It was a necessary disclosure.'

'Necessary how?'

'Necessary to stop Minty Hubbard blabbing to the whole island about old Mrs Campbell.' She turned to Mrs Hubbard. 'If you start gossiping about this, Araminta, it will be like a line of dominoes; they'll all go down. And one of those dominoes is a bit close to home and has been known to spend time in Len Hopper's shed when he tells you he's at the bowling club, if you get my drift. Now, that's all I'll say on the matter.'

Elsie pursed her lips and put the notebook back in her pocket, signalling that the matter was closed.

Mrs Hubbard gulped, stunned by the news that her Douglas was involved in the enterprise. She decided to drop the subject, instead hooking her arm inside Elsie's and giving her a friendly nudge.

'I'm very impressed that you can understand grams. I've never quite got my head around them. Give me pounds and ounces any day.'

Back on safe territory, Elsie beamed at her oldest friend.

'Thank you, Minty. My baking has fair come along now I don't have to convert everything. I'll treat you to some of my special brownies sometime.'

'Oh, that sounds fine,' said Mrs Hubbard. 'Are you making a batch for the church sale?'

'No. I'll just be helping Mrs Hay with her peppermint slices.'

Jim was just about to ask a very important question about the exact recipe for Mrs Hay's peppermint slices, when they were interrupted by another, smaller van pulling in behind Elsie's library van.

Gordon and Fiona, resplendent in matching denim dungarees, emerged and joined the group on the pavement outside the museum. Penny was struck by Gordon's appearance. He was always a little shabby and unkempt, with his bushy beard and old clothes, but that was to be expected when you were a smallholder working all hours to make a tiny living off your organic produce. And Gordon and Fiona's produce was definitely more organic than most, thought Penny, recalling the composting toilet. Today, however, Gordon looked as though he'd slept in his dungarees and hadn't had a rainwater bath in weeks. His red hair was lank, and his eyes were sunken, suggesting some rough nights recently. She hoped that Fiona hadn't been on the vodka again. Poor man could only spend so many nights holding back Fiona's hair after her now legendary drinking sessions with Captain Rab's brother, Kev. Although Penny doubted that this was the cause. Fiona was as perky as always, and Penny suspected that within the big yellow bag she was clutching were some plastic tubs full of delicious home-grown salad. Delicious if you could get past the thought of the composting toilet and the home-grown fertiliser, that is.

Penny gave a small shudder and switched on her smile. 'Thanks for coming. We're just missing Sandra Next Door and Eileen. As soon as they get here, Jim and I will explain what's going on.'

While they'd waited for the other Losers Club members to arrive, Jim and Penny had moved Colin Dogood's body to the ice cream van. He now lay on the floor, waiting to be loaded into the freezer just as soon as the stiffness wore off a bit and he became a bit more bendy. He was, as Jim had said, a little one and the freezer was a decent size, but they couldn't risk breaking anything by trying to jam him in there. Jim had guessed that things would be a little more pliable tonight, so that was something to look forward to.

Penny conceded that these were fairly gruesome thoughts to be having of a morning. What she wouldn't give to be back at Valhalla right now, hugging her father despite his vomity moustache, and bickering with her mother. She might even be nice to Alex over lunch. Anything other than this horror show into which they'd unwittingly stumbled.

Suddenly, she felt quite drained. It must have shown on her face because Jim looked concerned and said solicitously, 'Are you okay? Do you want to go for a sit down in the ice cream van?'

'Are you off your rocker?' Penny retorted. 'I mean, thanks for the concern, but…'

She let the sentence tail off as she saw the dawning look of comprehension in Jim's eyes.

'Aye,' he said, 'Sorry, not exactly a spot for quiet meditation. Look, here's Sandra Next Door's car coming up the road.'

He seemed relieved by the distraction, as if this would somehow grant him a "get out of jail free card" for having suggested that Penny go and relax next to the dead body. It wouldn't. Penny filed it away to add to the growing list of All

The Times Jim Has Been Annoying that she'd been compiling since he'd picked her up from the ferry. Top of that list was taking her to find the dead body in the first place. Yet she could see that he, too, was stressed, so there was no point in arguing right now. Far better to focus on the fact that Sandra Next Door appeared to have picked Eileen up on the way and Penny was delighted to see her best friend. She rushed to give her a hug.

'Hello, Winnie the Pooh,' she said, referencing the names they used for each other when they had been coordinating via walkie talkie during their investigation into Old Archie's death last year. Somehow, the nicknames had stuck.

'Are you okay, Rubber Duck?' asked Eileen, leaning back and regarding Penny's pallor.

'Just tired,' Penny told her. 'But now you and Sandra Next Door are here, we can go inside and explain what this is about. Alright there, Sandra Next Door?'

The older woman patted her neat, blonde bob, as if a stray hair might somehow have escaped the lavish attentions of the monster can of Silvikrin kept permanently on her dressing table. They had all agreed that if they were ever caught in a rockfall, everyone would hide under Sandra. Not even a two-ton boulder could make a dent in that hairdo.

'Your mother's cat has been doing its business in my begonias again. And don't even get me started on the dog. If you can't do something about the incessant barking, I'm calling the council.'

'Lovely to see you too, Sandra Next Door,' said Penny. She turned to the group and pointed a thumb in the direction of the museum. 'Shall we go in now?'

Penny had been dreading going back into the museum, but with her group of weight-loss buddies chattering away, the place felt lighter somehow, as if all it had ever needed was seven well-padded Scots and a little, skinny librarian to bring it to life.

Mrs Hubbard was tipping the contents of a carrier bag

onto the bench by the door, saying, 'When you told me you were putting together a makeshift kit to go and see Doc Harris' patient, I didn't realise it was to attend a death, so I've brought along some extras in case we need them.'

'It wasn't to come here Mrs H,' said Jim. 'I had to see one of his other patients at short notice last night.'

'Ooh,' said Mrs Hubbard, immediately sensing a tale to be had. 'Who were you going to see and is it anything to do with the ice cream van outside? Because I know Marie Knox is expecting soon. Is it the baby?' She suddenly looked worried. 'The baby is okay, isn't he?'

'Sorry, as Elsie says, confidentiality and data protection.' Jim saw the expression on Mrs Hubbard's face and relented slightly. 'But the baby's fine.'

'Ha!' said Mrs Hubbard triumphantly. 'So, it was Marie Knox.' A sharp nudge from Elsie interrupted her and she immediately looked apologetic. 'Sorry, dearie, take no notice of me. I'm just an old gossip. Here you go, anyway, every shower cap and rubber glove in the shop, free of charge.'

Jim thanked her then jumped, startled by Penny who suddenly clapped her hands and called for silence. There was an immediate lull in the conversation, with only Fiona's voice ringing incongruously loud as she berated Gordon.

'I don't know what's going on with you these days!' She regarded the silent group and looked sheepish. 'Sorry, Penny. Carry on.'

'Right. We are gathered here today to guard a crime scene. As I explained on the phone, it looks like Colin Dogood, the museum curator, has been murdered and it's our task to–'

'Investigate!' Eileen cried, sounding overjoyed at the news of the murder.

'–make sure that nobody accesses the crime scene until the police get here tomorrow evening.'

There was a babble of questions.

'Where *is* the crime scene?'

'Can we access the crime scene?'

'How was he murdered?'

'Is his body still there?'

'What are you going to do about Mojo shitting in my begonias?'

Penny clapped her hands again and the questions stopped.

'We've moved Colin's body and we're going to store it in Marie's ice cream freezer. Sorry, Mrs Hubbard. We don't mean to exclude you, and we know you are very good at frozen corpses. It's just that, well, what with the investigation and all.' Penny shrugged and gave Mrs Hubbard an apologetic look.

'It's alright, dearie,' said Mrs Hubbard. 'The big freezer's a no-go zone and the little one is packed to the brim with ice lollies. I have nowhere to keep the poor man. Anyway, my Douglas has already said we're to have no more corpsicles. Apparently, it's bad for business. Although I'm not sure how it can be any worse than me poisoning half the island.'

Gordon gave a small, strangled yelp at this and rushed forward to comfort Mrs Hubbard, whose eyes were now glistening with unshed tears. Elsie put an arm around her and with the other arm, shooed Gordon away.

'It's fine if you don't want to be here, Mrs Hubbard. We won't mind if you want to go home,' Penny told her anxiously.

Mrs Hubbard took a deep breath to steady herself and said, 'No. I'm better if I'm kept busy. Carry on.'

Penny didn't entirely agree with the elderly woman but respected her wishes and continued. 'The problem is that the cleaner who called in what was thought to be a heart attack has upped and vanished with the keys, leaving the door unlocked. If there are any spares, we don't know where they are. The police have asked us to preserve the scene as far as possible, so I propose we draw up a guard duty rota and look for the keys.'

'Where exactly is the scene?' Fiona asked.

'Good question,' said Jim. 'It's over by the Vikings video.'

'Oh, the Vikings in Vik video,' said Fiona. 'I can never say that when I'm drunk. Can we go and see it?'

A murmur of agreement spread around the group. They were all curious to see the crime scene.

Jim sighed and began handing out shower caps. 'Okay. Just this once and then we leave it alone, deal?' The others nodded. 'Aye, well, put these on your feet and follow me. When we get there, stand back and don't touch anything.'

If Sergeant Wilson had been there, they'd have been on the receiving end of a huge telling off for interfering with her crime scene, Jim thought. But she wasn't here, and the nosy buggers would only go and have a look the minute they were on their own anyway, he reasoned, so may as well get it over and done with.

He guided the group as they slipped and slid across the shiny floor towards the video display. Then they turned the corner and there was a collective "aw" of disappointment. Nobody knew quite what they'd expected to see, but the solitary pool of blood felt like an anti-climax.

'That's it?' asked Sandra Next Door. 'I'm to spend the next day and a half guarding a few pints of congealed blood on the floor?'

'Well deduced, Sandra Next Door,' said Jim. 'That's exactly what you'll be doing. So, maybe say a wee prayer that we find the keys.'

The group gravitated towards the benches furthest from the dark red puddle and sat down to formulate a plan.

'Just to be clear,' said Penny, 'we're not investigating.'

'But we always investigate murders,' said Eileen.

'One murder,' said Jim firmly.

'Cordon bleu! There has only been one murder, so technically that's always.' Eileen turned to Penny and winked. 'That's French for holy moly, in case you were wondering.'

'Your French is coming along a treat,' Penny assured her, as her eyebrows slowly lowered themselves back into place.

Eileen nodded enthusiastically. 'They gave me a part-time job at the tourist office, on account of me being cunnilingual.'

Penny stifled a laugh. 'We can have a tête-à-tête about it later. For now, I need to get everyone briefed.'

'Mange tout,' said Eileen, nodding solemnly.

'How was he murdered?' asked Fiona, who, at the mention of mange tout, had begun unpacking her yellow bag and handing out paper plates.

'We're not really sure,' said Jim, helping himself from the proffered box of tuna salad. 'His face was bashed into a bloody pulp and there was something sticking out of his mouth, so I'm guessing he was either battered or suffocated or both.'

Elsie dug around in her handbag and produced a block of low-fat cheese and some wholemeal baps.

'Cheers, Elsie,' said Jim, accepting a knife from Fiona and unwrapping the cheese.

A tub of vegetables, neatly sliced and diced, appeared from the depths of Fiona's bag and was passed around.

'We've had great results with our vegetables this year. Gordon has been adding hair to the soil to help it retain moisture,' she told everyone.

'I didn't know you could do that,' said Mrs Hubbard.

'Hair's great for composting, but it takes a long time to break down. If you take small pieces, though, and add them to the soil around the roots, it helps them stay hydrated.'

'And when you say small pieces?' asked Mrs Hubbard.

'We've been experimenting since last year and finally found the best ones. Gordon's been man-scaping like mad and storing it all in a box. His pubes are surprisingly fast-growing.'

There was an awkward silence as the others discreetly checked their vegetables for any strays. Fiona beamed proudly at Gordon and helped herself to a carrot stick. It was Penny who broke the tension.

'Are we seriously having a picnic in the middle of a crime scene?'

The others stared mutely at her. Eventually, Mrs Hubbard piped up with, 'We always share a meal at Losers Club.'

Everyone nodded and once more got stuck into the salad and cheese.

'But this isn't Losers Club!' Penny exclaimed. Then looked around the group, all of whom were studiously ignoring her, and sighed. 'Never mind. Give me a plate, Fiona. Sergeant Wilson would have a fit if she caught us doing this.'

Jim had the grace to look guilty. He'd been thinking the same thing, but there were times when it was matter over mind and the current rumbling of his belly signalled that this was one of them.

'Just as well I brought us a healthy pudding,' said Eileen, producing an enormous apple crumble and a packet of ready-made custard from the cavernous innards of her own bag. 'Fruit and dairy. My two favourite food groups. I learned that from you, Penny. Also, if he got his head bashed in, why isn't there blood all over the walls?'

'Have you been watching CSI again, Eileen? You know the entomologist gives you nightmares,' said Sandra Next Door kindly. Since investigating Old Archie's murder, the two had struck up an unlikely friendship. With Eileen being happily oblivious to the cruel world most of the time, Sandra's barbs simply bounced off her. As a result, Sandra didn't bother trying to provoke Eileen and tended to be a much nicer person around her. If only she could do the same for the rest of us, thought Penny.

Eileen looked delighted with herself. 'You can't do much with blood without there being cast-off or splatter of some sort. Either he was killed with the first blow, bled out but not from an artery, was shot and the bullet is still inside him or was strangled. Or maybe poisoned. So, his face must have been battered after he was dead.' She took a big bite of her cheesy bap and regarded her fellow diners, who had lapsed into a stunned silence. 'Or it could have been an alien probe,' she added, through a mouthful of bread.

Everyone relaxed. Normal Eileen service had resumed.

'Heard and understood, Detective Eileen' said Gordon, emerging from the self-imposed silence he'd been keeping since being rebuffed in his attempt to comfort Mrs Hubbard earlier. 'It sounds to me like it's overkill, pun unintentional. If someone has killed him then carried on after he died, that's anger. The attack on the face makes it personal. It's likely to be someone he knew who harboured strong emotions towards him.'

'Criminal Minds?' asked Mrs Hubbard. 'I like the older fellow in that. You know the one. Whatshisname. Beardy. Very distinguished looking.'

Gordon stroked his own ginger whiskers and nodded. 'Rossi. Aye, you can get them all on Amazon. Although I'm more of a Penelope Garcia man myself.'

'Jeeze, this is like déjà vu, only in a museum, with an ice cream van. We're *not* investigating,' said Penny.

'Ooh, déjà vu, voulez-vous coucher avec moi ce soir?' interjected Eileen.

'Eileen, I love you, but you're just babbling nonsense now. Before we start drawing up a guard duty rota, does anyone know the cleaner? It would make sense to see if we can at least ask her for the keys before any of us have to spend the night in this creepfest.'

There were shakes of the head all round. Nobody knew who the cleaner was.

'You could try Colin Dogood's cottage. He might have some spare keys there,' Elsie suggested. 'It's up near Hillside farm. The wee white house at the bottom of the big hill. You can see it from the main road.'

'I have a question,' said Sandra Next door, putting her hand up. 'Why has it taken until now for Elsie to tell us that she knows where Colin lived?'

Elsie remained unperturbed. 'I'm sorry, Sandra Next Door.

My hearing aid must be playing up again. I never seem to be able to hear a word you're saying.'

'Great idea, Elsie,' said Penny. 'Jim and I will head on up there and take a look.'

'We will?' said Jim, uncomfortably aware that Penny's disregard for locks and privacy had previously almost got them into very hot water.

'Yes, we will. Gordon and Fiona, would you mind taking the first watch? Then if we find the keys, Elsie and Mrs Hubbard don't need to make the trip back from the village, Eileen doesn't need to ask her mum to babysit and Sandra Next Door can…hmm…do Sandra things like…erm…call the council about Timmy's barking.'

'And the shitting cat,' Sandra Next Door reminded her.

'And the shitting cat,' Penny agreed.

CHAPTER 5

The drive towards Hillside farm didn't take long. It was a road with which Jim was all too familiar (Randy Mair the farmer practically having him on speed dial) and he handled the bumps and bends with practised ease.

'Slow down,' said Penny.

'That's the thing with you women,' said Jim, 'no appreciation for getting from a to b. You just tootle around, admiring the view, waving to your friends, planning your wardrobe.'

'No, slow down!' Penny repeated. 'We're almost there. Look, I think that's the turning up ahead.'

'Oh,' mumbled Jim, unable to think of anything else to say.

'Just as well one of us was admiring the view,' said Penny, smirking.

'Aye, well.'

For once, Jim had no witty rejoinder. Instead, he took the junction slightly too fast and felt a grim sense of satisfaction when Penny clung to the seatbelt for dear life. The satisfaction, however, was short lived as Karma sent a stone straight at his windshield. Watching a series of cracks spread across the glass, Jim did a quick calculation of just how much his bout of petulance was going to cost him. Quite a lot, and that didn't even include the humble pie.

'Sorry,' he told Penny. 'I'm being an arse and taking things out on you. I wish we'd never left Valhalla this morning. The only good bit was Eileen's apple crumble. Oh, and you calling me a genius.'

Penny gave him a wan smile. 'It's okay. We're just tired and things have been fraught. Let's see what we can find at Colin's cottage and get back to the museum.'

'You're not going to break in, are you?' asked Jim nervously.

'What? Little old me, with my head full of friends and wardrobes and nice views? Nah. Whatever gave you that idea?'

'You've got…what is it they say?…*form* for it. I'm not getting caught doing that again.'

'It would be a lot easier if we had Colin's keys. We never talked about him being naked. What do you reckon happened to his clothes?'

As they bumped down the narrow old track towards the cottage, Jim gave this some thought.

'The killer must have taken them. Unless Colin wandered round the museum at night, starkers. Come to think of it, he was an odd fish. Been on the island a few years but never really integrated. Like, you never saw him in the pub or at the football, so I wonder who his friends were.'

'No idea,' said Penny. 'I didn't know him at all. Only met him the once, when I took the kids to the museum. God, they were bored out of their minds, and he was doing his best to give them an entertaining personal tour. We were the only people in the place and there's him jumping around, pretending he was one of Prince Charlie's men, imaginary claymore at the ready. Come to think of it, he was the one who told me about the Vik treasure. I can't believe I grew up here and never heard of it.'

'Most of the islanders think it's nonsense; something cooked up for the tourists,' said Jim.

'He told me he was descended from Bruce Duguid, the first secret keeper. When the family emigrated to Australia in the early 20th century, the locals couldn't say or spell Duguid, so they changed it to the English version, Dogood,' Penny explained. 'I thought it was fascinating, but the twins were whining that they wanted to go home, so we cut the visit short. I wish I'd gone back to learn more. He was actually a very good storyteller. When we're in his house, it might be worth having a poke around to find out a bit about his life.'

Jim had seen this one coming.

'Oh no,' he said. 'We go straight in, get the keys and straight out. If we get caught meddling, it'll be us who are locked up. We're already in enough trouble if they find out we had a picnic at the crime scene. You said it yourself; we are *not* investigating.'

He pulled up in front of the small white cottage dwarfed by the enormous hill behind it. What had once been a garden surrounding the house, was now a tangled wilderness of stinging nettles and thorns. Someone had hacked a path to the front door and Jim could see what could only be described as a vague path leading from the door, round towards the back of the house.

'You stay here,' he told Penny. 'I'll go round the back and see if there's a way in.'

Penny waited by the front door while Jim bravely tackled his first patch of nettles. There were shouts of "ooh ya bugger" as his jumper snagged on thorns. He struggled on, vainly attempting to shield his face from the tiny barbs. Soon, any uncovered bits of flesh were a mass of scratches and raised hives where the thorns had torn at him and the nettles seared his skin. His hair stood on end and there was a long gash across the front of his jumper, where a particularly stubborn thorn had reluctantly ceded a game of tug of war.

Eventually, Jim fought his way through and emerged in a

cleared area by the back door. To his left was a small building; what had once been an outdoor toilet and was now used for storage, he presumed. He rattled the door, but it was locked. He peered through the small window to his right and found himself staring into a gloomy kitchen. A pile of dishes lay by the sink, waiting for a wash that would likely never happen. Unless Dogood had relatives who would clear out his stuff, of course. Jim realised that he hadn't given any thought to Colin's next of kin.

He gave up on the kitchen and moved along to the next window at the other side of the back door, expecting to see another gloomy room. Instead, to his surprise, the light was on, and someone was moving around in there.

Jim quickly ducked out of sight, then slowly raised his head above the windowsill, just in time to see the figure approaching the window. He ducked again but heard the window above him open. He tried to tuck himself into the wall, make himself smaller, as he said a silent prayer to whichever god was listening, to please, please, please make him invisible, then gave a high-pitched squeal when a voice above him said, 'For God's sake, Jim, get yourself in here. I'll open the back door for you.'

The window closed with a sharp clatter, and he heard a key turn in the back door. A moment later Penny was ushering him inside.

'You look like you should be standing in a field at Hillside farm, scaring the birds,' she told him.

'What the actual fuck are you doing?' said Jim, the words coming out in a high tremolo, as the sudden departure of adrenaline from his system left him shaking.

'Well, the front door was open, so I let myself in.'

'Was it actually open, or did it have a bit of assistance from you?' asked Jim, suspicious.

'Honest, it really was unlocked. I tried the handle and in I went.'

They were standing in a tiny kitchen. There was nothing

remarkable about it. Cupboards below, cupboards above, two drawers, small fridge, kettle, sink and cooker; purely functional and not so much as a herb rack or toaster in sight.

Jim peeked inside one of the drawers. Fork, knife, spoon and tin opener. Counting the cutlery by the sink, Jim reckoned there was enough here for two.

'He wasn't exactly living the high life,' he commented, sliding open the other drawer.

Where most people had an odds and sods drawer, full of stray playing cards, keys from two houses ago and a random selection of elastic bands, Colin had one neatly folded tea towel.

'It's like he barely lived here. How long had been on the island?'

Penny tried to recall her one and only conversation with Colin.

'I don't know, but he knew Granny Cairns and she died at least three years ago. I was telling him about Timmy, and I remember him saying how fond he was of Granny Cairns' sheepdog.'

'There's a blast from the past. I remember she lived in that cottage just outside the village, with no electricity or phone. She took water from a well. Used to walk the mile down to Mrs Hubbard's Cupboard for her milk and papers every day, rain or shine. Did she not end up in the old people's home?'

'No. She resisted all attempts to shift her. Said she'd go out the way she was born. That must have been a terrible birth because a spark from her coal fire set the whole place alight and she burned to a crisp. Mrs Hubbard told me all about it. Her nephew kept the dog and sold the land. There's a new bungalow there now, you know. Belongs to that twat with the white Range Rover who only visits twice a year. It's quite sad, really, to think that a woman spent ninety years on this earth and there's not a trace of it left.'

While they'd been talking, Jim had poked around the cupboards and cooker, finding nothing other than a few tins of soup and a handwritten note which turned out to be a scribbled recipe for fish pie. They agreed that this was hardly likely to lead them to keys or cleaner, so decided to repair to the living room.

'By the way, I had a look on Colin's computer while I was waiting for you. Unfortunately, it's password protected,' said Penny.

'Thank fuck for that,' said Jim. 'Sergeant Wilson would have had our guts for garters if you broke his computer,'

'Fortunately, Colin keeps all his passwords in a notebook in his desk drawer.'

Jim groaned. 'What have you done?'

'I've done gone and found out some interesting stuff, Mr Space.'

'What have you found, Ms Nosey Bugger?'

'A list of his favourite fences.'

Jim frowned. 'Well, I've heard of trainspotters writing down train numbers before, but I didn't know you could do it with fences.'

'Are you being thick on purpose?'

'Of course,' said Jim. 'How do you know they're fences?'

'Because he wrote "A List of My Favourite Fences" at the top. He wasn't exactly the brains of Britain, or even synapses of Scotland, was he? I mean, who leaves their password book next to their computer and evidence of their crimes lying about? Certainly not someone who was expecting trouble. Looks like it found him anyway, though. Do you think he might have been stealing from the museum?'

'Maybe...probably. Let's have a look at that list. Can you print it out?'

Penny bit her bottom lip and frowned. 'Won't the police notice if I print something?'

'That horse has already bolted,' said Jim. 'I'm no Bill Gates, but I think they'll probably notice that a dead man has somehow logged onto his computer.'

'Can't you erase it? There must be a way to delete the record.'

'Just print the damn thing and I'll ask Gordon later. He's good at stuff like this.'

Penny clicked the mouse a few times and the printer came to life with a whir. A minute later, they watched as a sheet of paper slid onto the tray underneath and the machine whirred and clattered its way back to standby.

Jim grabbed the printout and scanned the neat rows of black letters, running his finger down the list until it halted by a particular name.

'Well, bugger me with a prickle of hedgehogs.'

Fiona was in the back room of the museum. She'd never gone through a Staff Only door before and was quite disappointed to find a small office and a tea point with a small fridge, kettle and teabags. She wasn't sure what she'd expected, but Narnia would have been nice.

She pushed open a door at the back of the office and discovered what was clearly meant to be a storeroom for artefacts not on display, although currently it housed only a crateful of rocks, a deer's head and a silver tankard. Now, this was more like it. She took the silver tankard down from the shelf and went to switch the kettle on.

'I don't think we're supposed to be wandering round making cups of tea,' said a voice from the doorway.

Startled, Fiona jumped and gave a little squeal, spilling the sugar she was tipping into the tankard.

'Gordon! Look what you made me do. That's about nine sugars in there now. Never mind. I'll need it for the shock. There's only one cup, so we'll have to share.' She waggled the tankard at him.

Gordon knew there was no point in arguing. His motto with Fiona was "go with the flow." She was this kind, beautiful soul who grew vegetables and got off her tits on vodka once in a while. She made friends easily, far more easily than him, and was utterly loyal. Without her, he'd have been a hermit living on baked beans. And you certainly didn't want to be living in a wee hermit cave, dealing with the after-effects of a baked bean diet. Instead, this woman had shared her dream with him, become his family and given him the courage to set up a new life with her on Vik. Quite simply, she was his world.

Which is why he couldn't tell her about the terrible thing he'd done.

Losing her would mean losing himself again, and selfish as it was, he couldn't face life without her. These days, all he could see for his future was darkness. Rationally, he knew he had a great life. Yet the feeling that it could be swept away by this one monstrous deed made his stomach burn with anxiety. More than once, he'd thought about just driving his car over the cliff. Escaping this feeling. It was only a thought, but it was always there, ready to float to the surface no matter that he pushed it down as far as he could. It would almost be a relief to get away from what he'd done and the anxiety, the horror, the realisation that his life was built on quicksand and that any moment everything could be taken away. He couldn't do it, though. He looked at Fiona, sniffing a pint of milk, scrunching up her nose then deciding that it would just about do, and he knew he couldn't do it to her. He couldn't cause her that much pain, even though what was surely coming would devastate them both. Maybe if he'd told her at the beginning, but it had all gone too far. It was beyond saying "I did something stupid." His silence had made things a hundred times worse and now he was trapped in a nightmare of his own making.

'It's not bad,' said Fiona, handing over the tankard. 'Try a bit.'

Gordon obligingly took a tentative sip of the hot liquid.

'Jeeze, how much sugar?'

'I know,' said Fiona happily. 'Penny has us all minding our

healthy eating so much, it's quite nice to have a sweet hit sometimes.'

'You ate half of Eileen's apple crumble,' Gordon reminded her.

'Oh, right, yes. Funny how these things slip your mind. I could have sworn I've only had five calories all day.' Unrepentant, Fiona reclaimed the tankard and took a hefty swig. 'I'll do some exercise to work it off.'

She placed the tankard on top of the fridge and shuffled to the door, intent on giving herself a free tour of the museum.

'I'll come with you,' said Gordon from behind her.

'Are you admiring my bum in these dungarees?' she asked, turning to give him a cheeky wink.

'I'm admiring all of you. Always,' said Gordon, his eyes firmly on her bottom, his mind filing away this moment for the day when it all fell apart.

Fiona frowned. Gordon was the sort of man who expected her to know that he loved her, without it needing to be said. In fact, he never said anything unless it needed to be said.

'Seriously, what's going on with you? You're going around with a face like a smacked arse and you keep telling me you love me. Something's up.'

Gordon tried to smile and shrug nonchalantly, but the weight of the world on his shoulders turned it into a grimacing twitch.

'Nothing. It's like I told you. I just haven't been feeling myself.'

'You look like you've been feeling Eeyore. I don't mean physically. Not like a donkey pervert. More just channelling his spirit. What you need is a Pooh.'

'No, it's not an upset stomach. I'm a bit low and not sleeping right. Can we just leave it and go for a walk round the museum?'

'No, we can't "just leave it." I want to get to the bottom of this. Tell me what's wrong. Please?'

'Just leave it, Fiona, for God's sake.' Gordon could feel his stress levels rising in tune with his voice.

'I won't,' said Fiona, her own voice also rising. 'You've been like this for days. What am I supposed to do? Ignore it and hope you come round? You haven't even checked on the carrots all week and I've had to do everything in the greenhouse on my own. The greenhouse is *your* thing. It takes two of us to make a living and I'm starting to worry about paying the electric bill this month.'

'Aye, well, it would help if you didn't spend half of what we do make down the pub.'

'The pub?!' Fiona roared. 'Once a month I go out. It's not too much to ask. I know you'd be happy hiding away at home forever, but I need people. Which brings us back to what I was saying. I need *you*. So, you either tell me what's going on or I'll…I'll…'

Fiona couldn't think what she would do, but it was definitely something drastic.

Gordon deflated, instantly withdrawing back into himself and looking miserable.

'I'm sorry. I'll do better, I promise.' He tried a weak smile. 'Now, can we start this museum tour? You lead the way and I'll be behind you, admiring your bum.'

Realising that whatever was bothering Gordon, she wasn't going to get an answer, Fiona shuffled off on her shower caps, leaving him to follow. If shouting at him wasn't going to do the trick, she could at least try to cheer him up.

She led him to Living Vik, the museum's flagship interactive area where members of the public could dress up as eighteenth-century crofters and play with the items on display. Adopting the formal tone of a museum guide, she pointed at a heavy old flatiron.

'To your left, ladies and gentlemen, we have an instrument for extracting information from annoying husbands. The pointy bit on the end fits neatly between the bollocks when applied with force.'

Fiona smiled. Gordon went an interesting shade of grey and gulped.

'Step away from the iron,' he said.

'I was just joking,' she assured him, hefting the thing in the air and zooming it towards him in a mock stabbing motion.

'I mean it. Put it down.'

Fiona could feel her temper rising again. She laid the iron down on a table with a heavy thunk and started to say, 'Can't even take a joke?' but was interrupted by Gordon.

'Look at the pointy bit,' he said. 'It may not be for bollocks, but I'd swear that's been applied somewhere.'

Fiona bent over to take a closer look at the tip of the iron. Gordon was right; a layer of dried blood coated the dark metal. How on earth had Gordon spotted that? Suddenly, her heart was beating in her throat.

'Sergeant Wilson's going to kill me. My fingerprints are all over the murder weapon.'

'Give it to me,' said Gordon. 'I'll get my fingerprints on it and we'll both be in the shit together.'

For a moment, Fiona thought, Gordon had looked almost relieved. Curious.

CHAPTER 6

'Mac n Cheese,' announced Mary, pronouncing the 'n' as 'en'. 'What do you think the en stands for? Nutritious? Nom nom?' She smiled brightly at the six other people squeezed shoulder to shoulder around the dining table, before digging a large spoon into the glutinous mass and depositing it onto the plate of the guest of honour.

Johnny Munroe eyed the lumpy, yellow heap suspiciously and briefly wondered whether it was too late to claim he was vegan. Instead, he bravely lied through his veneers that it looked lovely and waited until everyone was distracted, before discreetly slipping it under the table, lump by lump, to a delighted Timmy. He was an actor after all.

'So, you guys got a murder on your hands. Any suspects?' he asked.

Penny and Jim exchanged glances and said in unison, 'We're not investigating.'

They had agreed to go back to Valhalla for lunch. Perhaps not exactly agreed. More conceded to a series of demanding texts from Mary and an impassioned plea from Len, "Please answer your mother's texts or I might have to get up from my sick bed and lock her in the shed. LOL."

Penny knew that in dad-text-language, LOL meant Love, Old Len. Other people, however, didn't know this, and it had almost led to a diplomatic incident at the Rotary Club when Len texted his condolences to the chairman upon the death of his dog, Bouncer, who had been somewhat of a club mascot; "Sorry to hear your bad news. Every club should have a Bouncer. LOL."

'You'll have to come with me,' Penny told Jim.

'I'd rather visit Hélène's Drawers,' he said.

'Of course you would. She's like the Nigella of the antiques world.' Bending over the computer desk and running her fingers along its length, Penny lapsed into a very bad French accent. 'Oh, Jeem, rrrrrub your 'ands over zee curves and feel zee wood.'

Jim really did try very hard not to look at the upturned bottom waggling in his direction. 'Aye, I'm definitely feeling zee wood.'

Penny immediately straightened up, her cheeks pink, and cleared her throat.

'Sorry. I didn't mean...I was just doing an impression.' Her protestation tailed off as she noticed the big grin on Jim's face. 'Shut up, you big idiot.'

'I could take Eileen as a translator,' Jim suggested, his eyes glinting with mischief.

'Oh dear, can you imagine it. She'd be like,' Penny once more donned the accent, '"Bonjour, Jeem et Eileen. Would you like to join me for déjeuner?" And Eileen would be like, "Ooh, I'll have the tuna salaud."'

'Why would the owner of the antiques shop and, according to this list, Colin's favourite fence, be asking us to join her for lunch?' asked Jim.

'It was a joke in French. Did you not have a misspent youth looking up swear words in the wee blue French dictionary with the plastic cover that the school made you buy?'

'I thought your youth was misspent round the back of the church hall disco snogging boys.'

'That as well. And on the subject of lunch, you're coming to Mum's. Alex will be there, and I can't do this alone.'

Now, here they were, sitting across from Alex Moon, eating the Americany food that her mother had cooked in order to extend an olive branch to Johnny Munroe for jube jube-gate. Privately, Penny thought an olive branch would have tasted way better than this muck, but her mother had gone to the trouble of stealing an entire block of Monterey Jack from the catering van and hiding it up her kilt, so to not eat the muck would seem churlish.

She braved a forkful, then took a swig of lemonade to unglue her back teeth, and said, 'You see, Mr Munroe, not so long ago we solved the murder of Old Archie the postman and nearly got ourselves killed into the bargain. This time, we've promised the police that we'll preserve the evidence until they get here tomorrow, and that's as far as it goes.'

'We're detective twins, Penny!' said the Hollywood legend who was, almost unbelievably and very surreally, sitting at her parents' dining room table and, Penny noted enviously, slipping his macaroni to the dog. 'I've solved murders too. I'm a seasoned professional, my dear. Didn't you see Death in the Palace?'

'That was a movie,' said Jim.

'Or that time I figured out who assassinated the Pope?'

'Also a movie.'

'And then there was my investigation into the death of the woman who memorised everything by repetition in Murder She Rote.' Johnny regarded Jim's blank look. 'Okay, that one went straight to DVD. My point is, I can help you. I want to help you. If we put our brains together, we can figure this out.'

Penny opened her mouth to remind Johnny that they weren't investigating, but Alex chose that moment to intervene. He reached across the table and laid his hand on hers, giving her the smouldering look that she knew he'd spent hours perfecting in the bathroom mirror when they were married.

'Penny, darling, you simply must let Johnny help. He's not needed on set for a couple of days, so you'll be doing the fellow a favour by giving him something to get his…I must say, Johnny, those are lovely teeth. Did you get them done by that man in LA?' Johnny nodded and Alex continued, 'If you give him something to get his excellent teeth stuck into, we might even be able to find another line for Mary. What do you say?'

I say you're a manipulative salaud, thought Penny, but she looked at the delight on her mother's face and relented.

'Okay, we do want to talk to the owner of the antique shop to find out what she knows about Colin. You can come with us, Johnny, but that's it. No more investigating after that.'

'Oh, thank you, Chunky,' Mary exclaimed, leaning across the table to hug her daughter and accidentally dipping both boobs in the macaroni. She sat back, beaming, seemingly unaware that she was now sporting two pasta nipples.

Johnny was grinning widely, his implausibly white teeth stark against the smooth caramel of his equally implausibly youthful skin.

'After lunch, I'm going straight to Costume for my detective outfit. Hey, twin dudes, you can help me pick something out.'

'Penny, you should come with us to see the set,' said Alex. He turned to Hector and Edith. 'What about that, you pair? Make it a proper family day out?'

Penny really, really wanted to say all the French swear words. You were allowed to say French swear words, weren't you? They weren't real swear words, after all. Not like proper English ones which sounded ten times more sweary in a Scottish accent. She knew this because she'd used her entire collection on Alex when she found out about him and the au-pair. And now the Chief Wankpuffin had her cornered. She saw the hopeful look in the twins' eyes and knew she'd say yes.

Hector and Edith had been weirdly silent over lunch and Penny could guess the reason why. They both had a huge crush on Johnny Munroe. Every time Johnny directed a comment their way, one or other of them would emit a high-pitched squeak. They were used to mixing with the rich and famous and didn't think of their father or their friends' parents as anything out of the ordinary. However, Johnny was a serious A-Lister and, despite the overly-white teeth, disturbingly perfect. The product of a Swedish mother and Puerto Rican father, he was a tall, dark-haired, chisel-jawed demi-god with piercing blue eyes. Ordinarily, Alex was the charismatic, handsome presence dominating the party and oozing pheromones wherever he went, but Johnny took sheer animal sex appeal to a whole other level. Once upon a time, Penny would have offered to snog the face off him, but these days, goodness knows why, she seemed more drawn to the Liam Neeson type. Nevertheless, Penny decided, he seemed like a nice man, and she didn't mind keeping him entertained for a day or two.

Jim was very busy staring at his plate, because punching people in the mouth tended to offend. He'd listened as Alex first manipulated Penny into babysitting Johnny, then into visiting the set with him. He was a slippery one, and Jim was sure Penny hadn't seen the look of triumph in the bastard's eyes when he'd cornered her into the "family day out." Or the sneer when, as an afterthought, he'd grudgingly said, 'Oh, and you can come too if you want, Jim.' Or maybe Jim was imagining the whole thing because he was insanely jealous and would rather get his balls trapped in Randy Mair's cattle grid than be sitting across the table from Alex Moon.

Johnny Munroe seemed okay, if you discounted the fact that the man was incredibly good looking. Hell, even Jim fancied him a wee bit. A thought struck him. What if Penny fancied Johnny? Shit. He glanced sideways at her. She was definitely smiling *a lot* at the man. Leaning forward. Flushed cheeks. Agreeing with everything he said. Noooooooo! All the signs of fancying. Jim shovelled some macaroni cheese into his mouth to distract himself.

Penny was dying a little on the inside. Johnny had just asked her a question, which she'd missed because she was concentrating hard on trying to swallow her mother's revolting macaroni without retching. He had seemed to be expecting an answer, so she'd leant forward, grinned like a maniac and nodded enthusiastically.

'Glad you agree,' said Johnny. 'I'll ask Costume to make one.'

One what? Penny had no idea, but if they were going to visit the set then get to Hélène's Drawers before closing time, they'd better get a wriggle on.

'Come on, you lot,' she said. 'Let's get going. We've got a movie set to see.'

Everyone ignored her and carried on talking, so she tried again.

'Chop, chop. Hector, go and put your shoes on. Edith, go and put your eyebrows on.'

The twins paid no heed.

Mary, however, frowned and said, 'Surely you don't need to go quite yet, Chunky. Now, who wants seconds?'

Penny didn't think she'd ever seen people leave a table quite so quickly.

The film set was far less glamorous than Penny had expected yet a hundred times more interesting. While Alex took the twins to his trailer, Johnny insisted that Penny and Jim accompany him to Costume.

He greeted a short, plump woman with an easy-going, 'Hey, Jenny, meet Jim and Penny, my detective sidekicks.'

Jim and Penny glanced at each other. They had considered Johnny their sidekick, not the other way around. Jim started to protest. However, years of experience had rendered Penny immune to the ego of actors, so she simply rolled her eyes and gave him a small shake of her head to indicate he should let it slide.

Jenny looked bemused as Johnny explained that he was investigating a murder and would require a detective outfit and, so nobody would recognise him, a beard.

'Penny agrees with me that a full beard and moustache would be better than a moustache alone.'

A flush bloomed on Jenny's neck and, frowning, she ran a hand across her brow.

'I'm sorry, Mr Munroe. I don't have time to make you a beard right now. I still have to alter the breeches for tomorrow and some woman has insisted I sew a large pocket on the inside of her kilt. I told her no, but Mr Moon said I had to. You can have a look through what we've got and see if there's an outfit there that suits. I'll try and make you a beard for tomorrow, but no promises.'

Penny felt quite sorry for Jenny. She could see that this was a woman on the edge.

'Johnny, it's okay. Why don't we skip the beard and just find you a nice mac, like Columbo. You remember him, don't you?'

'Columbo had a dog. Can I have a dog?' asked Johnny.

'You can borrow Timmy,' Penny offered.

'Alright. But you'll do the beard, Jenny. I want the beard.'

They left a fretful-looking Jenny and headed for a trailer containing row upon row of clothes. Penny and Jim flicked through the hangers, occasionally extracting something and holding it up for Johnny to inspect. Nothing passed muster. Eventually, rather tired of the whole business and remembering that she was actually supposed to be spending time with her children, Penny declared herself done and headed for the door. About to remonstrate, Johnny turned to follow her. Then stopped. There it was. It had been there all the time and he couldn't believe that they hadn't noticed. Really,

Penny and Jim were so unobservant, and it was just as well he had the keen eye of a three times Oscar-nominated actor. Johnny unhooked the mac from the coat stand by the door and shrugged it on. A perfect fit. He put his hands in the pockets and found three sticks of gum, a pen, a notebook and a cell phone. Excellent! It was like this coat had been made for Detective Johnny Munroe.

He closed his eyes, took a few deep breaths to get into character, then in a terrible Brooklyn accent said, 'Fuhgedaboutit, youse guys. This is the one. Badabing.'

Jim's lower teeth parted ways with his upper teeth, and he felt his eyebrows make a spirited dash for his hairline. He briefly wondered if the actor had done a line of coke while their backs were turned, maybe even heroin. He'd heard about these Hollywood types, with their Columbian and iced whites and herbal blends. Or was that the menu at Cuppachino in Port Vik? Whatever, he should warn Penny, just in case there really was fancying going on.

He rearranged his face and told the actor, 'Erm, I think that coat belongs to someone. You probably shouldn't take it.'

'On everything, this is *the* detective coat, capiche? Badabing,' said Johnny.

'I don't have a clue what he's saying, but we really should introduce him to Eileen,' Penny murmured.

The afternoon sped by, with a tour of the set given by Johnny in full detective mode. The twins were still somewhat dumbstruck, and Penny's toes curled when Hector finally plucked up the courage to ask Johnny, 'Are you um ooh eh erm seeing anyone right now?'

Edith whacked her brother over the head with a rolled-up script and said, in a far better Brooklyn accent than their tour guide, 'Fuck, little dude. Could you *be* any more obvious?'

Hector reddened, drew himself up to his full five foot eight (to his enormous relief, he had had a growth spurt recently) and said, 'Perhaps someone could direct Edith to the Willy Wonka set. They appear to be missing an oompa loompa.'

Edith, who (much to her annoyance) was now slightly shorter than her twin and had gone overboard on the fake tan that morning, immediately shot back with, 'And perhaps someone could direct Hector to the Star Wars set. I believe they're looking for Chewbacca's stunt double.'

Hector, whose growth spurt had come with a surprising amount of body hair, was about to deliver what he was sure would be a devastating comeback, when Johnny said, 'Sorry, little dude, I'm into girls. Or I should say,' he gave Penny a meaningful look, 'beautiful ladies.'

There was an awkward moment where Penny felt herself redden.

Alex, suddenly wondering if, in his fit of sycophancy, he had done the right thing by encouraging Penny to let Johnny tag along with her, cleared his throat and attempted a carefree laugh.

'Ha ha. I'm sure Penny isn't thinking of dating right now.'

Jim scowled and chimed in with, 'Aye, she's not interested in that sort of shenanigans.'

Penny glared at them both. How very dare they? Standing there like a couple of wee boys about to get their favourite toy pinched by the bigger boy. Telling folk what she did or did not think.

'Maybe I am,' she said defiantly, taking Johnny's arm. 'Lay on, Detective Munroe, lay on.'

Mrs Hubbard, Elsie, Sandra Next Door, Eileen, Gordon and Fiona stood in a huddle in the Living Vik display. Fiona, resplendent in an enormous pink bonnet that she'd purloined from the dressing-up box, was showing them the iron.

'Why would you stove someone's head in with an iron

then beat their face after they were dead and put the iron back where you found it?' she asked. 'It makes no sense.'

Mrs Hubbard patted her arm. 'I don't know, dearie. When you get to my age, very little makes sense. Wars, people who are unkind to strangers, pork scratchings. Didn't Penny say he has something in his mouth? That's very interesting.'

Beside her, Elsie stiffened. 'Araminta Hubbard, I know exactly what you're thinking and you're not going to do it.'

'Surely a wee peek wouldn't do any harm.'

Eileen shuddered. 'Cordon bleu, I don't want to have a wee peek.'

'Me neither,' said Fiona, who was trying to squeeze a mobile phone between her ear and the bonnet.

'Oh, for God's sake,' said Sandra Next Door. 'I'll do it. Who has the key for the ice cream van?'

Gordon produced a key from his pocket. 'I'll help you. It might be better if we moved him in here, though. More room to unwrap him and we can clingfilm him back up again afterwards. Has anyone tried Penny and Jim again?'

'Just rang them,' said Fiona. 'Still going straight to voicemail. They must be in a black spot.'

'Right, we'll have to try them again later. You lot put some of that clingfilm stuff down on the floor while me and Sandra Next Door get Colin out of the van.'

It took Gordon and Sandra Next Door a good ten minutes to manoeuvre Colin from van to museum. He was a little less stiff now, which made the operation more difficult. Gordon had the head end while Sandra, muttering darkly about the inside of that van being a health hazard even without the dead body, took the feet. Other than a brief interlude when Gordon dropped his end on the museum steps and Sandra Next Door stopped to call him a blithering idiot, they managed to deliver their human parcel onto the museum floor relatively undamaged.

The group stood gazing down at the bundle that was once their lively, helpful museum curator. There was a moment's silence as they let the fact sink in that they were about to unwrap an actual real-life corpse.

'Well, not a real-life corpse because that would be an oxymoron,' said Gordon.

'I don't know about the oxy part, but there are five morons here,' said Sandra Next Door. 'I'm just going to unwrap the head. Who has scissors?'

All five morons looked at each other then, with a reluctant sigh, Elsie opened her handbag. She extracted a ball of wool, two knitting needles, a bag of mints, a large magnifying glass and a framed photograph of her cat before finding what she was looking for.

'Here,' she said, passing an object to Sandra Next Door. 'And before anyone says anything, I only keep it in case I'm attacked when I'm doing my rounds in the library van.'

'Would a personal alarm not be better?' asked Fiona, eyeing the vicious-looking zombie knife doubtfully.

Sandra Next Door held the knife over the protrusion which she guessed was the object in Colin's mouth. 'If you're squeamish, look away now.'

Eileen took a step back and turned around, but everyone else stayed in place, their eyes on the woman about to interfere with a corpse.

Carefully, Sandra Next Door cut away at the plastic and folded back the material covering Colin's face. There was a collective gasp as the onlookers took in the mangled features then Mrs Hubbard shuffled in for a closer look.

She peered at the metal object in Colin's mouth, careful not to touch it, and said, 'I can't see it properly. Give me your magnifier, Elsie. Can someone shine a torch on it please?'

Fiona switched on the torch on her phone and held it over Colin's face, averting her eyes. Elsie, meanwhile, passed her magnifying glass to Mrs Hubbard, who bent once more over the object and emitted a long series of hmms and aahs, until Sandra Next Door finally snapped, 'Well? What is it?'

Mrs Hubbard straightened up, a satisfied look on her face, and said, 'I know exactly what it is. I've seen it before.'

Everyone looked at her expectantly, waiting for the big reveal. And waiting. And waiting.

Eventually, Elsie poked her in the ribs and said, 'This is the bit where you tell us, Minty.'

'Oops, sorry. It's…' Mrs Hubbard gave a dramatic pause, during which the others rolled their eyes in frustration, '…the Laird's Ladle.'

CHAPTER 7

Penny and Jim had eventually managed to extract Johnny from his tour of the set and get him into the back of Phil. He had objected to wearing a seatbelt until Penny had reached into the back seat, firmly clamped him in and threatened that if he didn't keep the thing on, he could go back to…

'Where *are* you staying?' she asked.

Johnny began to count on his fingers. 'The important people like me are at the Vik Hotel, some of the crew are in Bed and Breakfasts, then there's the runners at the trailer park by the ocean, Costume and Makeup in the village pub, stunt people also trailer park. Yeah, I adore your quaint little hotel and your pubs. Even your trailer park is cute.'

'That's because it's a caravan park,' said Jim through gritted teeth. The words "you idiot" were merely implied.

Since Penny had sashayed off with Johnny, he had been giving the actor some thought and reached the conclusion that the man was a fool; a fool that he just had to tolerate for a while then things with Penny would return to normal. Oh, she was a beautiful, warm, feisty little thing, with her perky bum and shiny hair. She'd let her short crop grow out since she arrived on the island, and Jim had more than once resisted the temptation to gently tuck a dark strand behind her ear. He gave himself a mental shake. Come on, Jim, old lad, she's your friend, nothing more. Of course men like Johnny and Alex were attracted to her. Men with money and fame and fancy cars and glamorous lifestyles. As opposed to vets who stuck their hands up cows' bottoms and drove ancient Land Rovers called Phil. It wasn't that he expected anything to happen between him and Penny, but she was too good for the likes of Johnny and Alex. Glumly, he released the handbrake and turned the car in the direction of Port Vik.

As they reached the outskirts of town, the car was filled with a cacophony of beeps. Their phones had once more connected to the world and the texts were flooding in. Penny was about to check her missed calls, when her phone burst into life with the dulcet tones of Chesney assuring her that he was the one and only and she couldn't take that away from him. She paused, not recognising the number, then decided to answer.

Sergeant Wilson's tones were on the other end of the line, and they were anything but dulcet.

'Do you know where Jim Space is? He's not answering his phone. Tell him to call me immediately.'

Penny donned her bestest innocent voice. The sort of voice she believed that a person not taking a famous actor to investigate something she shouldn't be investigating would use.

'Hello to you too, Sergeant Wilson. I'm with Jim now. Is there a problem?'

She switched the call to speakerphone and immediately had to turn down the volume. Sergeant Wilson was doing her bestest angry voice.

'There better bloody well not be. Maybe Jim can explain why members of the public have reported some people taking a body from an ice cream van into the museum.'

Penny and Jim exchanged a brief look of horror, then Jim fixed his eyes on the road. He decided to let Penny take this one. He was far too busy driving, and concentrating was very important.

Penny looked at her watch. 3pm. Mrs Hubbard and Elsie should be on guard duty by now. What the hell were they up to?

'I'm sorry Sergeant Wilson, we don't know anything about that. We set guards on the museum like we were asked, and we've put Colin in cold storage. Or at least we will just as soon as we can get his legs in the freezer.'

'So, you haven't left him in an ice cream van in front of the museum? And don't lie to me. I will fucking know if you're lying. They don't call me Polygraph Wilson for nothing.'

Penny was about to lie her head off about everything when she felt movement behind her. Johnny Munroe had unfastened his seatbelt and was leaning forward between the front seats.

'Excuse me, ma'am. Perhaps I can clear this up. Badabing.'

'Who the fuck is this?'

'Detective Johnny Munroe, at your soivice. But you can call me Johnny. No need to thank me, dear, it's a professional coitesy. May I call you Polygraph?'

'No, you fucking may not. Penny? Jim? What's an American detective doing there and why is my body in an ice cream van?'

'Calm down, Sugartits. We got it all under control heeya. When we've interviewed the antiques lady…why are you shushing me, Penny?'

There was a short pause, followed by the sound of a very ill woman retching, a faint splash then Sergeant Wilson was back on the line, sounding like the frontrunner at the Angry World Championships.

'Penny! Jim! Why is there an American sexist arsehole there and what the fuck is this about an antiques lady? You better not be investigating because if you're investigating, I'm going to take this bowl of sick and–'

'I'm sorry, Sergeant Wilson, you're breaking up. There's nothing to worry about. Oh, I think we're about to lose–'

Penny pressed the end call button, put her phone on silent and turned to Johnny.

'That was the actual police. I told you we're not allowed to investigate. Why did you have to open your big mouth?'

Johnny looked hurt and, still in character, said, 'Because youse guys never told me we couldn't trust our fellow officers.'

Penny instantly took pity on him. After all, they hadn't explicitly said not to tell anyone.

She put her hand on his and gently told him, 'Fuhgedaboutit. Now, put on your seatbelt and don't take it off again unless we tell you to. Jim's not insured for Hollywood legends going through the windscreen.'

Jim, who had given some consideration to braking sharply, nodded in agreement.

'Aye,' he said grimly, 'we wouldn't want any accidents. We're in enough trouble as it is.'

The remainder of the journey passed without incident. Penny had, she estimated, approximately fifty gazillion missed calls and messages to call Fiona. She tried to ring her back, but the call went straight to voicemail. Ho hum, she thought, she'd try Fiona again later. Hopefully, Fiona could fill her in on what was going on at the museum.

Miracle of miracles, they managed to get a parking space outside Hélène's Drawers. Jim was slightly relieved because, although the High Street did tend to be quieter towards late afternoon, he didn't want anyone to spot Johnny. It was half price for pensioners day at Cuppachino down the road, and pretty soon they'd be spilling out the door, hopped up on cheap scones and espresso, looking for trouble. Also, if anything reached Sergeant Wilson's ears, Penny and Jim might have a few awkward questions to answer about how they were definitely not investigating yet simultaneously visiting someone on Colin's list of favourite fences. Jim wasn't quite ready to be shouted at by Sergeant Wilson again. She was even better at swearing than him!

Jim and Penny exited the car and headed for the tasteful shop front, with its gold lettering on a green background. Jim paused at the door. It felt like there was something missing. He checked his pockets. Wallet, keys, phone – check. He checked his flies.

'I know Hélène's very attractive, but she's not going to be impressed by you fiddling with your bits,' Penny told him. 'Anyway, where's Johnny?'

They looked back at the car and there was Johnny, still sitting in the back seat.

'For goodness' sake,' said Penny, pulling open the rear passenger door. 'Why are you sitting there? I thought you wanted to come with us.'

Johnny looked somewhat befuddled. 'Youse guys said I had to keep my seatbelt on until you told me to take it off. So, here I am. Badabing.'

'*I'll* badabing you in a minute,' said Penny.

Johnny dropped the Brooklyn accent and reverted to his usual Californian drawl. 'You will, huh? Because my sex therapist says I shouldn't let things get backed up. I was kinda hoping the cute blonde waitress at the hotel might help a guy out, but that Martin dude is always hanging around.'

'That's because the cute blonde waitress is Rachel the hotel owner and Martin is her husband…oh, never mind. There'll be no badabinging or anything else beginning with b.'

'Not even a quick blo–'

'Not that, either. Now, come on, seatbelt off and let's get you inside before you get mobbed by randy pensioners.'

Their entry to Hélène's Drawers was heralded with a little tinkle from the bell above the door. Penny was quite delighted with the tinkle. The art of the tinkle was almost lost, she decided, subsumed by modern shops and their digital beep boops. If she had a shop, she'd definitely have a tinkle.

Unless it was a toilet shop of course, because that would never do. She'd once taken the twins bathroom shopping and Hector had relieved himself in one of the display toilets. And it wasn't a tinkle.

Her private musings were interrupted by the arrival of Hélène, who glided through from the back of the shop on a cloud of Gucci and, Penny noted enviously, an elegant pair of Jimmy Choos. She wore a figure-hugging white dress adorned with an ornate silver brooch, and her long, dark hair was tucked into a neat chignon. Standing next to the woman, Penny felt like a bag of used tampons.

'Ah, bonjour. How may I help you today?' said Hélène, her accent not nearly as strong as Penny's earlier parody.

Penny and Jim looked at each other in a "you go, no, you go" way. In all the hustle and bustle of macaroni and movie stars, they hadn't worked out what they were going to say. However, they were saved from saying anything by Johnny who, badabing still uppermost in his mind, practically threw Penny to one side in his haste to introduce himself.

'Bonjour, ma'am. Mon plaisir, mon plaisir. Detective Johnny Munroe, and these are my sidekicks, Penny and Jim.'

Beside Penny, Jim muttered, 'Man plays ear? Man plays ear? What's he on about bloody men playing with ears for?'

Penny ignored him. She was too busy watching in astonishment as the actor took Hélène's face in both hands and kissed each cheek…twice! That sort of thing could get you arrested in Scotland. Hélène didn't seem to mind, though, going by the enthusiasm with which she kissed him back.

'Alright, alright. That's enough of the kissy stuff,' said Jim. 'Hélène, would you mind if we asked you a couple of questions?'

'Sure, pas de problème,' said Hélène.

Jim took Colin's list from his pocket, unfolded it and cleared his throat.

'I believe you know uh knew erm have been acquainted with the museum curator, Colin Dogood?'

'Oui. Colin has been an acquaintance since he moved to the island. We have, how you say, a lot in common.' Hélène gestured towards the antique furniture filling the small shop. 'Mais, I haven't seen him since many months.'

'Right,' said Jim. 'Have you ever sold anything for him?'

'Oui, of course. He asked me to find a buyer for his grandmother's ring last year, and recently there have been a few small items. A silver snuff box, a pair of pistols, that sort of thing.'

'Which he stole from the museum!' exclaimed Johnny.

'Which he inherited or collected,' said Hélène, wagging a finger at Johnny. 'You are a very naughty boy to suggest such things.'

'Ba-da-bing, you know it,' grinned Johnny.

She turned away for a moment and opened the lower drawer of an old desk that was clearly still very much in use. Invoices, letters and office ephemera cluttered the surface and a large diary lay open at yesterday's date. At least, this was what Penny noticed. Jim and Johnny appeared to be in a hypnotic trance, their focus the woman in the tight white dress, her back to them as she bent over the drawer.

With a flourish, Hélène produced a blue, cardboard folder of the sort that used to fill filing cabinets before technology, with its hackers, ransomware and ability to delete years of work with a single accidental keystroke, came along and made everything so much more efficient.

'Voila. These are the sales records. Everything had provenance and I found private buyers for them.'

Jim took the folder and flicked through the contents.

'Why didn't he auction them?' asked Penny.

Hélène gave a very Gallic shrug. 'How should I know? You would have to ask him. He wanted quick sales and to be quiet. Perhaps he needed the money but didn't want his family to find out, non?'

'His family? What do you know about his family?'

'Nothing. I am guessing. I have known him for a long

time, but we are not close. Why are you asking these questions? You are police?'

'Eh, no,' said Jim. 'I'm the local vet, Penny here runs the slimming club and Detective Johnny is an–' Jim was going to say "idiot" but stopped himself, 'an actor.'

Hélène looked confused.

'Don't worry,' he assured her, 'it's all perfectly normal.'

'I don't think so,' said Hélène, her tone hardening. 'I think you are poking me.'

Sensing that things were heading downhill, Jim held up a hand to stop her. 'No, no. We're poking *into* you. God, that sounds even worse. Sorry, can we rewind? You probably won't have heard, but Colin died last night.'

Hélène gasped and held a hand to her mouth, her eyes wide. 'Sacre bleu!'

'That's it!' exclaimed Penny. 'Bloomin' Eileen. I knew it wasn't cordon bleu, but I couldn't think what the expression was.'

Jim gave her a sharp nudge with his elbow, his subtle way of telling her to shut up. He took a moment to think about his next words and decided to go with the abridged version.

'I'm sorry to bring you bad news, Hélène. I attended his body on behalf of the police and found this list of fences. Your name's on there.'

He handed over the folded sheet of paper. Holding it by the tips of her perfectly manicured fingers, Hélène unfolded the list and scanned the names. Then, with a cold smile, she handed it back to Jim.

'I think Colin has been having a little joke. I know some of the men on this list and they are as long as the day is honest. Perhaps he has been selling to other dealers.' She flicked a hand as if batting away any thought to the contrary. 'Now, excusez-moi, I do not know any more and I have my work.'

Penny and Jim understood that they were being dismissed and thanked Hélène for her time. Johnny, however, seemingly oblivious to the chill in the atmosphere, reached for her hand and gallantly kissed it.

'My detective salary don't stretch to much, but I'd sure push the boat out for you. I'll be in the bar at the Vik Hotel tonight, if you'd be kind enough to let a guy buy you champagne.'

Hélène gazed at him for a moment. She seemed to be calculating the benefits of going for a drink with this very strange American with the very irritating friends. Finally, she relented.

'D'accord. I will meet you there tonight provided *they*,' she gave a dismissive nod towards Penny and Jim, 'stay away. And it is only a drink. No funny business.'

'No badabing,' he gravely assured her.

Johnny practically skipped to the car, absolutely sure that there would be lots of funny business, if he had any say in the matter. The doll was smokin' hot. He was so happy that he didn't even argue about putting on his seatbelt. Just got in, pulled it on and waited for Penny and Jim to catch up. Voila!

Jim opened the driver's door and said, 'Get in the back.'

Gordon had had a very busy afternoon. Before she would tell them any more about the Laird's Ladle, Mrs Hubbard insisted they wrap up Colin and put him back in the ice cream van.

Once more, he and Sandra Next Door negotiated the museum steps with their grisly package. With Colin's neck being a little more pliable now, they decided to put him in the freezer, out of sight of nosey passers by who might peer in the window in search of a Soft n Whippy and find themselves faced with a Stiff n Whiffy.

That done, they returned to the museum to insist that Mrs Hubbard spill the beans.

'I must have phoned Penny about fifty times,' said Fiona. 'Either she has no signal, her battery's dead or she's on silent.'

'Well, there's no point in me telling the tale twice,' said

Mrs Hubbard, who was thoroughly enjoying keeping her audience on tenterhooks. 'I say we go to the village pub and wait for her there. Fiona, you do the text thingy and tell her.'

'Have you tried Jim?' asked Gordon.

Fiona shook her head. 'No reply from him either.'

'Pub it is, then,' said Mrs Hubbard.

Normally, she wouldn't be quite so keen to leave the comfort of her own fireplace, but with her Douglas in the hospital, the house felt empty and cold, no matter how many fires she laid. The thought that she'd done this to him was almost too much to bear. Yet she didn't have to be alone with her burden. She didn't believe in this new-fangled "talking it out" nonsense. One should never air one's dirty laundry in public, although it was fine to air other people's – that was just interesting news. She did believe, however, in keeping yourself busy so that for a little while at least, you could push the cold away and take comfort in the warmth of your friends. Goodness, she was getting philosophical in her old age.

'We can't leave the museum unlocked and unattended,' Eileen reminded her.

'We don't have to leave it unlocked,' said Elsie quietly.

'Does anyone want to stay here and not go to the pub?' Fiona asked.

'Well, my mum's picking up Ricky and Gervais from school and keeping them until Kenny gets home from work, so I'd like to make the most of it,' said Eileen.

'We don't have to leave it unlocked,' said Elsie, a little more loudly.

'If Eileen's going, I'm going,' declared Sandra Next Door. 'I'm not staying here with one of you numpties.'

'That leaves Gordon and Elsie, both of whom are the drivers. Without them, we can't go to the pub,' said Fiona.

'Four people can fit in my car, Einstein,' Sandra Next Door sneered.

'We don't have to leave it unlocked,' Elsie shouted, her voice an echoing boom in the cathedral-like space.

The others turned to stare at her.

'I don't think I've ever heard you shout before,' said Mrs Hubbard in astonishment. 'What brought that on?'

'People who don't listen. I didn't say anything before because…erm…because you were all so excited about investigating a murder again, but there's a chain and padlock in the library van. I use it to secure the…erm…special medicine. We could use it to tie the doors together.'

'But it's a library van. Why do you have medicine in there?' asked Eileen.

'Never you mind. It's for the pensioners and that's all you need to know.'

Eileen gave Elsie's arm a squeeze. 'You're so kind. Haven't I always said she was kind, Sandra Next Door?'

'Hmm,' said Sandra Next Door, eyeing Elsie suspiciously. 'Where do you get this special medicine.'

'None of your business.' Elsie fished in her handbag and produced a set of keys. Handing them to Gordon, she said, 'Top drawer at the back. It's heavy, mind.'

Five minutes later, the group stood watching as Gordon wound an incredibly thick chain through the museum door handles. The thing was so heavy, he was sweating despite the cool April breeze.

'It's a good job these door handles are so big. How on earth do you secure your medicine with this?' he asked.

'With great difficulty,' said Elsie. 'Now, put your back into it.'

He hefted the giant padlock and, after a bit of manoeuvring, managed to snap it into place. Then he sat down on the steps with a thump.

'What are we going to do about the ice cream van?' asked Fiona. 'We can't leave Colin here on his own.'

'I'll drive it,' Eileen offered.

'You?'

'Yes, me. I got my licence in the war.'

They all stared at her until, curiosity getting the better of him, Gordon asked, 'What war? You're not a time traveller from 1942, are you?'

Eileen regarded him calmly. 'No, silly. The Great Greengrocer war of 2003. I was working for Mrs Patel on North Street, putting vegetables out, minding the till, that sort of thing, when Jacobs and Sons started delivering vegetable boxes. That was the beginning of a decline in Mrs Patel's business, so she started doing vegetable boxes, only cheaper. Mr Jacob wasn't having that, so he undercut her. Pretty soon they were practically giving them away. Well, the islanders thought this was great and started ordering more and more vegetable boxes. Mrs Patel made me pass my driving test so I could drive the big van.'

'What happened to the greengrocers? Who won?' asked Gordon.

'Nobody. The council granted planning permission for the big supermarket, and eventually they both lost.'

'Alright,' said Gordon, 'I vote Eileen gets to drive the ice cream van.'

That agreed, they all left the museum, got into their vehicles and drove in convoy for the few miles to the village.

They parked up in the relatively empty pub car park and made their way inside. A light rain had started to fall and the temperature, generally on winter setting between September and mid-June, had decided that a burst of December was in order.

As they made a beeline for a table near the fireplace, Eileen said, 'I feel a bit sorry for Colin, out there on his own. What if somebody steals him?'

'No,' said Sandra Next Door, pulling out the chair closest to the fire, plonking herself on it and crossing her arms with an air of finality. 'Just no.'

'But it's cold and horrible out there. And the ice cream

van's quite old and people could get into it and it would be quite easy to steal Colin.'

'Firstly, he's in a freezer. The cold is the least of his problems. Secondly, it's the village. Nothing ever happens here. People leave their doors unlocked all the time,' Sandra Next door told her firmly.

'Could we not just…?'

'No.'

'I think she's right about the van being easy to get into,' said Gordon. 'There's a reason Elsie carries a big chain and a zombie knife.'

'It's called paranoia,' said Sandra Next Door.

Gordon folded his arms and scowled. 'Or being careful. The phone box was vandalised last year, and someone put poo through Jimmy Gray's letterbox.'

Fiona nodded. 'He's right, you know. And there was that shoplifter you caught, Mrs H.'

Mrs Hubbard shook her head sorrowfully. 'Five years old and stealing jelly snakes. What is the world coming to?'

'A village crimewave, then,' snapped Sandra Next Door.

'What about druggies?' asked Mrs Hubbard. 'They might get the munchies and break in, looking for a snack. You must have heard of the munchies. I've heard of the munchies. I think we might have caught them when we did magic mushrooms back in university, Elsie.'

'That wasn't me,' said Elsie.

'But you were there.'

'No, you hallucinated me. You, Ivor Space and Jeannie Campbell were so worried about the earbashing you'd get if I found out you were trying mushrooms, that you all hallucinated me telling you off. Then none of you would talk to me the next day. That's how I found out you tried mushrooms.'

'Oh,' said Mrs Hubbard, crestfallen. 'So, what are we going to do about all these druggies with the munchies?'

Sandra Next Door glared at everyone in turn. 'We'll send them to Penny for nutritional advice. Her broccoli goulash alone will drive them into rehab. Nobody, including you, is going near the van and Colin is staying put.'

With Johnny Munroe safely installed in the back seat, Jim fired up Phil and pointed him in the direction of the museum.

'I suggest we check in on the rest of Losers Club,' he said. 'God knows what they've been up to.'

It had begun to rain, so he switched on the wipers for the short drive. It was the sort of rain that wasn't heavy enough to have the wipers on medium yet was slightly too heavy to have them on low. He put them on low anyway and peered through the resulting smear, trying not to run over any stray metal-detectorists. The island bus had just decanted a group of them by Cuppachino and they'd starburst across the High Street, like a bunch of giddy teenagers fleeing an underage drinking raid. He'd seen it happen once in Turriff. The little buggers were practically paralysed with vodka, but they couldn't half move when the police walked in the door. The teenagers, not the metal-detectorists. He swerved to avoid a man in a bright yellow raincoat and received the middle finger for his efforts.

The rain was the reason why none of them spotted a slight problem until they were practically at the kerb outside the museum.

'Shit,' said Jim. 'Where's the ice cream van? Where's the van, Penny? Someone's stolen Colin.'

'Oh, youse guys have effed up big time,' said a voice from the back. 'It's just as well you got a professional on the case.'

'Hang on. Look at the doors,' said Penny, pointing to the handles which were practically buried beneath a length of chain. 'I think they must have gone somewhere and taken Colin with them.'

She checked her phone. Sure enough, there were approximately three gazillion missed calls and text messages from Fiona. Penny immediately felt guilty for not calling her back.

'Fiona's messaged me. They've gone to the pub.'

'Town or village?' asked Jim.

'Village.'

'In which case, we better join them.'

He once more started the car and this time pointed it towards the village.

As they trundled along, avoiding the post-winter potholes that the local council had been far too slow to fill this year, Johnny kept up a steady stream of chatter from the back seat.

He wanted to know what the car was called. Was it an SUV?

'It's called Phil,' Jim told him gruffly.

He wanted to know about caravan parks. What were they for? Why did people move out of their comfortable homes every year to trailers where they had to empty chemical toilets and use public showers?

'It's a holiday,' said Jim. 'You should try it sometime. Very relaxing.'

He wanted to know what the village was called because "youse guys always say the village, like there's only one village here, but it must have a name."

Penny could see Jim rolling his eyes, so she took this one. 'It's officially Foggy Harbour but nobody ever calls it that.'

'And the other villages?'

'They have names, but everyone just says "the village." I can't explain it. It's an island thing. We all seem to know which one we're talking about.'

'Youse guys are weird.'

'We are indeed, and we like it that way.'

The chatter died down as they pulled into the pub car park. Penny and Jim were relieved to see the ice cream van there, intact.

'Okay,' said Penny. 'We have a secure crime scene, and the body is safely stored away. Sergeant Wilson need never know that it's been in a pub car park. We'll have a quick case conference, then you can drive the van home and plug it in to charge the freezer. I'll follow in Phil and drop Johnny off at the hotel for his big date. All's well that ends well.'

Jim smiled for the first time in hours. Being in charge of all this stuff had been so stressful. He didn't know how Sergeant Wilson coped. Well, there was the swearing, of course, and he'd heard a rumour that she once wrapped a naked suspect in a duvet and duct taped him in before rolling him back to the police station. But all was safe and secure now. Everything was going to be alright.

They made their way into the pub and immediately spotted their friends at a table near the fireplace. Jim felt a rush of fondness for all six of them, no, seven, no six. No. Seven.

Because there between Eileen and Mrs Hubbard, a pint of bitter on the table in front of him, sat clingfilm Colin.

'Bugger me with a bag of lollipops!'

CHAPTER 8

'Shh! Keep your voice down,' said Fiona, correctly judging by the colour of Jim's face that an explosion was imminent.

Jim took a deep breath and imagined himself on an island, palm trees swaying in the gentle breeze, the sea lapping at his feet as, one by one, he held their heads under the water and drowned the lot of them.

Beside him, Penny watched with interest. She had never seen him *really* angry before. Irritated, yes. Mostly at her for making him replace his afternoon bag of chocolate buttons with fruit. But livid? No, he'd never come this close to losing his temper. She wondered whether now was a good time to mention that purple really wasn't his colour. Probably not. Maybe a drink would calm things down.

'Would anyone like a drink? My round. Come on, Jim, you can help me carry them?'

Jim ignored her. He grabbed the nearest chair and, in a series of jerky movements, pulled it next to Gordon and sat down. He realised he was biting his upper lip and made a conscious effort to relax. Aaaaaand breathe. He closed his eyes and took a few more deep breaths, ignoring the whispers of Penny and Eileen.

'He's all purple. What's he pulling the face for? Penny, is that his orgasm face?'

'Why are you asking me?'

'Because you and him…you know.'

'No, Eileen, I don't know. And if that *is* his orgasm face, I'm not sure I want to.'

'Who's the gadjee in the dirty mac? Did you find him outside the school with a big bag of sweeties?'

'It's Johnny Munroe. We can't get rid of him, but he's a nice man and he wants to help with the Colin thing. Shh, be discreet.'

Eileen gave a loud squeal, the pitch quickly rising to a level that only dogs could hear.

'Bugger Jim with a box of sharp pencils! You brought Johnny Munroe to the pub!' she shouted, alerting everyone in the bar to the arrival of a real movie star in their midst (if you discounted Alex's visits to the island, of course, which everyone did because they were quite used to him by now).

There was a rumble of chairs being pushed back, followed by some good-natured jostling as a crowd of drinkers surrounded Johnny, clamouring for autographs and selfies. He didn't seem to mind, happily chatting with the fans and posing for photographs with the ease of someone for whom this was an everyday experience. Alex had always loved this sort of thing, but Penny had happily stayed in the background, seeking to keep things as normal as possible for the twins. Penny couldn't imagine herself being unable to go places without being hounded. Then she corrected herself. Yes, she could. She recalled that awful period where Alex had been in the papers for tax avoidance and how she'd had to slip out the back door and climb into a neighbour's garden, simply to leave the house without being chased by paparazzi. That was the day she'd found out about the au pair; the final straw in a whole sordid packet of them.

Afterwards, when she came to Vik, she'd been running away, trying to find a safe place to lick her wounds. She hadn't thought beyond getting the twins settled somewhere peaceful and making enough money to find a place of their own. Yet here she was, over eight months later, with her little weight-loss empire spreading across Scotland, and now when she appeared in the papers it wasn't as the wife of a philandering tax dodger, it was as Scottish Entrepreneur of the Year and owner of Scotland's Favourite Start-Up.

She'd been offered ridiculous sums of money for Losers Club but had turned all offers down, the reason being the little gang of Losers in front of her. A group of friends who, with their banter and bonkers, fed her soul every day and had helped her little family rebuild their lives on this rock in the North Sea. Just over a year ago, she could not have imagined being where she was right now, and as she gazed at her merry band, sitting there open-jawed at the arrival of Johnny and completely oblivious to Jim's murderous glares, she felt a rush of love for them all. Except Colin, of course.

Jim was feeling slightly calmer now. Gordon had taken advantage of the other pub-goers' gravitation towards Johnny to slip to what was now a very quiet bar. He returned with a tray of drinks and slid a whisky onto the table in front of Jim.

'I think you need it, pal.'

'Aye?'

'Aye.'

'This body?'

'Aye.'

'Why?'

'Women.'

'Aye.'

'We asked the landlord first.'

'What did he say?'

'Aye.'

'Glad we got that sorted.'

'Aye.'

Penny shuffled her chair over and put a hand on Jim's arm.

'Are you okay?'

'Aye.'

'Shall we ask them what Colin's doing here?'

'No need. I've had the full story from Gordon.'

'Fair enough, but we still need to compare notes from today. We'll get no peace with Johnny here. Maybe Bertie the barman would let us use the back room. I'll go and ask.'

Jim took a sip of the whisky and grimaced. Nope. Twenty-five years since he'd last tried the stuff hadn't improved its taste. He'd rather have some of whatever Mrs Hubbard was having, he thought, looking over at the elderly woman.

She caught his eye, raised her lurid cocktail and said, 'Sex on the Beach, dearie. Would you like to try some?'

Beside her, Elsie rolled her eyes and sipped her lemonade.

Penny returned with the news that Bertie was giving them the back room, with the proviso that they tidy up after themselves. With the deftness of a woman who had regularly experienced her husband being surrounded by sycophants and selfie seekers, she plucked Johnny from his impromptu fan club and ushered them all into the back room. It was much cooler in there than the main bar and the room had a disused air. Spare chairs were stacked to one side and the only table, a large wooden affair with "EC Luvs KB" etched indelibly on the surface, stood on its own in the centre. Eileen ran a finger over the letters and smiled, recalling the night that Kenny Bates had stood on that very table and, in front of the whole pub, asked her to marry him. Then he blacked out from too much vodka, fell off the table and she'd had to call his mum to come and take him home. It was magical.

Penny, who had been there that night, noticed the initials and the look on her friend's face, and gave her a wink.

'At least he remembered it the next morning and sent you flowers, the old romantic,' she said.

Their moment was cut short by a bout of colourful language as Jim and Gordon tried to manoeuvre Colin through the door, with Johnny supervising from the rear.

Eileen rushed to fetch a chair and they lowered him into it, standing up to stretch their backs afterwards.

'He's a bit harder to move now he's not so stiff,' Gordon informed the group, 'so if we could hurry this up before the rigor mortis wears off completely, that would be fine.' He paused and shook his head. 'I never thought I'd hear myself saying that.'

Eileen put Colin's pint down in front of him and went to help the others pull chairs over to the table.

At last, they were seated, and Penny did a quick head count.

'We're missing someone. Where's Fiona?'

'In the bar. Where else? You need to have a word with her, Gordon,' said Sandra Next Door.

Johnny's head came up, one giant eye staring at the group. 'Wow. Youse guys are so tiny. Shall I go get Fiona?'

'I gave him my magnifying glass to play with,' Elsie explained, smiling at Johnny in a distinctly motherly fashion. 'No, you stay here. There will be too much fuss if you go back to the bar.'

'Och, leave Fiona be,' said Mrs Hubbard. 'She's a social butterfly, that one. Now, who would like to know what we know?'

'About time,' said Sandra Next Door.

'Well settle in, dearies, because old mother Hubbard has a tale or two for you. First, we found the murder weapon.'

She paused for dramatic effect. Penny, Jim and Johnny were suitably dramatized, their faces reflecting their surprise.

'How? What? Where?' asked Penny.

'Strictly speaking, it was Gordon and Fiona who found the murder weapon. They were playing in the Living Vik display and Fiona picked up one of those heavy olden days irons. I believe she was aiming it at Gordon's manly bits when he spotted the blood.' Mrs Hubbard turned to Gordon and whispered, 'I think I might know a bit more about you than I'm comfortable with.'

Unperturbed, Gordon whispered back, 'Don't worry, Mrs H. Your Douglas, or should I call him Mr Du Beke, has told me all about your Strictly Come Dancing nights. Your secret is safe with me…Katya.'

Mrs Hubbard cleared her throat and, in a voice that was slightly too loud, continued her tale.

'Anyway, as I was saying, the murder weapon. We think he must have been bashed on the head with the iron and maybe killed outright. The bit that doesn't add up, though, is the blood. Eileen's right. You'd expect there to be blood up the walls from when his face was battered, so Fiona googled it. The only way it makes sense is if he was killed and left to bleed out, then his face was battered after he was dead. And somewhere along the way, the killer hides the murder weapon in plain sight in Living Vik and shoves a ladle down his throat.'

Penny sat up straight as a light went on behind her eyes.

'Ladle! I knew I recognised it,' she cried. 'It's the–'

'Laird's Ladle. Yes, dearie.'

'The Layahds Ladle?' asked Johnny.

'In 1746,' Mrs Hubbard began.

The actor regarded her, open-mouthed. 'Seventeen fawdy six! That's like before America was invented.'

Mrs Hubbard ignored him. 'In 1746, the French sent a ship to the island, full of treasure to fund Bonnie Prince Charlie's army. Some say the ship sank in a storm without ever delivering its cargo, but others say that the treasure made it onto the island and was never sent to the mainland due to that same storm. By the time the storm died down, the battle was lost, and the treasure was hidden away. Legend has it that the whereabouts of the treasure has been handed down from one secret keeper to the next and that, even now, someone on the island knows where it's hidden. The last *known* secret keeper was a man called Bruce Duguid. There's a tale that he murdered someone for the treasure, but it's unlikely. The books say he died poor and is buried somewhere on the island.'

'That's weird,' said Penny. 'Colin told me that when his family moved to Australia, they changed their surname from Duguid to Dogood. Do you think he's related to the Duguid man?'

'Woo, spooky,' said Eileen. 'Psychic Penny.'

'He said it *before* he died.'

Eileen eyed Penny suspiciously and leaned forward, her blonde curls dangling in Colin's pint. 'How *long* before he died?'

'*Months* before he died.'

'That's *okay* then,' said Eileen and sat back, satisfied that her best friend in the whole world wasn't going around killing museum curators.

'So, what's this got to do with the ladle?' asked Jim.

Mrs Hubbard, who was three cocktails down and quite pink around the cheeks, gave a small burp and said, 'The ladle is the only part of the treasure ever known to have surfaced. It was a personal gift from King Louis the whateverth to Prince Charlie himself. Nobody is quite sure how or why it was separated from the rest of the hoard, but it ended up in the castle and has been passed down the Deer family ever since, right the way to your current man, Laird Hamish.'

'I remember that from a school trip to the castle,' said Penny. 'Wasn't there an old letter thanking the Laird for his kindness and bequeathing him the ladle?'

'Which school trip? Which castle?' asked Eileen. 'Was it the apple juice one or the septic tank one?'

'The septic tank one.' Penny noticed the curious looks of the others. 'She dropped her coat in the septic tank then went in after it.'

'That's disgusting. Why on earth did you do that?' asked Sandra Next Door.

'My sandwiches were in the pocket,' said Eileen.

'Okay,' said Jim, trying to bring the conversation back on

track, 'so we have Colin's head bashed in with an iron, then his face battered and the Laird's Ladle shoved down his throat after he was dead. Any clues as to why he was naked?'

There were silent headshakes all round, so he continued.

'Penny and I, sorry, Penny, myself and Johnny–'

'Detective Munroe,' Johnny corrected him.

'-Detective Munroe. Anyway, Penny found a list of fences on Colin's computer so we–'

'Fences? Who keeps a list of fences on their computer?' asked Sandra Next Door.

'I do,' said Gordon. 'We're having awful trouble with foxes just now, so I've been looking into fences. There's a place in Inverurie that does good chicken wire, but I don't think that will be enough to keep the little beggars out.'

Jim sighed. 'Fences as in stolen goods fences. Anyway, Hélène's Drawers was on the list, so we went to have a word with Hélène.'

'Ooh, did she talk sexy French at you?' Eileen pouted and, with a hand either side of her chest, plumped up her bosoms. 'Oh Jeem, mon chieur, you are so 'andsome.'

Penny stifled a giggle as Jim ignored Eileen and continued. 'She insists that everything she sold for him was above board. Showed us the paperwork and it looked okay, as far as I can tell. She said she hadn't seen him in months.'

'She's a lawyer,' said Johnny.

'No, dear, she's an antiques dealer,' said Elsie.

'She's a lawyer,' Johnny insisted. He looked around the group, all of whom who were staring at him, confused. 'Lawyer. Someone who tells lies!'

'Oh, a liar,' said Elsie. 'Sorry, it's quite hard to follow your accent. Which part of Texas are you from?'

Johnny sighed and, dropping the terrible Brooklyn twang, explained, 'It was in the diary on her desk. She was scheduled to meet Colin for lunch yesterday.'

Jim was astounded. Not so much by the revelation of Hélène's lie but by the fact that Johnny had actually done some proper detecting. Maybe the man wasn't such an idiot after all.

'Well spotted. Did it say where they were having lunch?' he asked.

'No,' said Johnny. 'I could try to find out when I meet her for drinks tonight.'

'Try to find out anything you can about their relationship,' Jim told him. 'Did either of you find it strange that she never asked about how Colin died?'

'Now you come to mention it, that *was* odd,' said Penny. 'Maybe she was involved in fencing stolen goods for him. I mean, she's hardly going to whip out a folder of "All The Stuff I Have Sold On The Black Market" is she? Of course she showed us the legitimate records. I'd say keep her as a suspect and let's see what Johnny finds out tonight.'

Jim nodded in agreement. 'I doubt she'll be honest with Johnny, but there's no harm in trying. In the meantime, Sandra Next Door, your Geoff knows all the café and restaurant owners through his work, doesn't he? Do you think you could phone around and discreetly try to find out where Hélène and Colin had lunch and whether they seemed close? Do they go there often? Did anyone overhear what they talked about? That sort of thing.'

'How about I do the Googling?' Eileen offered. 'You can give me the list of fences and I'll look into them. And I'll look into Colin.'

Gordon jumped in, eager to help. 'That's a lot of work. Fiona and I can take the list of fences if you do Colin.'

'What about me and Elsie? What can we do?' asked Mrs Hubbard.

Jim looked at Penny. He was out of ideas.

Penny smiled fondly at Mrs Hubbard, far too polite to point out that the woman was three sheets to the wind and could probably do with a good lie down.

'I expect you'll be going into town to the hospital to visit your Douglas later. Do you think you and Elsie could pop past the library and dig up anything you can find on the treasure and the Laird's Ladle? I know there will be information on the internet, but it would be interesting to see what the old books have to say on the subject.'

Mrs Hubbard gave another small burp and nodded, satisfied that she and Elsie were being included.

'That's sorted, then,' said Jim. 'And Penny and I will go to see Laird Hamish. Hopefully he can explain what the Laird's Ladle was doing at the museum when it should have been at the castle.'

'I see you've kept the best job for yourself,' Sandra Next Door grumbled.

'Aye, well, I know Hamish because I treat his dogs and horses. Does anyone else here know him?'

No one replied.

'Right, then it makes sense for me to go and see him. I nominate Penny to come with me as she's the only one without a task. Any further objections?'

Sandra Next Door looked like she was about to say something, but she was interrupted by Fiona who flung the door open and announced, 'I'm here. What did I miss?'

'Certainly not the vodka, going by the state of you,' sniped Sandra, taking her sour grapes out on the merry woman in dungarees and pink bonnet.

'Gordon will bring you up to speed,' said Penny. 'Now, how about we all meet at Cuppachino tomorrow morning to compare notes on what we've found out?'

Eileen looked delighted. 'So, does this mean we're investigating?'

'No,' said Penny and Jim in unison. 'We're not investigating.'

CHAPTER 9

Vik Castle stood in manicured lawns at the end of a long, pebbled drive. It was more long-term vanity project than fortification; a baronial style mongrel that had been added to by successive Lairds since the fourteenth century. Yet somehow the parts together made for a very impressive whole.

As Penny tiptoed across the gravel towards the enormous oak front door, trying not to kill her killer heels, she cursed her decision to go home and change into smart clothes. Jim had insisted that she was fine in jeans and trainers, but what did he know? He was still wearing a torn jumper and his hair, liberally decorated with bits of thicket, looked like he'd brushed it with a toffee apple. So, she'd sent him home to change as well.

Mary had been delighted to see Penny. The twins were still at the set with Alex and Len was asleep, so she was desperate for company and immediately tried to rope Penny into helping her paint Len's shed.

'It'll be a lovely surprise for him when he's better. He'll be so pleased.'

Penny regarded the yellow woman before her and said, 'Isn't the paint supposed to go on the shed, not you?'

'Yes, but it's so much more fun if you don't worry about the mess. Here, take a brush and slap some on.'

'No thanks. Where did you even get so much yellow paint?'

'Well, that's the funny thing. I found it on the pavement in the village.' Mary shrugged and tutted. 'Goodness knows what sort of person leaves large tubs of yellow paint lying around, just waiting for strangers with ideas about painting sheds.'

'Were there also a couple of men in orange jumpsuits by the side of the road?'

'Why, yes, the escaped prisoners. How did you know, Chunky?'

'And maybe some traffic cones?'

'Gosh, that's spooky. It's like you were there.'

'And could the escaped prisoners have actually been council workers painting road markings?'

Mary frowned. 'Ah.'

'Yes, ah,' said Penny. 'I can't believe you stole road paint, Mum.'

Mary's hackles rose at the mention of theft, and she became quite indignant.

'I didn't *steal* it. I...*repurposed* it. I pay my taxes and, anyway, it'll look far better on your father's shed than preventing people parking outside the bowling club.'

With that, she marched off, leaving a trail of yellow footprints across the kitchen tiles. Penny shook her head in exasperation and went to her room to rummage for decent clothes.

'Right, the Chezster and Sharlster, what do you wear to meet a laird in a castle? We want to get answers, so it has to be something that says professional and trustworthy. Yet just a little bit sexy and approachable.'

Chesney and Sharleen were annoyingly silent on the matter, leaving it to Penny's good judgement, so she turned to the wardrobe for inspiration.

'Okay, Mrs Wardrobe, in the words of the lovely Pat Benatar, hit me with your best shot.'

She reached in, sweeping aside a few eye-wateringly expensive gowns that she had once worn to premieres with Alex, and finally reached the Boring Section; the section which contained her old work blouses and plain skirts. Or at least it should have. Except they were all gone. The only thing left was an old school uniform that, for some bizarre reason, her mother had kept.

'Muuuuuum!' she shouted.

Penny stomped back through the house, out the back door and across Len's carefully tended lawn until she came to a stop by her mother and a pile of familiar-looking rags.

'Where are my clothes, Mum?' she said between gritted teeth.

Mary looked mildly befuddled for a moment then smiled. 'Oh, do you mean the old work stuff you never wear?' She pointed to herself, and through the yellow paint Penny could see a hint of grey chiffon.

'You're wearing my good blouse for painting!' she exclaimed.

'I'm only wearing the polyester stuff for painting. Anything cotton I cut up for rags. You haven't worn any of it since you moved in, so I thought I'd put it to good use. Plus, it's very handy that you have a large bottom. I was able to cut that skirt and put it over Sandra Next Door's begonias. I don't think she'd be too pleased if I painted them yellow. Although why that would make a difference, I don't know. Some animal's been in them, and there's so much poop in there it'll probably kill them off far quicker than a lick of paint could. It's really quite unhygienic. I shall have a word with her about letting animals poop in her begonias.'

Mary looked so pleased with her own ingenuity that Penny couldn't bring herself to scream at her. She really wanted to, but made do with growling, 'You owe me a new wardrobe.'

Back in her room, she examined the school uniform. If she unpicked the badge from the burgundy blazer, it might just pass muster as a suit jacket. Could she still squeeze into the blouse and skirt? There was only one way to find out.

Half an hour later, the front door of Valhalla opened, and Jim immediately took a step back.

'Whoa. Nobody told me it was fancy dress. Isn't the sexy schoolgirl look a bit inappropriate these days?' He gave her a lascivious wink. 'Maybe save it for when we're alone.'

Penny tried to take a deep breath to shout at him, but the waistband of her skirt threatened to slice her in two. Instead, she gasped, 'Bugger off, you big pervert. It's a suit. The… erm…latest designer thing. Yes, everyone's wearing it in London and just because you have no sense of fashion, it doesn't give you the right to criticise.'

She was glad that she had to step up into Phil. If she'd had to sink down into an ordinary car, she wasn't sure she'd ever have been able to make it back out again. As it was, her ability to step up was somewhat inhibited by the fact that pencil skirts appeared to have been in fashion during her teens and, despite her having had a rather ample adolescent bottom, the infernal thing was still a size smaller than her current bottom. Her thighs appeared to have blossomed too, resulting in what was once a demure, below the knee, slit skirt now being a slightly above the knee straitjacket for legs. She hitched the thing up a bit so that she could put her foot on the step, unaware that she was giving the world an excellent view of her knickers through the slit. Jim looked away and gave her bottom a less than gentlemanly shove to hoist her into the vehicle.

Now, here they were at the castle door, and she was starting to wonder if, instead of professional, trustworthy, sexy and approachable, she had simply achieved peak weirdo. Brazen it out, she told herself, brazen it out and pretend it's a thing. Everyone will be impressed if they think it's an actual thing.

Jim grinned at her. 'I like big knockers.'

Penny blushed and snapped, 'They're not big. It's just that the shirt was a touch small, and I had to squeeze them in.'

He looked momentarily taken aback then pointed at the door. 'I was talking about that.'

Penny took in the giant brass door knocker and mentally kicked herself. Jim was still grinning, and she couldn't help but shake her head and smile.

'Sorry, I feel a bit self-conscious. Okay, it's my old school uniform. It was the only smart thing I had, thanks to Mum painting Dad's shed with yellow road paint. Do you think they'll notice?'

'Road paint?'

'Long story. Honestly, do you think they'll notice?'

'Absolutely not,' Jim assured her. 'Smart black skirt, white blouse, burgundy blazer. Definitely sort of looks like a suit. You look very professional, in a…tight way.'

'Phew. Thanks,' said Penny. 'I was a bit worried when you said I looked like a schoolgirl earlier.'

'It was just a first impression,' said Jim. 'You look more like a–'

He paused as the door was opened then gave a sharp laugh. '–a member of staff. Hello, we have an appointment to see Laird Hamish.'

The woman in the burgundy blazer, white shirt and black skirt gave Penny a curious look then said, 'Follow me.'

She led them through a stone hallway, festooned with tapestries, and past the grand staircase to a small door marked "Private".

'This takes us through to the laird's own quarters,' the woman explained. 'Most of the castle is open to the public in spring and summer, but he keeps a few rooms in the east wing for family only.'

They walked down stone stairs, then through a narrow

passageway and up a further flight of stone stairs, finally emerging on a landing by a small window overlooking the gardens. The woman briefly knocked on a door ahead of them before opening it to reveal a bright, richly carpeted room, the walls lined with shelves straining under the weight of the books piled upon them. Penny was immediately struck by the fact that these weren't the usual musty old tomes bought by the metre by some long-departed lord of the manor. There were modern novels mixed with travel books mixed with gardening books mixed with DIY manuals, and even a battered old copy of The Essential Camping Cookbook. Laird Hamish certainly had eclectic taste.

The woman showed them to two chairs in front of a desk by the window and left, saying the laird would be along shortly.

Neither Penny nor Jim sat. They were too busy taking in the magnificent view of the gardens.

'I wouldn't mind an office like this,' Jim murmured. 'I have a desk at the back of the surgery. No windows and everything's covered in cat hair. Next door's cat is an escape artist and keeps coming in to visit the other cats. I can't tell you the number of times I've found her asleep on my keyboard. I don't know how she did it, but she once updated my Facebook status to "in a relationship" and posted a picture of a German Shepherd. Jesus, you can't have that as a vet. Cameron Smith owns three of the buggers and I never heard from him again.'

Penny gave a snort of laughter and was about to respond when she was interrupted by a door opening at the other end of the room. A tall man of about sixty, wearing what appeared to be gardening trousers and a motheaten jumper, entered and immediately headed for Jim, hand extended.

'Jim m'boy. Lang time nae see. How are you?'

He didn't wait for a reply, turning to Penny and saying, 'You can go now.'

'But–' said Penny.

The man rolled his eyes and smiled. 'You canna get the staff these days. Away you go.'

'But I'm not–'

'You must be new. If you want to keep your job, GO. NOW.'

Penny looked at him, startled. She had no idea why, but she did want to keep her job. Good lord, she thought as she bustled out the door, her new boss was a bit of a meany pants. It was only as she was about to close the door behind her that she heard the uproarious laughter.

She went back inside to find Jim and the man who was clearly Laird Hamish collapsed on the sofa by the fireplace, tears streaming, biting sofa cushions to stifle their howls.

'Ha bloody ha!' she shouted, lobbing a spare cushion at Jim.

'I'm sorry,' Hamish gasped between giggles, 'you shouldn't have come dressed as staff. I couldn't resist.'

'Pleased to meet you too,' said Penny tartly.

The laughter quickly subsided under her withering gaze and the two men looked contrite.

'I really am sorry, Penny. Pleased to meet you. I'm Hamish.'

Penny gave him a tight smile and shot Jim the sort of look that said, "I'll deal with you later."

Hamish gestured to her to join them on the sofa and offered them some tea.

'No thanks,' said Jim. 'We won't stay for long. We wanted to ask you a few questions about something we're looking into, if you don't mind.'

Hamish leaned forward, curious to hear more.

'Do you know Colin Dogood?' asked Penny, getting straight to the point.

'The museum curator. Yes, of course. He's done me a few favours over the years. Why?'

'He was found dead this morning.'

Hamish's eyes widened in shock.

'Dead? What happened? He wasn't even that old. What was he? Forty?'

The cynic in Penny watched Hamish's reaction closely. Was it real? She couldn't tell. Part of her wished they'd brought Johnny along instead of sending him back to the hotel to get ready for his date. He would have spotted whether Hamish was acting.

'He was murdered,' she replied.

'Murdered! How? I mean, when? Why? Why would anyone murder Colin?'

Jim, who had also been monitoring Hamish's reactions, chimed in.

'We don't know. It looks like someone bashed his head in.'

'Good God. So, what has this got to do with me? More to the point, what does it have to do with you?' Hamish asked.

'Fair question,' said Jim. 'We were asked by the police to secure the crime scene, and we couldn't help noticing something. Something in Colin's mouth.'

Hamish looked genuinely confused. 'What in his mouth?'

'Your ladle,' said Jim.

'My what? My ladle? How do you know it's my ladle? We've probably got hundreds of them in the kitchen. Hang on.'

'No, I mean–' said Jim, but Hamish held up a hand to stop him and walked over to the desk, picked up his phone and dialled a number. They could hear the ringtone, followed by a muffled voice.

'Is that you, lovey? I can't talk right now. I'm at the hairdressers and they're about to blow dry me.'

'Just a quick question, my wee angel. Are we missing any ladles?'

'What are you talking about? How would I know? What about the Laird's Ladle? Didn't you take it to that man to get valued?'

Jim could see the light go on behind Hamish's eyes as he

suddenly put two and two together. The laird said a quick goodbye to his wife and returned to the sofa.

'Sorry. I'm so stupid. Was it the Laird's Ladle? Was that what you found in his mouth?'

Jim nodded grimly. 'Aye. More like stuffed down his throat. Any idea what it was doing there?'

'Jesus, no! I took it to him yesterday morning. He has… had some good contacts in the antiques world and was going to get it valued for me. I left it with him. That was the last time I saw him *and* the ladle.'

'Fair enough. Obviously, it's none of my business, but why were you getting it valued?' asked Jim.

Hamish leaned back on the sofa, arms crossed, and gazed at them, clearly weighing up how to answer this question. Penny watched his expression change as he came to a decision, and she wondered whether his next words were going to be the truth or a politician's answer.

'Okay. I'll be straight with you. I'm in a bit of financial trouble and Colin was helping me out. The upkeep on this place,' he gestured towards the rest of the castle, 'is horrendous. I'm mortgaged to the hilt and just about keeping us afloat, but I want to start a glamping business in the grounds. The banks won't lend me any more money, so I started selling off a few things. It was my new factor who suggested the Laird's Ladle. It's quite well known, so it should fetch a good price.'

Hamish pointed to a portrait above the fireplace, which showed him in army uniform standing next to a beautiful woman in a long, white dress. Penny's breath caught in her throat as she recognised the stunning woman she'd spotted on the ferry.

'It doesn't help that I'm a cliché. The typical older man trying to keep up with the young, glamorous wife. Cara's never out of the bloody shops.'

Jim nodded sympathetically. 'Does Cara know about any of this?'

'No, and I'd prefer we keep it that way, if you don't mind. If I manage to get this glamping thing off the ground, she'll never need to know.'

Penny, no stranger to the impact of financial secrets on a marriage, said, 'Surely if you tell her, she'd be supportive.'

'I don't think so,' said Hamish firmly. 'It's hardly an exciting life, stuck here with an old man who spends his days gardening. I think she might be having an affair. I suspected Colin at one point. She always refers to him as "that man", never by his name, yet she's met him here many a time. It's almost like she deliberately distanced herself from him to throw me off the scent.'

'Yet you still did business with him,' said Jim.

Hamish hung his head and sighed. 'Not much choice, really. It was him or that Hélène, and…erm…me and Hélène…let's just say we have a past, and we stay out of each other's way.'

Deciding to take a chance that the man was telling the truth, Penny said, 'Hélène was on a list of fences on Colin's computer.'

'That doesn't surprise me,' said Hamish. 'She always just about skated on the right side of the law, and things are not exactly buoyant in the antiques market at the moment. People are tightening their belts. It's too tempting for business owners to do what they need to do to survive, even if that does mean the odd shady deal. I'll tell you what, time's ticking on, so why don't you two stay for dinner and I'll look out the records of everything I've sold through Colin? I don't know if it will be of any help, but at least you'll know something of Colin's legitimate business dealings. Laird knows if there were any illegitimate ones.'

Hamish smiled at his own little joke and looked at Penny and Jim expectantly.

Penny took a millisecond to consider the alternative (mac n cheese leftovers, bleurgh) and nodded.

'Thanks. We'd love to stay.'

'Great,' said Hamish. 'I'll let the cook know and get someone to take you for a private tour of the castle while we're waiting.'

Penny had expected dinner to be a fairly grand affair, given that they were in a castle, but it was quite ordinary. They were shown into a dining room, only slightly larger than her parents' albeit with an elaborate stone fireplace and wood panelling, where the cook had laid dishes on the table so that they could help themselves.

Hamish was already seated at the head of the table, alongside a woman who Penny recognised as his wife, Cara. To his other side sat a man Penny didn't recognise.

As Penny and Jim entered, the trio immediately stood to greet them.

'I hope you enjoyed your tour. Come in, sit down. Have you met my wife? Cara, this is Penny and Jim. Jim looks after our animals and Penny…?' Hamish looked at Penny quizzically.

'I'm Jim's friend,' said Penny, holding out a hand.

Cara ignored the hand and leaned in, air kissing Penny. Three times. Penny, not sure when the air kissing would stop, went in for a fourth and almost headbutted the woman.

'Oh! Sorry, are you alright? I'm a bit out of practice with the kissy thing.'

Cara smiled warmly and said, 'Don't worry about it. Have you met our factor, Chris Spencer?'

The man, who had been shaking Jim's hand a moment before, turned at the sound of his own name. He proffered the hand again and Penny obligingly shook it.

'I don't think I've ever met a factor before,' she said.

Chris gave a mock bow and, in an accent Penny thought of as Posh Edinburgh, said, 'I'm honoured to be the first. Technically I'm a property manager but in reality, I'm Hamish's business manager.'

'I stole him from Burdocks,' said Hamish. 'Ha! Best broker they had, and I pinched you from right under their noses. His father's an old friend, you see.'

They were interrupted by the chimes of the clock on the mantelpiece. Hamish, brimming with bonhomie and, Penny suspected, a few pre-dinner whiskies, clapped his hands and invited them all to sit down "before Mrs Goggins in the kitchen shouts at me for letting the food get cold."

Jim sat next to Chris and Penny took the chair beside Cara, who kept up a steady stream of chatter. She was delighted to discover that Penny was the owner of Losers Club and rhapsodised about a friend whose life had been changed by Penny's programme.

'She put on so much weight during her illness and it's wonderful to see her full of life again. She said she's made friends for life in her little group and the online support is amazing. You must be so proud of your business.'

'Thanks. I am proud,' said Penny. 'It feels good to be making a difference.'

She realised that, despite feeling like a drudge next to the glamorous beauty, she genuinely liked Cara. She'd been expecting a shallow shopaholic, but the woman had gone out of her way to put Penny at her ease.

'So, I've been thinking,' said Cara, 'I don't have many friends on the island, and I would like to eat healthier. Would I be allowed to join Losers Club?'

Penny imagined this svelte sophisticate sitting next to Sandra Next Door in the church hall of a Wednesday. It would drive Sandra mad.

'Of course! We'd love to have you. Give me your email address and I'll send you details.'

Chris leaned over the table to help himself to more roast potatoes.

'I'm in pretty much the same boat. I haven't heard of Losers Club, though. Maybe I could take you for a coffee sometime and you could tell me all about it?'

Ooh, forward, thought Penny. She regarded Chris, smart-casual in his jeans and white shirt, with his tousled fair hair and strong jawline, and decided that she quite liked forward.

'Yes, that would be lovely,' she said.

'Great,' said Chris, his eyes twinkling with mischief, 'but you're not going to turn up in school uniform, are you?'

'You can go off people, you know,' snapped Penny, although there was also a little twinkle in her eyes.

CHAPTER 10

Penny and Jim left the castle in high spirits, having had a wonderful evening. Jim was clutching a list of items that Hamish had sold through Colin, although neither he nor Penny were quite sure whether it was at all useful. A quick glance had revealed none of the items mentioned earlier by Hélène.

'You know,' said Penny, 'Hélène wasn't exactly forthcoming about what she'd sold for Colin. She was a bit cagey, even.'

'Aye,' Jim agreed, 'she knows a lot more than she's letting on.'

'Which is why I was thinking, well, what with her being out with Johnny for the evening, we might take a wee peek at her records?'

Jim braked far more sharply than the bend warranted.

'No. God, what is it with you and breaking into places?'

Penny sighed. 'You're right. I'm hardly dressed for it. Drop me off at Eileen's and I'll see what she's managed to dig up on Colin. Oh, and can we stop at the supermarket on the way? This is going to involve wine.'

'Alright, Miss Bossyknickers,' said Jim, relieved that she'd dropped the subject so easily. 'Why can't I come to Eileen's?'

'I thought you'd be going home to charge up the ice cream van.'

'I hate to say this, but you're right. I need to get Colin tucked in for the night.'

'Also, Eileen and I are long overdue for a girly chat. Just wait 'til she hears that Chris asked me for coffee. For goodness' sake, Jim, will you stop braking so hard!'

'You're not actually going for a coffee with him, are you? I mean, have you heard the man speak? Sounds like he's got… got… the Queen shoved up his arse.'

'Oi! You do not mess with her Maj,' Penny warned him.

'Sorry,' said Jim, 'She was the poshest person I could think of. But seriously, you're not going out with him, right?'

'Jeeze, it's only coffee. It's not like we're getting married. Although,' Penny grinned, 'can you imagine if I did a Harry Met Sally in the middle of Cuppachino?'

'That's not even funny. You can't go out with him. The man's an arsehole.'

'You liked him fine at dinner. I heard the two of you making plans to go for a pint.'

'Well, that was then, and this is now. He's an arsehole. Connard, arschloch and gilipollas. Ha! See? I was paying attention at school!'

They bickered all the way to Port Vik harbour, where Penny slammed the car door and stalked towards Eileen's cottage.

'And I'm not fucking giving you a lift home!' Jim shouted after her.

'And I'm not flippin' asking you to, you big twat,' Penny shouted back, before stomping up the lane to let herself in Eileen and Kenny's back door.

Eileen looked up from her laptop at the sound of the door. She watched Penny kick off her shoes in the porch and noted that her friend had a face like thunder. Jim again. Why couldn't those two just admit they fancied each other and have a good snog? Why did they have to make it so complicated? In Eileen's opinion, if you fancied someone, you snogged the face off them. Simple as. Unless you were married, of course. She didn't think her Kenny would take too kindly to her snogging the face off Jimmy Gupta the baker. Mind you, he wouldn't say no to a lifetime of free fondant fancies, so she might get away with it.

'What's the matter and is that wine for me?' asked Eileen as Penny plonked herself into a kitchen chair, groaned and pretended to headbutt the table.

'It's for us. Bloody Jim. I said I'd go out for a coffee with Chris and now he's acting like I've offered to shag the man on the good table in Cuppachino on pensioner day. Sorry, let's not talk about it. How are things with you?'

'Oh, let's do talk about it,' said Eileen, reaching into the cupboard for two glasses. 'Who's Chris?'

'Nobody, really. Laird Hamish's factor, business advisor, whatever.'

'And is he top totty? Does he have the x factor? Cordon bleu, don't tell me he looks like Simon Cowell?'

'*Sacre* bleu, no he doesn't. He's quite handsome and seems nice enough. Okay for a coffee and a wee flirt but nothing more. You know me. I'm not ready for–'

'Another relationship. Yes, yes, but you're going to have to do something before your fanny heals itself. That can happen. Sean Harrow told me.'

Penny snorted. 'That was when you were sixteen and he was trying to get you to sleep with him. Are you telling me that you've believed it all this time?'

'Um, no,' said Eileen, shifting uncomfortably in her chair. She unscrewed the cap off the bottle of wine and poured them both a generous measure.

'I love you Winnie the Pooh,' said Penny, raising her glass.

'Love you too Rubber Duck,' said Eileen, clinking her glass on Penny's. 'Now, what did you find out up at the castle and why are you wearing school uniform?'

Penny told Eileen about Hamish having left the Laird's Ladle with Colin for valuation. Swearing Eileen to secrecy, she explained about Hamish's financial difficulties and how he'd suspected Cara of having an affair with Colin.

'So,' she concluded, 'Hamish seems pretty straight up and, even if his wife was having an affair with Colin, why would he kill the golden goose?'

'What goose?' asked Eileen. 'I didn't know about any goose. Where does the goose come into things?'

'No, I mean Colin. He's the golden goose. It's just an expression. It means Hamish was relying on him to get him money.'

'Why didn't he go to Hélène?'

'He hinted that they'd had a fling way back and that things hadn't ended well between them. Also, he pretty much said she's a dodgy dealer. If Colin was selling stuff through her then it probably was stolen. Sounds like he was legitimately selling things for Hamish but had a little deal going on the side with Hélène.' Penny slapped her forehead. 'Oh, I've just remembered, Hamish gave us a list of things he'd sold via Colin, and I put it in my handbag when we were in the car.'

'Or is it in your schoolbag?' asked Eileen with a cheeky grin.

'Ha, ha. Do you want to have a look?'

'In a minute. Let me tell you what I've found. Remember last time, when we did all those ancestry and news searches? Well, I did them again for Colin. There's nothing under Dogood. That one was simple because there aren't too many Dogoods in Australia. The bad news is that there are loads of Duguids, so I've asked my contact on the dark web to look into him.'

'Your what now?' said Penny, astounded that Eileen had even heard of anything beyond Google.

'My dark web guy, Spartacus. It's amazing how many

different people you meet when you work in the tourist office.'

'That sounds a bit scary. Is Spartacus even his real name? Just how friendly are you?'

'Ivan Kimov.'

'Well, that's a wee bit more friendly than I'd expected.'

'I gave him a picture of Colin and he's running it through some sort of photo recognition thingy. I really struggled to find a photo, but then I remembered they did an article in the Parish newsletter when the museum had that Vik - Religion Through the Ages exhibition a couple of months ago.'

'That's brilliant, Eileen. You clever thing!'

Eileen flushed with pleasure. Or it might have been the wine. Penny wasn't sure. She rummaged in her handbag and brought out the envelope that Hamish had given Jim.

'I doubt this will be of much use,' she said, pulling out the contents and handing the list to Eileen. She rifled through some additional pages. 'I didn't realise, but he's given us photographs of the items he sold through Colin.'

Penny fanned the photographs out on the kitchen table and stared at them. She was vaguely aware of Eileen oohing and aahing over some of the precious items Hamish had sold, but something in one of the photos had caught her eye. She picked it up and looked at it more closely.

'Well, bugger Jim with a wonky pineapple.'

Johnny was living his best life; sipping champagne waiting for a beautiful woman and planning how to go from polite conversation to badabing.

Truth be told, he'd been bored on the island. What did you do for fun around here? Everyone seems obsessed with walking and scones, he mused. Goddamn scones everywhere and you have to call them scawns, not scohns. They probably have to do the walking to stop the scawns from killing them. And WTF is it with the people? Nobody's busy and they have time for everything. Oh yeah, and the endless chatting, my God, you can't even buy a stamp without a discussion about whether it's a good drying day and how Mrs Hay's bunions have grown. Johnny wasn't sure what a bunion was or how you cooked them. Maybe he'd ask that cute little waitress, whatshername Raquel-Rachel-Rochelle, if they had them on the menu. Or were they a bar snack?

'Excuse me, bartender,' he asked the barman, 'could I have a bowl of bunions?'

The barman's double take was almost imperceptible. 'Do you mean onions, sir? I have some pickled onions.'

'No, I mean–'

Johnny's train of thought was stalled by the sight of the woman in the figure-hugging green dress who had swept into the dining room and was making her way towards him, seemingly oblivious to the fact that every head in the place had turned to watch her pass.

'Bada-freaking-bing!' he exclaimed. 'You look hot.'

Hélène slid gracefully onto a bar stool and smiled at his reaction.

She gestured at her dress. 'Oh, zis old thing. I'm sorry, I didn't want to overdo it on our first…what would you call it? Not a date. Our first get together.'

'Honey, you'd look like a million bucks in a sack. Champagne?'

Over the next hour, they chatted amiably about Johnny, then some more about Johnny, before he remembered that he had two missions. The first and most important was, of course, badabing, but the second was to find out about Hélène's relationship with Colin. He decided to impress her with his local knowledge.

'Hey, barkeep, what about those bunions, huh?'

Deciding that discretion was the better part of valour, the barman sighed and placed a bowl of small pickled onions on the bar.

Johnny picked one, pressed it to his lips and bit down

seductively, all the while maintaining eye contact with Hélène.

'I can't get enough of Mrs Hay's bunions.'

He reckoned he must have done something right because, after that, she opened up a little. She asked his opinions on fresh lumbago and whether he preferred his quinsy chopped or julienned.

The conversation soon turned to Colin. He asked how they met, and she told him that Colin had asked her opinion on a nineteenth century armoire donated to the museum. Her speciality was furniture, she said, although she sold a range of fine pieces. Perhaps Johnny was looking for something Scottish to take back to America?

Johnny thought that was a fine idea. But about Colin, were she and him friends or was there a little more going on?'

Hélène assured Johnny that they were merely friends and that she hadn't seen Colin in over a week. Now, how would he like to come to the shop tomorrow and choose a few pieces to take home?

'That's weird,' said Johnny. 'You said months before.'

'Pardon?'

'You said you hadn't seen him in months.'

Hélène airily waved a hand and leaned over, giving him a tantalising glimpse of cleavage.

'Ah, months, weeks, days. Who knows? But I am sad that he is gone. Now, let us have some more champagne and I will tell you all about how the coupe glasses in my shop were modelled on Marie Antoinette's breasts.'

Johnny Munroe, fine actor and dogged detective, was easily distracted. Ba-da-bing.

'We definitely should not be doing this,' gasped Eileen as, standing on an overturned wheelbarrow, she winced under the weight of Penny's foot on her shoulder.

Penny scrambled atop the low roof of the extension behind Hélène's Drawers and turned to pull her friend up after her.

'Shh! Be quiet. Give me your hands and I'll pull.'

After a few heaves and some muttered curse words, Eileen finally arrived panting beside her friend on the roof of what appeared to be Hélène's kitchen. Both women were dressed in an odd assortment of black clothes, scavenged from the drawers of Eileen, Kenny and their children, Ricky and Gervais. Eileen was wearing a little black dress tucked into Ricky's pyjama bottoms. Penny had squeezed herself into Eileen's yoga pants and one of Kenny's old sweatshirts. It smelled of motor oil and Lynx.

'What if she's here?' Eileen asked.

'Relax,' Penny assured her. 'She'll be out with Johnny.'

'I don't think we should be doing this. Especially not after almost two bottles of wine.'

Penny hiccoughed and giggled, 'This is exactly when we should be doing it. Courage, mon ami, courage.'

'Cooooraaaage,' Eileen echoed. 'Okay, let's va te faire footer.'

'Or on y va perhaps?' Penny gently corrected her.

'That as well. But I'm more interested in how we get your backside through that little window. You've pulled, now it's my turn to push.'

'It's a sash window. It should slide up a bit more.'

Penny put her hands beneath the window and heaved upwards. It didn't budge. Bugger. She bent over, stuck her head through and looked up. Something in the mechanism was blocking it and the window could only be opened from the inside. Double bugger.

She turned over and tried to squirm through the gap. Half in and half out, she felt Eileen's hands on her bum.

'You're not kneading dough. Give me a shove,' she hissed.

Eileen obliged and a moment later, Penny slid face first

onto the plush bedroom carpet and found herself nose to nose with a white cat. The cat growled at Penny, tensing as though it was about to lash out. Penny growled back and sprang to her feet, wondering how she'd have explained a scratched face in the morning. She stepped back as Eileen made her own inelegant entrance and sent the cat scurrying under the bed. So far, so good.

'Winnie the Pooh to Rubber Duck. This feels wrong,' said Eileen, taking in the four poster bed and the ornate dressing table with its clutter of lotions and potions.

'Rubber Duck to Winnie the Pooh. When we met her, the woman was wearing Hamish's brooch. Either she stole it, bought it or Hamish gave it to her and they're having an affair. Someone is lying and we have to find out what's going on.'

'We should have waited for Sergeant Wilson. I'm a bit scared.'

'Scared? The house is empty, there's nothing to be afraid of.'

'I'm afraid of Sergeant Wilson. That woman scares the merde out of me.'

Penny groaned. 'Me too. Look, we'll just have a quick scout around, see what we can find and be on our way. Neither Hélène nor Sergeant Wilson will ever know we've been here.'

She went to the bedroom door, followed by a reluctant Eileen, and together they crept downstairs.

The shop was eerily silent, lit only by the faint glow of the streetlights outside. Wardrobes and dressers lined the walls, their looming presence reminding Penny of lurkers at a funeral. The myriad of cabinets and chests of drawers were dark boxes in the gloom, and more than once Penny cursed softly as she caught a hip on a corner while trying to thread her way between them. Behind her she heard Eileen, who by now had convinced herself that the place was haunted, stifle a squeal as a tablecloth moved, stirred by a draught stealing beneath the shop door. This was followed by a louder squeal when a small ball of white fur shot past them to take refuge under the desk.

'Bloody cat. Did you leave the bedroom door open?' asked Penny.

'Mm hmm,' said Eileen, not trusting herself to speak. She was so frightened that she was on the verge of screaming and she thought she might have done a little wee in Ricky's pyjama trousers.

Penny took her hand and said, 'It's alright, lovey. Come with me. Sit here by the desk and I'll capture the cat. We have to put him back or Hélène will notice someone was here.'

Eileen sat with her feet up, knees tucked under her chin, while Penny lowered herself to the floor and spoke gently to the frightened animal.

'Here kitty. It's fine. Come and see your Auntie Penny. She's got something nice for you.'

This cat was not for coaxing. Once again, it growled and gave a hiss for good measure. Penny could see its tail twitching and knew that if she tried to put a hand under the desk to grab it, she'd come away with shredded fingers.

She stood up, telling Eileen to stay where she was, and followed the furniture maze back to the house behind the shop. A quick check of the kitchen cupboard revealed a packet of Dreamies.

'Also known as cat heroin,' she said with a satisfied smile.

Back at the desk, she once more bent down and shook the packet of Dreamies. The tail stopped twitching and the cat looked mildly interested. Penny took one of the small treats from the packet and rolled it towards the cat. Tentatively, the cat sniffed the treat, just in case the strange lady was trying to poison him. He gave it an experimental lick and gently batted it with a paw. Looks like Dreamies, smells like Dreamies, scoots like Dreamies. Definitely Dreamies, he decided, before wolfing it down and looking expectantly at the strange lady. This time she laid another Dreamy down, just out of his reach, the minx. The cat took a step forward and ate the little treat.

Inch by inch, Penny coaxed the cat out from his hidey-hole until at last she was able to pick him up. Hopped up on Dreamies and well aware that the strange lady had a bag of the things, the cat chose not to object.

'Yessssss,' Penny hissed, holding the creature aloft. 'I am the cat whisperer.'

Her joy, however, was short-lived. The floor above them creaked, the noise cracking loud in the shroud of the night.

'Not a ghost. Just a creepy old building,' Eileen babbled.

'Eileen, shush!'

They listened for a moment, then relaxed. Just a creepy old building.

Creak. Creak. Creak.

Footsteps!

Clinging on to the cat, Penny beckoned Eileen to follow her and bundled all three of them into a wardrobe by the shop door. She closed the wardrobe doors and pushed until they were all squeezed into a corner. Thank goodness they made their wardrobes big in the old days.

Creak. Creak. Creak.

Footsteps on the stairs. A muffled "oof" as a body collided with furniture. Shit! Someone was in the shop with them.

The cat chose this moment to object to the sudden withdrawal of Dreamies. The strange lady had a full packet of the things and hadn't given him a single Dreamy since she'd picked him up. He squirmed and scratched at her hand until she dropped him and, with a thump, he landed on the wardrobe floor.

Penny and Eileen sank even further into the corner, trembling and silently praying that the intruder hadn't heard the noise. Or, if they had, they wouldn't open the wardrobe. Or, if they opened the wardrobe, please God let it be the other door and not the one that Penny and Eileen were cowering behind.

Creak. Creak. Creak.

The footsteps stopped outside the wardrobe.

Penny hastily clamped one hand over Eileen's mouth and the other over her own.

The door clicked open.

The other door.

Penny closed her eyes and entreated her holy father and all the angels. For the love of fudge, don't open this door as well. Not this door. Please, please, please. I'll tell Mum I stole ten pence out of her purse when I was six and the tooth fairy didn't come, even though she probably figured it out because she was the forgetful tooth fairy and where the feck else would I have got the small fortune that was ten pence? I'll confess to Mrs Hay that when she asked me to deliver her peppermint slices to the church sale, only half a box made it that far. I'll move out of Mum and Dad's so that Hector can bring his new boyfriend home without Mum putting him off boys forever by asking them who's the postman and who's the letterbox. I'll tell Jim I fancy the pants off him and had a fantasy about shagging him in the front seat of Phil, only the fantasy ended when the gear stick went up my…Jesus, did I say that out loud?'

'Ah, so you do fancy Jim,' whispered Eileen. 'It's okay. Whoever it was has gone. Do you think we could get out of here and you can tell me all about that gear stick?'

Penny could almost feel her friend smiling in the darkness.

Johnny was beginning to feel quite frustrated. Every time he tried to turn the conversation towards Colin, the woman deftly steered it back to something else. He'd learned nothing and, even worse, she seemed immune to his hints that she might like to enjoy her champagne somewhere more relaxing. Like his bedroom, for instance. And now, to top it all off, she'd abandoned him to take a phone call. He wasn't used to people abandoning him and not fawning over him. He didn't like it.

Hélène came back into the bar, hips swaying in that tight dress, and for a moment Johnny forgot that he was irritated.

'I am so sorry,' she purred. 'There has been an emergency and I must go. Our little chat has been very interesting. How you say…enlightening.'

She reached out to stroke Johnny's cheek then bent forward and softly kissed the spot on his jaw where her hand had rested.

Johnny breathed in the delicate scent of her perfume as she raised her lips to his ear and whispered, 'Perhaps we can have another get together and chat some more.'

And, with that, she was gone, leaving Johnny to ponder whether it would appear on his hotel bill if he went to his room and spent some quality time watching a particular pay-per-view channel.

Back safe and sound at Eileen's kitchen table, a third bottle of wine in front of them, Penny slumped in her chair and said, 'I'm really sorry, Winnie the Pooh. I put you through all that for nothing.'

Eileen grinned. 'Not nothing,' she replied. 'At least we know your true feelings about Jim. And then there's this.'

She lifted the little black dress and there, tucked firmly into the waistband of Ricky's pyjama trousers, was a large black book.

'I grabbed it just before we hid in the wardrobe. I had to wedge the bottom into my knickers, and I should warn you that I might have done a little pee in them when that cat jumped out.'

Penny plucked Hélène's diary from Eileen's waistband.

'I've said it before and I'll say it again, you're a bloody genius.'

'Derrière.'

'De rien.'

'Don't mention it.'

CHAPTER 11

Screwing her eyes closed against the enemy that was daylight, Penny reached out to switch off her alarm clock. She pressed all the buttons and still the thing was beeping. Oh God, she was going to have to open her eyes. Two was slightly ambitious. Maybe she should start with one eye.

'How much did I have to drink last night?' she groaned, once again pressing all the buttons.

Beep beep. Beep beep.

She opened her left eye just a tiny little bit. Sod. It wasn't even her alarm. She peered through the slit and spied her phone on the floor, still attached to its charging cable, the screen merrily flashing up another text message.

Beep beep. Beep beep.

For flip's sake, who can be this desperate to get hold of me at…Penny peered blearily at her alarm clock…eight o'clock? She rolled over and caught the cable, reeling the phone in like an expert angler. She'd just got to the part where she was about to detach it, when gravity took over and the little silver devil dropped to the floor, leaving her holding an empty cable. Jeeze, no wonder fishing's a rubbish sport she thought, dangling a hand over the side of the bed and vainly scrabbling around the carpet.

She cursed as she felt her hand hit the side of the phone and she knew for a fact that she'd just sent the thing scooting under the bed.

Beep beep. Beep beep.

Alright already! Penny opened the other eye and tentatively sat up. Okay, sitting was fine. She swung her legs over the side of the bed and stood up. Standing not so fine. Oh no. Head flying. Stomach pointing out the emergency exits. Oh no, no, no. Stomach contents requesting permission to land. She grabbed her wastepaper basket just in case she didn't make it to the loo in time and ran.

Beep beep. Beep beep.

Penny returned to her bedroom with a large glass of water and two paracetamol. They were more belt and braces really, as she felt much better having rid herself of the remnants of last night's excesses.

Her phone went again, this time accompanied by a loud banging on her bedroom wall.

'Alright, Edith. Keep your eyebrows on, I'm getting it.'

She reached under her bed and retrieved the offending object. One missed call and forty-two missed texts, all from Jim.

Sorry.

Sorry. Sorry.

Sorry. Sorry. Sorry.

She stopped reading at that point, fairly sure she'd got the gist.

She texted back.

Where r u?

The reply came almost immediately.

Sitting in Phil outside your house

Like a big, hairy stalker?

Exactly like a big hairy stalker. Can you forgive me?

Do u freely admit u r a twat?

My name is Jim Space and I am a twat
Why did u text me 42 times?
I didn't want to knock on the window and wake you
And u thought my phone going off 42 times wouldn't wake me?
My name is Jim Space and I am a twat
Ok I forgive u. Come in.

Penny padded through to the front door to let him in. This time there was no cheeky joke at the expense of her outfit, only a contrite man bearing two newspapers and a pint of milk.

'I brought my own paper for a change. Thought your dad might want to do the crossword now he's feeling a bit better.'

'He's still a bit peely-wally, but I expect he'll want to get up today.'

They went through to the kitchen and Penny did a double take. Her mother appeared to have taken care of yesterday's footprints by painting the whole floor yellow. She looked out the window. Holy guacamole, Dad's shed was like a beacon.

'Oh, Sandra Next Door will be pleased,' she said wryly. 'Mojo shitting in her begonias, Timmy barking and now Dad's back garden shrine to Ra.'

'Och, leave her alone,' said Jim, settling himself at the table and opening his newspaper. 'She likes complaining. It makes her feel she's in the right. Sandra goes through life thinking the rest of us mere mortals are useless and Jesus wants her for a sunbeam. You just have to take her how she is.'

'That was very wise and insightful.'

'Aye. Jim Space. Not such a twat after all. Now, where's my bacon sandwich?'

'I have a confession to make,' said Penny, her back to him while she obligingly put a frying pan on the hob. 'This probably isn't the right time, but something happened last night, and I promised that I would tell you how I feel and I thought I should get this out of the way as quickly as possible so if you don't feel the same way then we can carry on as normal and it doesn't have to affect anything.'

Behind her there was silence. Avoiding looking at Jim, she took a packet of bacon from the fridge and began to lay slices into the pan.

'You see,' she continued, 'Eileen and I did something stupid after quite a lot of wine and it made me realise that it's about time I moved on with my life. After all, I can't stay with Mum and Dad forever. The twins and I need a place of our own. I think I'm ready to close the last chapter and start the next. I wondered if you might want to be part of the next chapter in a…erm…more than friends sort of way. Does that make sense?'

'Waste of time!'

'Oh. Okay. Sorry, I just thought…'

'Three across. Pointless to refuse clock. It had me going there, thinking about clock hands and pointing at the right time. Refuse – rubbish – waste. Ha! Waste of time.'

'Have you been listening to a word I…oh never mind. How do you want your bacon done?'

Any further discussion was stymied by the arrival of Len, who was feeling much better and had been tempted from his lair by the smell of bacon. Realising they had company, he fastened the top button of his pyjamas then sat down at the table across from Jim.

'Is that my crossword?' he asked, steeling himself to give Jim a good telling off.

'Morning, Len. I brought my own paper today. Yours is here. How are you feeling?'

'Almost back to normal, thanks. I think I might be able to try a bacon sandwich. Is there something different about the kitchen?'

'I'll give you a clue,' said Jim. 'Cowardly level below.'

'Oho!' exclaimed Len triumphantly. 'Too easy, Mr Space. Yellow floor! And you thought you were so clever.'

Then he was silent for a few seconds, before…

'Dear me, what has she done now?'

Penny placed a bacon filled roll and a glass of orange juice in front of him.

'You might want to have this before you take a look outside.'

It was after ten by the time Jim persuaded Penny to put some proper clothes on and "get your big backside in the car." Consequently, they happily bickered all the way to the Vik Hotel, where they'd promised to pick up Johnny.

They were still bickering when they entered the lobby and bumped into Rachel.

'Do you two never stop arguing?' she asked.

'Shh, Rachel,' said Penny. 'This is important. I'm telling you, Jim, it was 1998.'

'Definitely 1999,' said Jim.

'What's 1999?' asked Rachel.

'The year Geri Halliwell left the Spice Girls,' Jim told her.

'Except it was 1998,' said Penny.

'Are you here for breakfast? Because you're a bit late. 1998,' said Rachel.

'1999 and we're here to pick up Johnny,' Jim told her.

'1998 and you've just missed him. He went up to his room with someone from the film crew.'

'1998. We'll wait here for him,' said Penny, grinning and giving Rachel a high five. 'Girl power.'

Jim summoned Google on his phone. A few taps later, he sat down heavily on one of the leather wingback chairs, looking dejected.

'I'll let him know you're here,' said Rachel, throwing Jim a pitying look. A look that said "Suck it up, fella. She's never going to stop reminding you that she was right."

'Ah, it feels good to be right,' Penny gloated once Rachel had gone. 'How does it feel to be wrong?'

Jim simply shifted a little in his chair, smiled and waited.

A moment later, Penny wrinkled her nose then dashed to the other side of the lobby, crying, 'You absolute midden!'

The lift next to her pinged, the doors opened and a ginger-bearded man in a beige mac stepped out, followed by a short woman she recognised as Jenny, the costume lady from the set. The man sniffed the air and eyed Penny in disgust.

'You had too many eggs for breakfast, lady?'

Before Penny could reply, Jim sprang out of his chair, exclaiming, 'Wow, great beard, Johnny. Nice to meet you again, Jenny. I see you had time to sort out the facial hair. Amazing job.'

Jenny beamed at the compliment and gave a self-conscious giggle. 'Oh, it was a stroke of luck, really. I met a woman called Fiona in the village pub last night and she said she could sort me out with some hair. Even sent her husband home to get it. He came back with a whole jar of the stuff.'

Johnny blew on the patch of red hair above his lip. 'Yeah, great job, Jen, but would you mind trimming the moustache a little? It keeps getting in my mouth.'

As Jenny got to work with a pair of nail scissors, Penny and Jim exchanged horrified glances. Then Penny shrugged.

'Well, at least nobody in Cuppachino will recognise him.'

They led Johnny to the car, Jen peeling off to return to the set in her own hire car. Cuppachino was only a short distance down the High Street, but neither Penny nor Jim had wanted Johnny on the loose. If people found out he was going to the coffee shop, the place would be rammed, and they'd get no peace to discuss the case.

Jim managed to find a parking space nearby and a quick glance across the road told them that Hélène's Drawers was closed. Penny wasn't surprised. Eileen pinching that diary last night meant they had hardly covered their tracks. Hélène was bound to have noticed it missing this morning and no doubt Sergeant Wilson would be shouting and swearing down the phone shortly. Ho hum, she thought, there isn't much I can do about it now. Here's hoping that the coffee shop isn't too busy, and we can get a table big enough for us all.

As it was, Cuppachino was relatively quiet. Mr Hubbard, Elsie, Fiona, Gordon, Sandra Next Door and Eileen had pulled two tables together to make one larger one and sat waiting, oversized cups and a plate of scones in front of them.

'Love the beard, Johnny,' said Fiona, giving the actor a wink.

'You look grand, dear,' said Elsie, patting the empty chair to her right. 'Come sit here, I've saved you a place. I brought some knitting for you to try. I thought you'd find it relaxing. Knit one, purl one.'

'Hey, knit one, poil one. I can do that,' said Johnny, settling in next to Elsie and making an eager grab for the knitting needles.

As Elsie took Johnny through the basics of knitting, Jim and Penny ordered their coffees.

Finally, with everyone duly fed and watered, the discussion turned to the case.

'I got nuttin',' Johnny declared, clacking away in the corner. 'The broad said she'd seen Colin last week, not months ago like she said before. She was only there to sell me things. That's the problem with being a famous guy, all the other guys want your money. They don't wanna be friends no more, not like Elsie. You get me, dontcha Elsie doll? You're like my Scottish mom.'

Elsie went pink and buttered his scone for him.

Mrs Hubbard rolled her eyes heavenward and said, 'Me and Elsie have found some very interesting information but, before I tell you, let's hear what everyone else has got.'

'Surprise, surprise. Mrs H holding out for her big moment again,' said Sandra Next Door. She pointed at Penny. 'And you have certainly got some explaining to do. I'm reporting your father's shed to the council again. The police, if needs be. He surely has to have some sort of planning permission to paint it bright yellow. It stands out like an infected thumb. I'll be insisting that they come round and take a look.'

Penny caught Elsie's eye and gulped. The last thing they needed was the authorities poking around Dad's shed.

'It was Mum's idea of cheering him up,' she told Sandra Next Door. 'Don't worry, we'll get it sorted. It'll be green again by next week. What did you and Geoff find out?'

Sandra Next Door sniffed, somewhat mollified, and took a sip of her coffee.

'I don't think any of you will be shocked to learn that Hélène *was* lying about her relationship with Colin. She met up with him at the café out by the loch the day before he was killed. She had the salmon salad, and he had a bowl of Cullen Skink. Then they shared the cheesecake. *Shared* the cheesecake. One cheesecake, two spoons. Not very hygienic if you ask me. I wouldn't even share my deodorant with my Geoff that time we went to Edinburgh for the weekend, and he left his soap bag at home. It's a roll-on and who wants man hairs in their roll-on?'

'And?' Penny prompted her.

'And he had to buy a toothbrush. Complete waste of money when he had a perfectly good electric one lying at home.'

'And what about Colin and Hélène?' asked Fiona.

'Oh, they were all over each other. Mrs Mearns, the woman who runs the café, said they were there every week, kissing and plotting how they were going to find the Vik treasure. Apparently, Colin had found some old map at the museum, and they'd been on the internet trying to figure out what all the symbols meant.'

Gordon leaned forward. 'Did she say what the symbols were?'

'No. She's a café manager, not a cryptologist.'

Johnny looked up from his knitting. 'Perhaps I could help, what with me being Pickles the spy and all.'

Elsie gave him a fond smile. 'That's just a character in a

movie, dear. You carry on with your knitting. Goodness, by the time we leave, you'll have the world's longest Barbie scarf.'

'Right, so we know Hélène and Colin were in a snoggy relationship and they were looking for the treasure,' Fiona summed up. 'Gordon and I didn't find much when we googled those dealers. They exist. They seem to be genuine antiques dealers. What about you, Eileen? What did you find out about Colin?'

'I'm still waiting for Spartacus to get back to me,' said Eileen.

'Spartacus?' asked Fiona.

'My dark web contact. I couldn't find Colin, so he's running a facial recognition thingy.'

Fiona frowned. 'That sounds a bit dodgy. Do you even know his real name? How did you meet him?'

'At the tourist office. Ivan Kimov.'

Jim's face lit up and he gave a short bark of laughter.

'Vonce a veek or just at veekends?' he asked.

Eileen was confused. 'No, he came on holiday.'

'I bet he did,' Jim chuckled.

'Enough,' said Penny, leaping to her friend's rescue, although she wasn't sure that Eileen actually needed saving. Penny could tell by the woman's face that Mr Joke was knocking but there was nobody home. Never mind, it would dawn on her eventually. 'Tell them what else we have, Eileen.'

From her bag, Eileen drew the large diary and Penny heard Jim's sharp intake of breath as he recognised it. He didn't look pleased. Suddenly, a thought struck her. Jim had been very reluctant to let her break into Hélène's to see that diary. Where exactly had Jim been last night? Could he have been doing a little breaking and entering of his own? Was he the other person in the shop? Probably, she decided. He must have gone in himself, like some bloody knight in shining armour, because he didn't want her getting into any trouble. Well, he'd wasted his time. She was perfectly capable of being a burglar without his help and now she was quite glad he wasn't listening this morning when she'd tried to tell him she fancied him. Breaking into places and scaring the bejesus out of other people who'd broken in. The man had no consideration.

Penny tuned back into the conversation. Eileen was explaining how they'd sneaked into Hélène's and been disturbed.

'And when we got back home, I had Hélène's diary in my knickers. It was damp, but Penny didn't mind.'

Mrs Hubbard, who had picked up the book to examine it, immediately dropped it back on the table.

'When you say damp, dearie?'

'Oh, it was just sweaty from all the excitement. Don't worry, it didn't touch my lady bits. Anyway, about the symbols. I didn't think anything of it before, but if you have a look in March, there are some pictures.'

Mrs Hubbard flicked through March, stopping at the sixteenth. Everyone leaned in for a closer look at what appeared to be doodles at the top of the page.

$$\pm \triangle \, \Omega \int$$

'Do you think those could be the symbols Mrs Mearns was talking about?' asked Eileen.

Sandra Next Door gave her a friendly nudge with an elbow.

'For someone who's not very bright, you're a wee genius.'

Eileen looked pleased. 'Murky buckets. That's what Penny called me.'

'Why did you call her murky buckets?' asked Sandra Next Door, glaring at Penny.

'I didn't. She means merci beaucoup. The third symbol is

Omega, last letter of the Greek alphabet. Could the last symbol be like how they used to write s in the old days? You know, where it almost looks like an f?'

'Oh yes, dearie, we know all about that,' said Mrs Hubbard. 'Do you remember, Elsie? The minister once brought out the old King James bible for a special Easter service. Job 3:12 "Why did the knees prevent me? or why the breasts that I should suck." Except he didn't say suck. He was looking directly at Mrs Mackay in the front row with the Sunday school when he said it. Now, there's a woman who hasn't seen her feet in years.'

Mrs Hubbard could hardly finish the tale. By the time she got to the last sentence, her silver curls were shaking, and the final few words emerged in a wheeze of laughter. Even Elsie, normally the disapproving one of the pair, gave a small titter. The mirth was infectious and soon everyone had joined in, drawing the attention of the other patrons.

'Okay, okay, we have to calm down. Everyone's looking,' said Fiona.

Gordon took a few deep breaths and wiped his eyes. It was a relief to laugh again. He'd been so miserable recently, after what he'd done. The thought quickly sobered him and the cloud once more descended.

'If Hélène and Colin had the map and couldn't figure it out,' he said, 'there's not much chance we will. We don't even know if it has anything to do with Colin's death. Let's put it to one side for a minute and hear what Mrs Hubbard and Elsie have to say.'

Mrs Hubbard looked at Elsie, who nodded, giving her silent permission to go ahead.

'You probably don't realise,' she began, 'that the library has old books and documents that can only be accessed with special permission. They're usually accessed for research and such like, but this is Vik. Nothing momentous has ever happened here and the big libraries have all the important things, so there's not much call for research. In fact, nobody knows when any of the material was last accessed. Certainly not during Elsie's tenure, and she's been there almost fifty years.

'Last night, Elsie and I had a good rummage through the old stuff and found some contemporary accounts of the treasure, along with old parish records, wills and deeds. In the mid nineteenth century, the old Union Bank took over the branch from the British Linen Company. I don't think either company found Vik a very profitable place, but the government of the day decreed that the islands had to have banking services, so the people lodged their important documents at the bank. Elsie thinks some of these documents were, I suppose you could say, naturally inherited when the old Union Bank closed in 1952 and the building was turned into the library. Then, when the hideous "new" building was completed and the library moved again, everything moved with it.

'Remember, we didn't have a museum until 2008, so anything written about Vik was stored in the library. Some really important documents, like the Royal Charter, were later moved to the museum, but the rest lay untouched in boxes. It's doubtful anyone but Elsie even knows it's there.

'We spent most of the night trying to decipher old handwriting. It was a nightmare, and we haven't even scratched the surface, but we've come up with some important clues.

'In 1746, James Alexander Macrae was murdered at Hillside Farm. There's an old court document sent to Bruce Duguid at Burnie Croft regarding the transfer of property from James Alexander, known as James-Alec, Macrae to him. Parish records show that Bruce Duguid died on the 5th of May 1748 of intoxication. The Aberdeen Journal from the 10th of May 1748 notes his death and recounts the story of Bruce and James-Alec being the leaders of a band of Jacobites smuggling French loot to the prince. The journal repeats local suspicions that Bruce kept the treasure to himself but adds one interesting fact. James Alec was never buried in consecrated ground. He was buried at Burnie Croft, which was very unusual for the time. Bruce's wife, Mhairi, went on to remarry and lived to a ripe old age.

Now, she would be the obvious choice for secret keeper, and you'll never guess who her last direct descendant was. Och, I'll just tell you. It was Granny Cairns. Remember her? The old woman who lived near the village in the house with no electricity or running water.'

'Oh my word,' said Penny. 'Colin knew Granny Cairns. He told me that time I visited the museum. He was talking about her dog. I bet she was a secret keeper and that's why he got to know her.'

'It's possible that he found out the same information as Mrs Hubbard and Elsie but by different means,' said Jim.

Elsie nodded. 'I agree. You can get a lot of old newspapers and birth records online. However, Burnie Croft is a different story. Tell them, Minty.'

Mrs Hubbard wet her whistle with a sip of her, by now cool, coffee and continued.

'You might think that Burnie Croft is where Granny Cairns lived, but it's not. Burnie Croft was owned by the Deer Estate. The laird at the time, a man called William Deer, was a childhood friend of Mhairi. Her father worked on the estate and the two of them played together. Mhairi even had reading lessons from William's tutor, suggesting that she was treated as almost a member of the family. There are some old letters between the two of them, and it's clear he let her stay on there, rent free, after Bruce's death. Bruce had no children, but the records show that Mhairi and her new husband went on to have six.'

'So, all this guff Colin told me about being a descendant of Bruce Duguid was, well, guff?' asked Penny.

'He must have made it up to explain why he was so interested in the treasure. Or because it sounded exciting. Or because his real name is Twatty McTwatface,' said Eileen.

Mrs Hubbard ignored her and carried on with her tale.

'By 1760 the family had outgrown Burnie Croft and moved to a larger cottage near the village, which was the one Granny Cairns lived in. No wonder Granny Cairns refused to move, with that much family history attached to the place.

'Colin would have struggled to find any information about Burnie Croft, unless Laird Hamish told him something, because when it was handed back to the Deers, they renamed it. All the old deeds and records from it being Burnie Croft through to the change of name are at the library. It was too insignificant to be marked on any map, and there were barely any maps of the island anyway. All the locals knew where everything was, so why bother? In 1824 the croft was sold by the Deers to raise money for taxes. It's doubtful Hamish even knows they ever owned the place.'

'Let me guess,' said Jim. 'By some massive twist of fate, the croft is the cottage that Colin lived in.'

'No, the name of the cottage is–' Mrs Hubbard paused for dramatic effect.

Everyone groaned and there was some light heckling. With a mischievous grin, she relented.

'Braebank.'

The stunned silence that followed was eventually broken by a squeak from Fiona.

'But that's *our* cottage.'

CHAPTER 12

None of the Losers Club members had ever visited Gordon and Fiona at home. Those who lived in the village and town popped by their friends when passing, to share a drink or, in the case of Elsie, to harvest you-know-what from Len's shed. However, Gordon and Fiona's smallholding was quite remote; not exactly popping in territory.

Now, as they stood in front of the small cottage, surveying rows of neatly planted vegetables, polytunnels and a vast greenhouse, it occurred to Penny that they had been rather selfish, always expecting Gordon and Fiona to come to them.

She wasn't sure what they had expected to find. Gordon and Fiona had dug up most of the place several times over, so there was unlikely to be treasure under the tatties. If James-Alec Macrae was buried here, it had to be somewhere away from the cottage where he wouldn't be disturbed. Penny's mind went back to the symbols.

'Fiona, I wonder if that cross symbol could have been James-Alec's grave. Have you ever seen anything that could have been a grave?'

'I don't think so,' said Fiona. She took a moment to ponder the question. 'We haven't dug everywhere yet though. There's still the bit at the back of the house, at the bottom of the hill. It's overgrown and quite rocky, so we left it while we focused on farming the flatter areas. We thought we might get goats or sheep at some stage, and they'd go at the back.'

She led the group down the path towards the front door then veered off around the side of the cottage.

'Sorry, it's a mess back here. We haven't had time to do anything with it.'

Mess was an understatement. The ground to the left of the cottage was a testament to Gordon and Fiona's passion for farm auctions. It was filled with obscure agricultural equipment and half-finished projects, giving it the air of an al fresco torture chamber. There was even an old-fashioned plough and harness, although Penny had no idea where the couple had planned to find a horse to pull it. Maybe it really was some sort of kinky torture chamber, Penny mused, and Fiona popped the harness on Gordon of a weekend. She shuddered at the thought, knowing that now she would never be able to unimagine a naked Gordon, with his shaven man bits, gambolling around the field in a harness.

Behind the cottage was the thickest of thickets. A tangle of thorns and weeds as high as two men, spreading from the back wall of the building and beyond the confines of what would once have been a garden to meet the trees on the hill.

'It would probably be a good idea to search it,' Penny commented.

'No, it wouldn't,' said Jim. 'I've already ruined one jumper.'

'What about one of them weed whackery thingies?' suggested Eileen.

'I have a scythe and a chainsaw,' said Gordon.

Jim sighed. He really, really didn't want to do this.

'The police will be here later. We could leave it to them,' he said.

'They're not going to do anything,' said Sandra Next Door. 'They're looking for a murderer and, even though he was searching for the treasure, it's obvious Colin was never here. They'll question whatsherface, the French one, and Hamish, do some CSI in the museum and Colin's cottage, then be on their way.'

'So, why are we lookin' for the treasure and not the moiderer?'

Everyone turned to Johnny, who was gazing around him, a long, inch wide knitted "scarf" looped around his neck, two knitting needles and a ball of blue wool stuffed into his pocket. He'd insisted that it gave him a British Doctor Who vibe and nobody had had the heart to tell him that he looked like a diehard fan of auto-erotic asphyxiation.

'We're at a dead end with the moiderer, so to speak,' Penny reminded him. 'We agreed to point the police in the direction of Hélène and follow the clues to the treasure instead.'

'Fiona, dearie, would you mind if we went inside and made everyone a cup of tea?' asked Mrs Hubbard. 'I don't think Elsie and I will be much good to you out here.'

Fiona, still somewhat amazed that her little cottage was the epicentre of so much drama, nodded distractedly.

'Scone's are in Gordon's old wellies by the front door,' she mumbled.

Mrs Hubbard looked askance at Gordon.

'She hides the scones from herself so she doesn't eat them all,' he explained. 'I found a bag of them in my underpants drawer the other day.'

Mrs Hubbard screwed up her face and said, 'I think we'll just stick with the tea. Come on, Elsie. Let's make ourselves useful.'

Elsie tucked a hand into the crook of Johnny's arm and gently steered him in the direction of the front door.

'You come with me,' she said, 'and I'll show you how to cast off.'

'I'm great with a cast. And the crew. They love me,' said Johnny, allowing himself to be guided inside.

When they'd gone, Penny turned to Jim and Gordon.

'What do you think? There are six of us and loads of sharp implements. Can we clear this?'

'We can have a go,' said Jim doubtfully. 'Gordon, do you have any big shears?'

Gordon nodded and went off to gather what they'd need.

Four hours later they had cleared the patch immediately behind the house, but a sizeable area was still covered in thick bushes.

Penny and Eileen sat on upturned, rusty buckets and surveyed their progress.

'We could be here for days, and I don't think we'd finish. Has anyone seen Jim?'

Jim's voice sounded from behind a bush. 'Sorry. Too much tea, thanks to Mrs Hubbard. What goes in must come out.'

A trail of liquid emerged from under the bush, trickling in the direction of Penny's feet, and she quickly shuffled the bucket to one side.

'You're a heathen, Jim Space.'

'You know you like a bit of rough, Penny Moon,' he replied.

'Gordon, bring your scythe over here. There's something that needs lopping,' Penny shouted.

'It's weird that you two have space-sounding names. Although you should change your name back to Hopper,' said Eileen.

'Why?' asked Penny.

'So that when you get married you can be Penny Space-Hopper.'

'For goodness' sake, don't tell Mum that. She'll take a full-page advert out in the Vik Gazette for the Space-Hopper wedding. Anyway, what am I saying? We're not even together.'

'You will be,' said Eileen with an air of smug certainty, 'when your planets align.'

'Ha ha, very funny. Moon, space, planets,' said Penny.

'No, it's true. I've done the astronomy.'

'I didn't know you were interested in stars.' Penny nudged her friend. 'Has Kenny got a big telescope in the bedroom?'

'It was in the Gazette. You're a Libra and he's a Gemini. Very compatible.'

'Astrology, not astronomy,' interjected Sandra Next Door. 'Honestly, Eileen, you're so…you.'

Eileen winked and told Penny, 'I'm right. You'll see.'

Then she wandered off to speak to Gordon.

Penny lowered her voice. 'You were about to say stupid, weren't you?'

'Aye, but I didn't,' said Sandra Next Door.

'That's as maybe, but you've a sharp tongue and if you ever hurt her, I'll take out a full-page ad in the Vik Gazette telling everyone on the island that you were the one who backed into the minister's car and drove away.'

Sandra Next Door's eyes widened in shock, and she took a step backwards.

'How…how did you know?'

'You took your car to Kenny's garage to get fixed. The minister took his car to Kenny too. Kenny may be no genius, but he can put two and two together and come up with four. He told Eileen, she told me. Now, Kenny and Eileen might be far too nice to say anything, but I'm not. And you might also want to think about that when you're considering reporting Dad's shed.'

Sandra Next Door's face crumpled, and she sank onto the bucket recently vacated by Eileen.

Eyes brimming with tears, breath trembling, she told Penny, 'God, I'm such a terrible person. I felt so guilty about that. When the church did the fundraiser for refugees, I donated half my savings. Geoff couldn't understand the sudden fit of generosity, and I had to lie and pretend to have come over all religious. I started going to church every Sunday and even volunteered to clean the place. And I've been stuck cleaning it every week ever since. Good job I like dusting. The man who did it before me was useless. Couldn't see the organ for all the dust!'

Sandra Next Door had recovered some of her bravado towards the end of that monologue, but it was a brittle thing. A bitter eggshell concealing a hot mess. Something in what Sandra had said struck a chord with Penny. Perhaps it was a recognition that she herself had been a bitter, hot mess in those weeks following her discovery of Alex's dalliance with the au pair. Perhaps it was a better understanding of why the woman was driven to criticism and judgement of others. Outwardly asserting control when you're churning on the inside, thought Penny.

She put an arm around Sandra Next Door and said, 'Kenny and Eileen will forever be grateful for what you did last year, saving Ricky and Gervais, and so will I. That's why none of us will ever tell anyone about the minister's car. You did a bad thing, but you've also done some very, very good things that made a difference. I'm sorry I spoke in anger. Eileen's been my best friend since we were four and I couldn't bear anything that burst her happy little bubble.'

Sandra Next Door ran a finger under her nose and sniffed. 'She's my friend now, too, and I promise I'll never be the one to burst her bubble. She's a wee angel. Look at her.'

Penny looked over at Eileen, who was staring into Gordon's teacup and loudly declaring that she could read teabags. He had been so miserable recently that Penny felt almost relieved to see him crack a smile when Eileen assured him that he was going to be the father of three goats.

A sudden shout from the bushes made everyone stop what they were doing and look up.

'Come here and see this, you spiky little fuckers,' Jim yelled. Followed a moment later by a contrite, 'Sorry, I was talking to the thorns. That's another jersey ruined. Seriously, though, come and see this.'

Fiona laid down the tray of cups she'd been gathering to

take indoors and wandered over, closely followed by Gordon and Eileen. Penny stood and held out a hand to help Sandra Next Door off her bucket.

'He's probably found an interesting beetle or something,' she said, 'but shall we?'

They joined the others by the big bush and peered through a gap. Jim bent down and peered back at them.

'Are you nae coming in?'

'How do you suggest we do that without scratching ourselves to death? How did *you* even get in there?' asked Penny.

'No idea. It's amazing what a man can do when he really needs a pee and doesn't want anyone to see his willy. Gordon, can you give it a wee whack?'

'Your willy?' asked Gordon.

'Aye and when we're done, maybe you could get the scythe out and whack the bush.'

'Well, as Fiona will tell you, it's been a while since I whacked the bush.'

Between Gordon's scythe and a large pair of shears expertly wielded by Sandra Next Door, who had years of experience of maintaining immaculately precise gardens, they managed to clear a path to Jim.

He was standing beside a small stone object. It was slightly lopsided and, after decades of being shrouded in greenery, covered in moss. But it was most surely a cross.

'My, it's freaky that we've been living next to a grave all this time. Scratch that. It's amazing. Just think of all the history here, and we've been right on top of it,' said Fiona.

Out of all of them, she had been the most determined to clear the thicket and find out what lay behind. To that end, she had worked tirelessly and now stood, hands in the pockets of her soil-stained dungarees, exhausted yet clearly elated at their find.

Gordon laid a hand on her shoulder and said, 'Aye, darlin', it's pretty amazing.' He handed her a trowel. 'Do you want to knock some of that moss off and see what's underneath?'

Fiona took the trowel and gently removed the moss to uncover some lettering engraved deep into the surface of the cross. It was weathered yet still legible.

J.A.M 1720-1746
△ Ω ∫

'James Alexander Macrae and the same symbols we saw in Hélène's diary,' said Fiona. 'Do you think the treasure's buried here?'

'The only way to find out is to dig him up,' said Jim.

Gordon visibly balked at the thought.

'I'm not digging up a dead body. It was bad enough carting one up and doon the museum steps.'

'Tell me about it,' said Penny. 'It's not the only way to find out, though.'

The others looked at her expectantly.

'Metal detectors,' she explained. 'The island's full of them.'

'Aye, attached to metal detectorists hunting this very treasure. How long do you think it will take before word gets out and Braebank is swarming with the buggers?' asked Jim.

'Good point. We can't ask one here to help us but maybe we could borrow their equipment?' said Penny.

'I could say me and Fiona are looking for underground pipes,' Gordon offered. 'Does anyone know how to work a metal detector?'

'I do,' said a voice behind them.

Johnny stood there, mug of tea in hand, gazing at the cross.

'Don't tell me,' said Jim, closing his eyes and putting his

fingers to his temples. 'Hang on, it's coming to me now. You once played a metal detectorist.'

'No, it's my hobby. Civil War relics.'

'Oh. Right. Sorry,' said Jim. He pointed at the gentle mound of the grave. 'Okay, so if we can get hold of a metal detector, can you tell if there's gold in them thar hills?'

'Yeah, I can do that,' said Johnny.

'If James-Alec was buried with other metal, like a belt or something, wouldn't it also beep?' asked Penny.

'Yeah,' said Johnny, 'but it's all to do with frequencies. If you get your frequency right, you can eliminate things like iron and find high conductivity metals like gold. You get me a good metal detector and if there's gold in that grave, I'll find it.'

'Will someone please get the man a metal detector and put us all out of our misery?' groaned Sandra Next Door. 'Does anyone here know any of the metal detectorists?'

'I do,' said Mrs Hubbard, emerging from the back door of the cottage. 'Quite a few of them are camping near the village and they come into the shop for their milk and papers. I shouldn't really say this, but there's one lad, you know him Elsie, the one with the limp and the funny eye. Well, he's never worked a day in his life. His dad has been funding him since he finished university and the dad must be loaded. Now, I know what you're going to say. Minty, how can you tell? Well, I'll tell you how I can tell. Andrex. He never buys the value loo roll. His dad has rented him a caravan until October and that boy has the most pampered bum on the island. I'll bet you a bag of my pick and mix that his dad has bought him the best equipment as well.'

'Good thinking, Mrs H,' said Jim. 'Do you think you and Gordon could find this lad and persuade him to lend you his metal detector?'

'I could manage that. Johnny, you come too. You can tell us if it's the right thing.'

Elsie folded her arms and pursed her lips. 'And what about me?'

'I just assumed you were coming. We'll take the library van, if that's okay. Gordon's van would be a tight squeeze.'

As Mrs Hubbard, Elsie, Johnny and Gordon walked towards the odd assortment of vehicles parked at the entrance to the smallholding, Jim turned to Penny and reminded her, 'We have to meet the police off the ferry, so we can't be here until late.'

Penny looked at her watch. 'Goodness, it's almost teatime. No wonder I'm hungry. Is anyone else feeling a bit peckish?'

Fiona nodded. 'I'll go and see what we have in Gordon's old wellies.'

Johnny was like a small child who had been let loose on the sweetie jars in Mrs Hubbard's Cupboard. He arrived back at Braebank clutching a metal detector unlike anything his detective sidekicks had ever seen.

'That guy's father has too much dough. The kid has more equipment than The Fixing Man.' He caught the blank looks all round. 'Come on, youse guys, The Fixing Man? I played a serial killer who repaired computers for a living. No? Okay. This is a two-box detector. It goes deeper than your standard detector and will find anything big. It ignores the small stuff. I figured if they'd buried the guy a couple of metres down then the treasure might be at the same depth. I love this baby. She musta cost a thousand bucks easy.'

None of them had ever seen Johnny so fired up or, for that matter, so knowledgeable. They watched, rapt, as he switched on the receiver and transmitter boxes then held the transmitter box over the grave, slowly sweeping it towards the cross. They listened intently as the machine squawked and buzzed, buzzed and squawked. They held their collective breath. Nothing. No high-pitched signal, just a steady buzzy-squawk.

Johnny was crestfallen. He laid the machine on the ground and sat on one of the upturned buckets, head down, dejectedly fiddling with the ends of his scarf.

'I'm sorry. I guess it ain't there.'

Elsie picked her way across the yard and sat next to him, tugging gently on his coat sleeve until he looked up at her.

'Furgedabootit,' she told him. 'We're all grateful to you for trying, aren't we everyone?'

They all nodded, except Fiona. She was standing by the little cross, looking up at the hill where the rich evening sun had painted the landscape in rich hues of yellow and green, the rocks picked out in pinks and deep shadows. She lowered her gaze to the cross then stared up at the hill again.

'Look up there at the rocks. I've never noticed it before, but does that look like a cave to you?'

The others came to stand beside her, Johnny bringing up the rear, and gazed upwards.

'You're right,' said Gordon, 'A small cave.'

Hands in pockets, Jim rocked back on his heels, giving the matter some thought.

'Aye, and if you follow the line of the rocks, it looks like a snake, with the cave as its head,' he said.

'The symbols,' said Penny. 'It's not Omega. It's a hill, a cave and a snake.'

'Well, duh. I think we figured that out for ourselves, Einstein,' said Sandra Next Door.

'How much light have we got left? Do you think we have time to get up there? Penny asked.

'*We* don't,' said Jim. 'We're meeting the police, remember?'

Penny was tempted to tell Jim that he could meet the police by himself. She was staying to find the treasure. But she couldn't do that. There was an awful lot of explaining to do and some slightly illegal activities that needed to be glossed over. She couldn't leave him to do that on his own.

'Alright,' she sighed. 'We'll go up to the cave in the morning.'

'No, we bloody well won't. We'll go up there now,' said Sandra Next Door. 'You and Jim can go to the police. Elsie and Mrs Hubbard, sorry, you're not really fit for climbing, so you may as well go home. Me, Fiona, Gordon, Eileen and Johnny will take a walk up that hill and see what's there.'

She was like a blonde-helmeted, purse-lipped field marshal, gathering her troops and setting out the plan. Within minutes, Fiona and Gordon were scouring the cottage for torches and Johnny had swapped his Italian leather loafers for a pair of Gordon's walking boots.

Penny, Jim, Elsie and Mrs Hubbard left the scene, the sound of Sandra Next Door's voice urging everyone to "get a bloody move on, you useless maggots" ringing in their ears. They wondered if the power might have gone to her head, just a wee bit.

CHAPTER 13

A chill wind blew in off the North Sea, carrying with it the cries of seagulls circling above, the grey and white scavengers loudly proclaiming success as they swooped to snatch an unattended sandwich aboard the evening ferry.

It had been an unseasonably warm day but now, as evening closed in, Penny found herself pushing her hands deep into the pockets of her coat, sealing off the sleeves from the breeze that seemed determined to find any gap in her defences. Jim looked down at her, wrapped up in the winter coat, her face hidden in the depths of a fur trimmed hood, and his heart did something. He wasn't sure what it did, but it felt like it had suddenly filled up. He had to resist the urge to put an arm around her and pull her close to stop her shivering. He wondered what would happen if he tried. His imagination presented two scenarios. One where she sank gratefully into his warmth and looked up at him as he lowered his head to kiss her. The other where she kneed him in the balls, and he left the harbour in the back of the very police car they were here to meet. Only in handcuffs. His heart shrank back to normal proportions, and he felt quite annoyed with her for kneeing him in the balls. Bloody woman could freeze for all he cared. It really was cold. What he could do with right now was a warm sausage roll. He'd gone past the supermarket on his way home from the pub yesterday and had popped a packet of frozen sausage rolls in with Colin. He ought to grab those before the forensic bods made off with them.

Penny glanced up at Jim. She wondered what he was thinking. For a moment he had looked almost tender, then he looked quite annoyed. Then deeply thoughtful.

'What are you thinking about?' she asked.

'Sausage rolls. I left a packet in with Colin, and I don't want anyone pinching them.'

'Fair enough,' she said, satisfied that sausage rolls explained the full range of emotions. He had once become almost orgasmic over a slice of lemon drizzle cake, after all.

'You shouldn't be eating sausage rolls,' she commented.

'Aye, but it would be a waste to leave them. Colin's nae needing them where he's going.'

'Don't try and blame Colin. It wasn't Colin who bought them and he's certainly not going to eat them.'

'How do you know? He didn't buy that pint at the pub, but the sneaky fucker drank it.'

'That was Fiona. Look, here's the police.'

A small procession of vans and cars left the ferry and drove slowly towards them, the lead car swerving to avoid a large woman, laden with bags, who had made a surprisingly sprightly dash towards a waiting BMW.

Jim grunted. 'That was Margaret Bell. I'd have given them fifty points if they'd ran her over. She fed her dog on chocolate for years and wondered why the poor animal was a mass of sores.'

Penny said nothing. Merely shook her head at the sheer stupidity of folk.

The police car drew up beside them and a window slid down.

'Jim Space?' said a thin, dark-haired woman in the passenger seat.

'Aye. And this is Penny. Penny Moon. She's my…my… partner in crime. No, not crime. Definitely not crime. My partner. Not that sort of partner. The other sort. Where you team up, like. Friends with benefits. But not those sort of benefits. I mean, it's not like we're sleeping together. She'd knee me in the balls if I so much as put an arm round her to keep her warm. Bloody woman.'

'Good to know,' said the woman. 'I'm DCI Muriel Davis. Just call me Muriel. Hop in, both of you, and you can direct us to where we're going.'

'Where exactly are you going?' asked Penny once they were settled in the back of the police car. It was surprisingly comfortable back here she thought, although possibly less so if you were wearing handcuffs. She hoped she never found out.

'Museum, police station and wherever you're storing the body. Sergeant Wilson said you'd commandeered an ice cream van. I don't think we've had a body in an ice cream van before.'

'It's parked at my house,' said Jim. 'Colin's not going anywhere at the moment, so if you want, we could start at the museum.'

'Perfect,' said Muriel.

Wow, thought Penny. She seems a nice, normal person. Not sweary at all.

'You what the fuck now?' shouted Muriel, shaking a box of neatly cut carrot sticks at them.

'We had to have our lunch. It's not like we stood over Colin, dropping crumbs,' said Jim.

'You had two jobs. Store the body and secure the scene. At what point did anyone say you could invite your friends over for a fucking picnic and a tour of the museum?'

They were standing by the benches beside the crime scene, this time properly kitted out in booties and paper suits. Jim had just finished explaining how they'd wrapped the body and organised a rota to guard the scene, before Elsie had remembered the giant chain and everyone had buggered off to the pub. He shifted uncomfortably.

'To be fair, you wouldn't have the murder weapon if Fiona hadn't been messing around. Not unless you examined every item in the museum. It's not like it was sitting there with a big note on it saying "murder weapon."'

Muriel sighed deeply. 'And where was Colin while this was happening?'

'Mostly in the ice cream van,' said Penny.

'Except for the bit where they took him out to have a look at his mouth,' said Jim sheepishly.

Muriel managed an even deeper sigh.

'And why were they looking at his mouth?'

'To see the thing in it. Obviously.' Jim caught Muriel's menacing look and cleared his throat. 'It was the Laird's Ladle. To be fair, you wouldn't have known it was the Laird's Ladle if Mrs Hubbard hadn't recognised it.'

'Did they touch anything?'

'I've no idea. We weren't there.'

Muriel sighed, if possible, even more deeply.

'Where were you?' she asked, a definite chill in her voice.

'Erm. We thought it might help if we went to Colin's house. It's just as well we did. The front door was unlocked. Anyone could have gone in.'

'Did you touch anything at Colin's house?'

'Eh…Penny might have accidentally nudged the mouse on his computer and seen a list of his favourite fences on the screen.'

'This computer. Password protected?'

'Oh aye, but the idiot had left his password book beside it.'

'And Penny's fingers slipped? She just accidentally keyed in the password before she accidentally nudged the mouse?'

'You're quite good at your job, Muriel,' said Jim.

'I am. And you can call me DCI Davis. Now, what happened next?'

It was Jim's turn to sigh.

'We picked up a famous movie star, dressed him up as Columbo and took him to have a chat with Hélène. She owns the local antiques shop, Hélène's Drawers, and she was on Colin's list of fences.'

DCI Davis shook her head in frustration and put her hands in her pocket, just in case she should accidentally find them around Jim's throat.

'This little investigation of yours. Find anything interesting?'

'Only that Hélène was lying. She claimed to be merely an acquaintance of Colin, but Johnny Munroe saw in her diary that she'd recently had lunch with him. When we phoned around, we found out that they often had lunch and that they were hunting for the Vik treasure.'

DCI Davis' interest was piqued. Could this be a falling out over treasure?

'What about the Laird's Ladle? What is it?'

Jim and Penny explained how it belonged to Laird Hamish's family and that he'd taken it to Colin to be valued. They told the real detective how they'd had dinner with Hamish and that he'd given them a list of all the items he'd sold through Colin.

'He said he didn't sell through Hélène because they had a history and hadn't parted on the best of terms,' said Penny. 'Except, I'm not sure that's true. When we went to her shop, Hélène was wearing his brooch. Hamish also told us that he suspected his wife had been having an affair with Colin.'

DCI Davis looked thoughtful. Perhaps this was some sort of love triangle...quadrangle...was that the right word? Love square. Love rectangle.

'Hmm,' she said, 'Could be some sort of lovers' tiff gone wrong, I suppose. You said Hélène and Colin were hunting for treasure. Had they found any?'

'We don't think so,' said Penny, preparing herself to give an abridged version of the truth. 'Johnny spotted some symbols in her diary, and we've tracked them down to the grave of the first secret keeper. The man who originally hid the treasure. We don't think Colin and Hélène could possibly have known where to look. Some of our friends are there now, following the clues to a possible hiding place.'

'So, while you were gallivanting around with movie stars and finding clues to buried treasure, where was Colin?'

'Oh, he was down the pub with our friends,' said Jim. 'Not like *in* the pub. Just outside in the car park. In the ice cream van, all safe and secure and locked up. Ha! It's not like anyone took him into the pub and gave him a pint or anything. That would be ridiculous. Right, Penny?'

'Ludicrous,' Penny agreed.

'We know all about chain of custody,' Jim assured the detective. 'Eileen watches CSI. That's also how we know Colin was killed by a single blow to the head and his face was bashed in after death.'

'He's right. There would be a lot more blood spatter if the man was beaten when he was alive,' said a voice from behind them. 'It must have been a good while later before they bashed his face in, going by the lack of blood. Maybe twelve hours. Looking at the crime scene photos, he was probably turned over. You can see the blanching on his chest where it was in contact with the floor and that takes about twelve hours to set in.'

DCI Davis turned to the scene examiner and gave him her iciest glare. The man held up his hands and backed away, deciding that now might be a good time to examine something at the other side of the crime scene, where he couldn't eavesdrop on other people's conversations.

'Okay,' said the DCI. 'I think we've got the bare bones of

it, but you'll all have to come to the station tomorrow to give your statements. Your *full* statements. So, you might want to have a chat with each other and agree how you did not compromise my crime scene with fucking carrots. Take my word for it, you do not want to be standing in court explaining you had a picnic here'

She paused for a moment then said, 'Mrs Hubbard. Where have I heard that name before?'

'Poisoned half the island, allegedly,' said Jim.

'And half of Police Scotland,' said DCI Davis. 'Allegedly. I need to check on something, but I will probably want to talk to Mrs Hubbard tomorrow. Now, come on, let's gather the troops and go see Colin.'

'Just to warn you, the sausage rolls are mine. I left them in with him after we went to the supermarket.'

DCI Davis rolled her eyes. 'Is there anywhere Colin hasn't been? Have you signed him up for the local football team?'

'He couldna be worse than our current goalie,' Jim muttered.

Sandra Next Door herded her troops through the woods and up Bosie Brae. She was in charge. She loved being in charge. All her school report cards had called her a bossy boots, and Mr Wright had gone so far as to say that if they did exams in being a know-it-all, Sandra Sharp would pass with flying colours.

Sandra had been clever at school, but her personal qualities didn't win her many friends, a theme that had repeated itself as she grew older. Her father, a large man who ruled the roost with his sharp tongue and blunt fists, had demanded unquestioning obedience from Sandra and her mother. God help you if you had an opinion of your own. The bastard knew where to aim for so the school wouldn't see the marks. At school, though, she ruled the roost. It never occurred to wee Sandra Sharp, with her wicked tongue and hectoring ways, that she was her father all over. Only later in life, when the world of work delivered a few knocks of its own, did she realise to her horror that she had become a bully, just like the man she hated.

Resolving never to repeat the sins of the father, Sandra made the decision to forgo having children. She didn't believe in that namby-pamby therapy nonsense, but she had read some self-help books and done her best to curb the intolerant, domineering side of her nature. Meeting her Geoff had been the saving of her. He was a laid-back, decent man who liked nothing more than a round of golf and a pair of size ten stilettos. If he'd been able to combine the two, Geoff would have been sorted for life. He recognised that underneath the shrew was a frightened lass who could be tamed with kindness and a quiet word now and then when she was going too far. As she yelled at the group to "pick up the pace, sheeple" and gave Eileen a prod with a big stick, Sandra Next Door wondered if Geoff would call this going too far. But she really, really liked being in charge.

Huffing and puffing their way up the hill, the others silently cursed Sandra Next Door. They hadn't minded being organised into pairs and told to look out for their partners. They hadn't even minded the yelling. After all, it would be dark soon and nobody wanted to be stumbling about Bosie Brae in the pitch black. Making everyone hurry up was probably a good thing. What they did mind, however, was the stick.

'If she pokes me one more time with that bloody thing, I'm going to force feed her your jar of ginger pubes,' Fiona told Gordon. 'Or I would, if Johnny wasn't wearing most of them on his face. Sorry about that, by the way. I decided his need was greater than ours.'

Gordon looked miserable. Head down, focusing on the ground in front of him as he dully put one foot in front of the other, he mumbled, 'S'okay. It wasn't really working anyway. Most of the stuff died.'

'At least you can let it all grow out again,' said Fiona. 'I prefer you fluffy.'

The group trudged on, their muscles beginning to ache as the hill grew steeper.

'Bosie Brae. What does that mean?' gasped Johnny, his breathing laboured as they navigated around some large boulders.

'Cuddle Hill,' Eileen told him. 'The story goes that a pair of lovers used to meet here. The woman was from the village and the man was from the village. The other village. They were from these huge families that had been fighting for years, probably centuries. They're still fighting to this day, though none of them knows why. It's just accepted that if you're born into the Campbells you hate the Wallaces and vice versa.

'Anyway, while the families were at church, the pair would slip away and meet here for a kiss and a cuddle. It all went fine until they were spotted by a shepherd, who told her father. He locked her in the house until, a few weeks later, the lad sneaked in and rescued her. They hid on one of the fishing boats and escaped to Aberdeen.

'Their escape added fuel to the flames and the families met here for a pow wow, which ended in a declaration of peace, sealed with a hug – a bosie - between the two fathers. The peace didn't last long but the name stuck, and this place became Bosie Brae.'

In front of them, Sandra Next Door roared, 'We're nearly there, maggots. Stop your blethering and get your feet moving.'

She turned to give Johnny a poke with the big stick, but he was too fast for her. Grabbing it and tossing it into the heather, he said, 'I don't know you, lady, but you sure are a pain in the ass. Did nobody ever teach you no manners?'

'That's a double negative, you idiot,' snapped Sandra Next Door. She adopted a fake Brooklyn accent to match the actor's own. 'Now quit your whining and walk.'

'There's no point in arguing,' Eileen told him. 'She's having the time of her life. I'll speak to her later.'

Johnny stopped, took Eileen's hand and kissed it, giving her one of his best smouldering looks.

'You, ma cherie, are quite the opposite of her - a true lady.'

Eileen was not immune to the actor's charms, despite the fact that he was wearing a rather disgusting beard. Of course, she was utterly devoted to Kenny, but there was no harm in window shopping so long as you didn't get your credit card out.

She giggled and curtsied, the bob made somewhat awkward by the fact that she was balancing on the side of a hill.

'Enculé, monsieur.'

'For crying out loud!' roared Sandra Next Door.

They climbed on, tramping through the heather, until they reached the small gap in the rocks that Fiona had spotted earlier. Johnny attempted to rest on a boulder, but Sandra Next Door was fired up, the treasure almost in her grasp. *Our* grasp, she reminded herself. She wasn't interested in the treasure for profit, but the idea of finding it before anyone else and telling all those metal detectorists they could eff off home filled her shrivelled heart with joy.

Sandra Next Door eyed the opening with some doubt. Then she eyed her companions, equally doubtful.

'There's no way we'll fit through there.'

'Aye, we will,' said Eileen. 'Take it from me, I've had experience of squeezing large bottoms through tight spaces.'

'When did you do that?' asked Fiona.

'It was when Penny and I–' Eileen stopped, realising she was about to blurt out their secret late-night visit to Hélène's Drawers. '–were drunk and we tried to crawl out the dog flap at my Mum's.'

She wasn't sure whether Penny would thank her for her quick thinking or be mortified that she'd made up a tale about her best friend getting her backside stuck in a dog flap.

Nevertheless, it worked. As the slimmest one who was not a world-famous movie star, therefore could be sacrificed without someone getting sued, it was agreed that Eileen would attempt to enter the cave.

Johnny unravelled the scarf from around his neck and handed it to her.

'Tie this around your wrist. I'll hold the other end. If you get in trouble, yank hard.'

'Or I could just shout,' suggested Eileen, but she tied it round her wrist anyway and gave him a grateful smile.

Fiona handed her a torch, and she approached the entrance to the cave, trying to decide whether to go in feet first or head first. Feet first, she decided. She didn't fancy crawling in, getting stuck and having to breathe cave air for hours until the fire brigade arrived to free her. How much air even was there in a cave? Her bum might plug the gap so thoroughly that the air ran out and she died doggy style, a queue of people behind her desperately trying to pull her out. Somebody would put it on YouTube and Kenny would be embarrassed and the boys would have to move schools for the shame of it. No. She couldn't have the boys changing schools, so feet first it was.

This turned out to be a good decision. Once she had wriggled and squeezed her hips through the opening, she found herself sitting on a ledge at the top of a scree slop. She shone the torch downwards. It wasn't a long drop, no more than a couple of metres or so, but it was steep, and she'd have been unable to navigate it head first.

'There's a drop,' she shouted back to the others. 'Johnny, I'm going to leave your scarf dangling here because I'll need it to get back up again.'

A hand nudged her on the back and handed her a pair of gloves. Sandra Next Door might be a sour cow, but she did care.

Grateful for the fact that she was wearing a thick pair of jeans, Eileen shuffled off her stone platform and, knees bent, used her hands and feet to slow her descent as she slid down the rubble.

When she felt her feet hit solid ground, she stood up and took the torch from her pocket. Pointing the beam at the walls and ceiling around her, she could see that she was in a small cavern with an opening at the other end.

'I'm in a cave,' she shouted up to her companions.

'No shit Sherlock,' Sandra Next Door replied. 'Is there any treasure in there?'

Before Eileen could respond, Fiona's voice came through the gap above.

'Be careful. There could be loose rocks in the ceiling. Honestly, I think this is the most stupidest thing we've ever done. We shouldn't have sent her down there, Gordon. You should have gone.'

'Why me? Are you trying to bump me off for my fortune?' Gordon sounded quite miffed.

'No, of course not. I don't need fifty pence right now. Finding the treasure would have cheered you up, though, and you do have a very thick skull. Remember that time we were in bed and–'

'No!' Gordon yelped, cutting her off before she could do any more damage to his good standing with their friends. 'Anyway, what about her? Silvikrin Sandra over there? You could throw a lorry at her head and it would bounce off. Geoff probably uses her for target practice at the driving range.'

'That was uncalled for. She may be a pain in the ass but there's no need to get poisonal aboud it,' said Johnny.

'Poisonal,' sneered Sandra Next Door. 'Your accent is rubbish, and as for you, Gordon, you can keep your comments to yourself. You've been tripping over your bottom lip all week and I haven't even mentioned it once. Maybe we *should* have put you in there. It would have been a relief to get rid of your miserable face.'

'Oho, you listen here, you sarky bitch,' said Fiona.

Eileen didn't catch the rest. She had made her way across the cave and was now standing at the entrance to a second cavern. Once more, she pointed her torch at the walls around her and gasped as the beam of light picked out a shape on the floor. It appeared to be a lump covered in some sort of cloth.

Heart hammering, Eileen made her way towards the lump. She was so focused on her goal that she didn't notice the dip in the cave floor. As her foot went down and found nothing, she overcompensated for the uneven surface, instinctively bending a knee and twisting to help her foot find purchase. She felt something in the knee ping and a sharp pain lanced through her leg.

The others stopped arguing at the sound of Eileen's cry.

Gordon stuck his head through the gap and boomed, 'Are you okay in there?'

'No, I think I might have twisted my knee.'

'Well, that's a bugger.' Gordon turned to Sandra Next Door. 'One of us is going to have to go in there and help her out.'

'I'll do it,' said Johnny.

'You can't,' said Sandra Next Door. 'We'll have an international incident if you get injured.'

'And even worse,' said Fiona, 'Sergeant Wilson will shout at us.'

'I'm the only one who can easily get through the gap,' said Johnny. He handed Gordon the end of the scarf. 'Here, we'll need you to pull us up.'

'Do you mind if I video this?' Fiona asked him. 'I can sell it to the Vik Gazette, no, the Turra Squeak, no Fiona, think bigger, much bigger…the Banffie! The money will help us through the winter.' She put a hand in the air and ran it across an imaginary headline. 'Famous movie star rescues damsel in distress.'

'The Hero of Bosie Brae,' Johnny grinned. 'Yeah, why not. But youse guys need to think national.'

'You mean like the Inverurie Herald? Oh, that's a big step

for us. I'm nae sure we're ready for that kind of exposure,' said Gordon, frowning.

'Hello, injured lady here,' echoed a voice from the cave.

'Sorry, I'm on my way,' Johnny shouted back.

He lowered himself to the ground and bottom-shuffled through the narrow entrance, before sliding downwards and coming to a halt at the bottom of the scree slope. There was a clatter as Sandra Next Door rolled a torch down to him.

He shone the torch around the cave, immediately spotting the entrance to the second chamber that Eileen had found just ten minutes before. Picking his way carefully across the uneven floor, Johnny quickly reached Eileen.

'Bonjour, ma cherie. Are you able to stand?' he asked.

'Probably, but I'll have to lean on you.'

Johnny made to put his hands under her arms to help her up, but she stopped him.

'Before we go, check this out.'

Eileen shone her torch at the cloth covered object at the back of the cave and Johnny started forward, curious to see what it could be.

'Careful,' she warned him. 'We don't want you falling as well.'

With his torch beam lighting the ground before him, Johnny safely reached the object and pulled on the cloth.

'Aagh!' he squealed, his voice a few octaves higher than was comfortable.

Startled, Eileen gave a small scream of her own.

'What? What is it?' she gasped, once her heart had removed itself from her throat.

Johnny cleared his throat and adopted a tone a couple of manly octaves below his normal voice.

'Spider,' he said gruffly.

'Aw, that's so cute. A wee spider out doing its spidery business. I love spiders,' said Eileen. 'What about ghosts, though? Do you think there are ghosts down here?' She put her torch below her chin and shone it up her face. 'Wooooooo.'

If Johnny hadn't been pointing his torch at the object, she'd have seen him look at her like he regretted ever coming to her rescue. What was that expression he'd heard someone in Port Vik use to describe an eccentric neighbour? One slate slipping and another one slidey. Mad, he thought. They're all mad.

He looked back down at the cloth and, this time not waiting for tiny, terrifying creatures to catch him unawares, he swept it aside. A cloud of dust rose, turning the torch beam to thick fog and filling his throat. Eyes streaming, torch bobbing, he coughed and spat to clear what he imagined to be centuries of desiccated mouse droppings from his mouth.

When his vision cleared, he directed the beam once more at the object.

'What is it?' asked Eileen, craning her neck to peer around him.

'It's a chest,' he whispered, in awe that he was touching something that had lain undisturbed since before America was invented.

He ran a hand across the top, and the dust came away to reveal a fleur-de-lis stamped into the ancient, cracked wood.

'I think it's a French chest,' he told Eileen.

'Ooh la la,' said Eileen. 'Can you help me get a bit closer. I want to see.'

Johnny walked back to her and put his hands under her armpits, heaving her onto her feet. She put an experimental foot on the floor and winced. Leaning on him, his arm around her waist, she slowly hopped towards the treasure.

With Eileen clinging to his shoulder for balance, Johnny shone his torch on the chest.

'Locked,' he said. 'There's no way we can open this.'

'Or so you think,' said Eileen. She slipped off her coat. 'Help me take my top off.'

'Honey, I don't know what you think I came down here for, but this wasn't it.'

'Just take my damn top off, man.'

'To be clear, this is consensual badabing.'

'It's not badabing, you twit. We're going to pick that lock.'

Confused, Johnny helped Eileen remove her top.

'And now the brasserie,' she told him, indicating her bosoms.

'Hold on, I don't want no accusations.'

'For flips' sake, I can't do it myself. I'll fall over.'

'Okay, but I'm not doing the panties.'

'You won't need to, you feel gype.'

'Feel what? I'm not feeling anything.'

'Feel gype. It means idiot. Now undo me.'

Johnny reluctantly fiddled with the hooks of Eileen's bra, his fingers slipping as he tried to hold the torch in place. Just as he hit upon the solution of tucking the torch beneath his chin, a voice boomed through the cave.

'What's going on in there?' Gordon shouted.

'Johnny's taking my bra off,' Eileen shouted back.

'There's an old chest,' shouted Johnny.

'She's only in her forties. They should still be quite bouncy,' yelled Fiona.

'A French chest.'

'She's not really French. She just knows all the swear words.'

'No, we found an old French chest. A box,' Johnny clarified.

'Does it have any treasure in it?' Sandra Next Door wanted to know.

'We don't know. That's why Johnny's taking my bra off,' Eileen replied.

'What? Did the two of you just get a bit bored or something?' asked Gordon.

'No, I'm going to use the underwire to pick the lock,' said Eileen. 'I saw it on CSI.'

Johnny looked relieved and undid the last hook.

'Don't point the torch at my tits,' warned Eileen, slipping the bra off.

She chewed at the end of a cup until the stitching holding the underwire gave way and she was able to pull the long, thin piece of metal from its channel. Then she did the same with the other cup then, holding the underwires up for Johnny's inspection, she triumphantly announced, 'Lockpicks and I said don't shine the torch on my tits.'

Johnny hastily moved the torch beam upwards and apologised. He swung the beam away, scanning the floor until he found her discarded top and coat.

Handing them to her, he asked, 'How do you wanna do this? You'll need to bend down to look at the lock and I'll need to hold the torch and support you.'

'I'll squat down on the good leg. You sit on your knees behind me, and I'll use you as a chair. That way you can still hold the torch.'

They shuffled into position and Eileen bent to her work. Behind him, all Johnny could hear were scratches, clicks and what he considered to be some very unladylike language.

Eventually, with a small yelp, Eileen sat back and said, 'I did it.' She had surprised even herself.

Johnny helped her to stand and together they tugged on the lid of the chest. The dry conditions in the cave had prevented rust, but the lid was still reluctant to shift. With a "one, two, three, heave!" they finally managed to dislodge it and reveal the glorious contents within.

Three things lay in the chest: a dead beetle, a button and a small, gold coin.

'So, that was worth it,' said Eileen, her voice flat.

'Yup,' said Johnny. 'Shall we get you back?'

With Johnny's help, Eileen hopped and limped back to the cave entrance, where she tied his woollen scarf around her waist.

Feeling the tug on the scarf, Gordon bent down and peered into the dark hole.

'Did you find the treasure?' he asked.

'No. Just a button and a coin,' said Eileen.

'That's a shame. Up you come, then. Johnny, you push from your end, and I'll pull. Fiona, start the camera rolling.'

With Johnny behind her, giving her bottom a good shove upwards, Eileen leaned back on the makeshift rope and hopped her way up the scree slope. As the wool stretched, she could feel it slipping up from her waist to her breasts, taking her top with it. It'll stop when it gets to my boobs, she thought. A few seconds later, she took those words back as first one treacherous boob, then the other, popped through the loop. With her coat and top bunched around her ears, she clung to the scarf, ignoring the pain and propelling herself upwards.

Behind her phone camera, Fiona was gleefully narrating the scoop of the century.

'Johnny Munro, the hero of Bosie Brae, bravely went down into the cave, risking life and limb to bring the injured Eileen back to the surface. Oh, there's movement. Here she comes. Any minute now, we'll see the bonnie, smiling face of the lovely Eileen as Gordon pulls her up. One last pull. And look at that bonnie…pair of boobs. Oh, my word. They really are quite perky for her age. Aaaaand here comes Johnny, the triumphant hero. He's waving something. A white flag? Ah, no, it's a bra. Och, bugger. Eileen's going to make me delete this.'

The group gathered around Eileen, who lay panting on the grass in the dying evening light. Sandra Next Door had hastily pulled down her top and coat to cover her modesty and everyone was fussing over the sore knee.

'Don't worry,' she said, 'I'll get Jim to take me down the vets for an x-ray in the morning. I think it's just a sprain.'

'You went through all that for nothing,' said Fiona.

'Not completely nothing,' said Eileen, reaching into the pocket of her jeans. 'We found these.'

She held out the coin and the button to show the others.

'The coin looks gold,' said Gordon, picking it out of her hand and holding it up to examine it.

Johnny helpfully shone his torch on the object while Gordon turned it over. He rubbed it between his thumbs to remove some of the dirt then placed it on his palm, where it glinted in the beam of light.

'I could be wrong,' he said, 'but I think that's a Louis.'

He looked at his companions, who gazed back at him, none the wiser.

'An old French coin,' he explained. 'I was reading about Bonnie Prince Charlie last night and I disappeared down the Wikipedia rabbit hole. This is pretty much definitive proof that the treasure was here. Although I suppose that's the end of the trail as far as we're concerned. It must have been moved sometime, probably centuries ago. We'll never find it now.'

'Not centuries ago. Century.' said Sandra Next Door.

She had taken the button from Eileen and was squatting down beside her, peering closely at the tiny, white disc.

'This button's plastic. Someone had a key to that chest, and it's been opened in the past century, maybe even the past sixty years.'

Sandra Next Door looked up at the group around her.

'There's still a secret keeper on the island.'

CHAPTER 14

'Order! Order!'

Jim clinked a fork against his glass and the group settled down. They were in the upstairs room of the village pub again and had just finished a slap-up meal of chicken in a basket, scampi in a basket and chips in a basket. Not exactly on the approved healthy eating list for Losers Club, but Bertie the barman had created the pub menu in the 1980s and saw no reason to change it.

The conversation over supper had been all about Johnny and Eileen's discovery of the coin and button. All agreed with Sandra Next Door's assessment that the treasure had been moved in modern times and that they were unlikely to ever discover its current location.

Jim gave the glass another clink. 'Let the record show that this is approximately the forty-nine-billionth meeting of Losers Club, and today we welcome a guest, DCI Davis.'

DCI Davis smiled warmly at the faces around her and said, 'You can call me Muriel. Except you. You can still call me DCI Davis.' She glared at Jim then turned to Penny. 'And maybe you. The jury's out.'

Mrs Hubbard, Elsie, Sandra Next Door, Fiona and Gordon introduced themselves. Johnny, who had removed the beard and was now sitting next to Elsie, knitting a new scarf to replace the one he had declared ruined by their adventures in the cave, looked up momentarily from his clacking needles and grunted a hello. He was thinking of adding a second colour to his scarf and couldn't wait for this meeting to end so that he could get Elsie back to his hotel room for another knitting lesson. His fellow Hollywood A-listers wouldn't recognise him right now, he thought. These people had changed him. Perhaps everyone should spend time on this crazy island.

'Time to share developments,' said Jim. 'I've briefed DCI Davis on events as far as this afternoon, the main points being that Hélène lied about her relationship with Colin, she and Colin were hunting for the Vik treasure, she was probably having an affair with Laird Hamish and Hamish's wife, Cara, might have been having an affair with Colin. Colin was selling antiques through Hélène and other people he called fences so there was probably a bit of skulduggery going on there. Does that about sum it up?'

There were nods all round, so Jim continued.

'He was killed when he was bashed over the head early evening, then got his face smashed and the Laird's Ladle rammed down his throat. Now, here's the interesting bit. The police have confirmed that the face smashing, and presumably the ladle ramming, took place hours after the head bashing. He died face down and twelve hours later, whoever did the smashing and ramming turned him over to do it. That would be about the time that the cleaner called it in.'

'So, the cleaner did the smashing and ramming?' asked Fiona.

'Looks like it,' said Penny. 'Which means it's unlikely that the cleaner is the killer. Why would you kill someone, return to the scene of the crime, smash up the dead person's face and shove a ladle down his throat, then phone the police? The only thing we can think of is that the cleaner had some sort of grudge against Colin and took it out on him after he died.

Unless someone else did the smashing and the cleaner found his body straight afterwards. In which case, we're looking for a killer, the cleaner and a third smashy party.'

'Which is why we need to find the cleaner,' said DCI Davis. 'I have someone going through the staff records now, but the museum computer is password protected and it seems Colin was more careful about keeping his work password secure. It'll take some time to get answers. In the meantime, can you all please ask around the island to see if anyone knows the name of the cleaner?'

Jim beamed happily at them all. 'I don't think any of us had understood the significance of the cleaner. You see, this is exactly why we need the professionals. Excellent deductive reasoning.'

'You can stop sucking up,' said DCI Davis.

'Yes, DCI Davis, but you truly have done a fine job,' said Jim.

'Oh for God's sake, call me Muriel.'

Jim grinned. Annoying vet one. Muriel nil.

'Plan of action on finding the cleaner?' asked Sandra Next Door.

'It's not just the museum which needs cleaning. Other places have cleaners too. I could check with the library,' Elsie offered. 'They have cleaners in at the weekend when we're closed.'

'How do people employ people around here? Are there any agencies on the island?' asked Muriel.

Everyone looked at her like she had two heads.

'There's the notice board in the supermarket in town, and I have one in my shop,' said Mrs Hubbard.

'Could you look through old cards?' asked Muriel. 'What about the internet? Do people advertise on the internet? Do you have a community website or something?'

Mrs Hubbard looked doubtful. 'There's the parish newsletter and sometimes the Vik Gazette has adverts for important jobs, like with the local council. We're a wee bit more traditional here compared to you mainlanders, dearie. The internet signal blows hot and cold, if you get my meaning. Sorry, I don't know all the right computer words.'

She took a sip of her Slow Comfortable Screw and looked to her companions to back her up.

'Everything's word of mouth,' Fiona agreed. 'It was one of the reasons we moved here, the slower pace of life. The Warrior Islanders have a website. And the Vik Historical Society. Have you thought about all the strangers on the island, like the treasure hunters and the movie folk? If a treasure hunter knew Colin was trying to find the treasure, there could have been some rivalry.'

Muriel helped herself to a cold chip from one of the baskets while she gave this some thought. She was enjoying this bouncing around of ideas. Normally she'd be in a room with other police officers, following protocol and dishing out tasks. Yet these Losers Club people were quite insightful and worked well together as a team. Nothing was getting done strictly by the book, but progress was being made and they were remarkably persistent. She wasn't sure what her superiors would make of her "harnessing their talents", as she would call it when she eventually told them, but for now, it made more sense to work with Losers Club rather than exclude them.

'It should be straightforward to find out where the cast and crew were when Colin was killed, but I'm not sure how we identify all the metal detectorists,' she said.

'I can help with that, dearie,' Mrs Hubbard told her. 'They all come to my shop for their milk and papers, and they mostly pay by card. Unless the internet's down, of course. I can give you the card payment records.'

'Isn't that against data protection or whatever?' asked Gordon.

'It's a murder investigation,' Elsie told him.

'But you refused to share your records yesterday when we–'

Penny cut him off. 'That was library records. This is different.'

She gave Gordon a look that said now would be a good time to shut up and turned back to Muriel, who had sensed some sort of subtext and was looking bemused.

'Sorry, we had an argument about the library van yesterday. Nothing to do with this. It seems to me that all of the checks you'll have to do will take ages. Is there anything else we could be doing? Can you think of any other leads to follow up?'

'Not at the moment,' said Muriel. 'You've done what you can. Myself and one of my colleagues will be interviewing Hélène this evening. We don't have enough to arrest her, but I'll be very interested to hear what she has to say about her relationship with the deceased. And I wouldn't mind taking a look at that diary.'

Penny squirmed slightly in her seat. Hélène would no doubt tell Muriel that the diary had been stolen. All the evidence to corroborate the lunches with Colin and the treasure symbols were currently under Eileen's bed. She'd suggest to Eileen that they break in to put it back, if it wasn't for the fact that her BFF was currently lying on that very bed with a bag of frozen peas round her knee.

'I suppose that's it then,' said Sandra Next Door, standing up to put on her coat. 'Can someone give me a lift home?'

'There is one more thing,' said Muriel. 'Mrs Hubbard, could I have a word in private?'

Mrs Hubbard immediately donned the appearance of a rabbit caught in headlights. After all, her experiences with the police thus far had hardly been pleasant. She looked at her friends, then at the door, desperately seeking a way to avoid any one-on-one conversation with a police officer that didn't end with her spending the night in Port Vik police station.

'Anything you have to say to me can be said in front of my friends,' she told Muriel stiffly.

'Even Sandra Next Door,' added Elsie, giving Mrs Hubbard's arm a supportive squeeze.

The others shifted their chairs around the table towards Mrs Hubbard, leaving Muriel isolated at the other end. Even Johnny put his knitting down.

'Okay,' said Muriel. 'I have some good news for you. I made a few calls earlier and can confirm that you're no longer a suspect in the island poisonings.'

This pronouncement was followed by a long silence until, her eyes brimming with unshed tears, Mrs Hubbard said, 'But it was my ice cream that poisoned them. I don't see how anyone else could have done it.'

Elsie stuck a hand up the sleeve of her cardigan and withdrew a tissue, which she handed to Mrs Hubbard.

'How long have you known this?' she asked the detective.

'The lab results came through just before you were released, but DI Mitchell and the rest of the local force came down with food poisoning before anyone could make a decision on what to do about them.'

'But it was my ice cream,' Mrs Hubbard repeated.

'It may have been your ice cream, but the salmonella was in the strawberries, and they weren't your strawberries,' said Muriel.

'What do you mean not my strawberries?' asked Mrs Hubbard. 'They came from Gordon and Fiona. They were the same ones I always use.'

'Shit, shit, shit. Quite literally. Was it the composting toilet? We're always really careful, but if you don't get the composting process right, well, things can get messy,' said Fiona. She buried her head in her hands and howled, 'I can't believe our strawberries poisoned everyone and got you into so much trouble. I can't tell you how sorry I am, Mrs Hubbard.'

'It was my fault, dearie, not yours,' Mrs Hubbard reassured her. 'Gordon always washes them before he delivers them and I usually give them a second wash, but I must have forgotten.'

'This is what I wanted to talk to you about,' said Muriel. 'The strawberries in question didn't come from Fiona and Gordon. They came from the Aberdeen fruit and veg market, and before that they came from China. Some salmonella cases popped up in Huntly and Portsoy that were unconnected with your ice cream. Sergeant Wilson may be stuck at home throwing up, but she refused to believe you were a mass poisoner. As soon as the lab report came in, she got on the phone and tracked down the fruit seller. As she put it, "that arsehole has a lot to answer for, labelling them as organic Scottish strawberries". The lab says the things were so riddled that even if you'd washed them twice, there's a chance the salmonella would have slipped through.'

Mrs Hubbard allowed the tears to fall. She sat upright at the table, silently looking around at her friends, as a steady stream of tears flowed freely down her cheeks.

'The other good news,' said Muriel, leaning forward, 'is that nobody died.'

'What about Mrs Taylor?' asked Elsie.

'Carbon monoxide poisoning from her gas fire.'

'Mrs Hubbard, not guilty. Hooray and all that. What I want to know is how the strawberries got into her ice cream in the first place,' said Sandra Next Door. She stared malevolently at Fiona and Gordon. 'Because, if you'll pardon the pun, they sure as shit didn't come from Braebank.'

Penny couldn't help noticing that throughout this conversation, Gordon had been sitting perfectly still, rigid in fact, staring straight ahead. He hadn't even stirred to comfort his wife, who was sitting next to him, her eyes swollen and red from rubbing away her tears.

So rapt in his strange behaviour was she, that she jumped and almost knocked her wine glass over when Gordon suddenly yelped and sprang to his feet.

'It was me. I did it. I poisoned everyone!'

He swung his head from side to side, wild-eyed, finally settling his gaze on Mrs Hubbard.

'I'm sorry. I'm so sorry. I should never have let it get this far. When the strawberries died, I went to the mainland and got some off a market stall. It said organic! I thought nobody would ever know the difference! Oh God, it's all my fault and I'm sorry…just…sorry.'

He sat back down with a thump and lay back in his chair, staring at the ceiling, taking short, deep breaths to control the tears. Next to him, Fiona realised that her jaw was hanging open and she clamped it shut, the click of her teeth clearly audible in the silence that had followed Gordon's confession.

'Gordon, pal,' Jim started to say.

'No, don't talk to me,' said Gordon in a strangled voice.

'We gotta talk to you, man. If we don't talk this out, you're gonna make yourself ill,' said Johnny. The fake Brooklyn accent was gone, and he spoke gently to Gordon. 'You owe it to Mrs Hubbard, you owe it to Fiona and, most of all, you owe it to yourself to tell us what happened.'

Gordon sat up straight again, sniffing loudly and mashing the heels of his hands in his eyes. It took a very long minute for him to regain sufficient control to talk and even then, he couldn't bring himself to look at his friends.

Staring resolutely at his glass of lemonade, he mumbled, 'I'm so ashamed. I didn't know there was anything wrong with the strawberries and even when folk started getting ill, I didn't make the connection. Then, when they arrested Mrs Hubbard, I thought they'd realise their mistake and it would all blow over. Only it didn't.

'I should have come forward then, but I was worried about the business, about Fiona and, I'll be honest, I was worried about myself. You see, long before I met Fiona, I spent some time in prison. I was young and stupid. You know what they say about having the temper to match the red hair. Well, I had the temper. I got into a fight in a pub, and someone got seriously hurt. I was sentenced to eighteen months and did nine months, but those nine months nearly broke me.

'My mum died when I was inside, and my brother was in a car accident. Not being able to be there for them, fuck, it tore me apart. I railed against the system, the people who put me in there, the lad that I hurt, everything and everyone who had kept me from my family. But I went to the anger management classes and I got a job in the prison garden, which is what helped me accept that it was my own fault. Working in that garden and bringing life to things helped me make peace with myself. By the time I met Fiona, I was a changed man.

'Then I did this and suddenly I could see everything I'd built being taken away again. I couldn't face it. Couldn't lose Fiona. We don't have much, but we're happy.'

Gordon turned to Fiona, tears in his eyes. 'We are happy, aren't we?'

Her own eyes glistening, Fiona put a hand on his and nodded.

'I wouldn't have left you over one mistake, you big eejit.'

'It wasn't just that,' said Gordon. 'It was the not telling. I can't believe I put you through the very thing I was terrified of, Mrs Hubbard. I'd like to think I'd have stepped up and confessed eventually, but I just don't know. The longer it went on, the more guilty I felt. I know it's no consolation, but I've spent days punishing myself. You remember when I put my fingerprints on the iron, Fiona? So we could both get a bollocking off the police? I thought it was something small I could do for you. Something you'd maybe remember when all the bad things came out.'

'Jesus,' Fiona breathed. 'I thought maybe you'd killed Colin and were trying to cover it up! I thought that was why you were so miserable. All this time, I've been planning how I was going to lie for you if you needed an alibi. Sorry, Muriel. I'm sure you understand.'

'Not really,' said Muriel. 'And I think we'll be having words about this iron.'

Gordon looked directly at Mrs Hubbard. 'That's it. That's all there is to say. I was a stupid man, who did a stupid thing, and I hope that one day you'll forgive me.'

All eyes were on Mrs Hubbard as she considered her response.

After a few seconds thought, she said, 'I understand why you did it and I can see how sorry you are. You know me. I'm a woman of few words.'

'You're the biggest gossip in the village,' said Elsie.

Mrs Hubbard ignored her and continued. 'This has been one of the worst times of my life, no doubt about that, yet the friendship of everyone here kept me going. I think you've tortured yourself enough and friendship is what you need. Let's put this behind us, dearie, and appreciate what we have – good people who'll get us through thick and thin. I choose to believe that you're one of those good people and you would have told the truth in the end.'

She paused to let that sink in, then added, 'At least there's one thing to celebrate. Elsie made me watch all those episodes of Orange is the New Black and I don't need to be a lesbian anymore. I'd have been rubbish at it. Now, who's going to buy me a woo woo?'

In the general hubbub that followed, nobody noticed Penny slip out onto the landing outside. She quietly closed the door and put her phone to her ear.

'Sorry, Eileen. Can't hear a thing in there. You'll never guess what's happened.'

'Never mind that,' said Eileen. 'I have some exciting news. This is going to blow your mind, like BOOM. Brain exploding all over the walls and Sandra Next Door getting out the big cloth to clean them up.'

'Okay, you tell me your news and I'll tell you mine. We can explode together,' said Penny.

She listened intently as Eileen explained, then...

'Well bugger Jim with a bicycle rack!'

CHAPTER 15

Penny rushed back into the room and yelled for quiet.
'Sit down, everyone. Eileen's on the phone and she has big news.'

Penny put her phone in the centre of the table and stabbed at the screen.

'Eileen? Can you hear me? You're on speakerphone.'

'That's a ten four, Rubber Duck. Over.'

'Speakerphone, Eileen. Not walkie talkie.'

'Roger that. You forgot to say over, over.'

'Oh no. We're not doing this radio speak again. If you try that, we're over.'

'We're what? Over.'

'Over. Over.'

'Over or over over? Over.'

'Shut up, Winnie the Pooh. In the room are Jim, Sandra Next Door, Johnny, Elsie, Mrs Hubbard, Fiona and Muriel. You haven't met Muriel yet. She's a real police detective.'

'Enculé, Murielle.'

Penny leaned over and whispered to Muriel, 'She means enchanté. Just go with it, we do.'

'Where's Gordon?' asked Eileen.

'He's nipped downstairs to get Mrs H a woo woo. Says he owes her a lifetime supply.'

'Ooh, what do I need to do to get a lifetime supply of booze from Gordon?'

Penny rolled her eyes heavenward. 'Trust me, that's not a prize you want to win. I'll tell you later. For now, tell everyone what you told me.'

'Exciting news, my friends. My dark web contact called.'

'Your what?' said Muriel.

'My dark web contact.'

'Who is this dark web contact and, more to the point, how does someone like you even have a dark web contact?'

'Ivan Kimov.'

'Yes, but what is his name?'

Penny caught sight of Jim out of the corner of her eye. He looked ready to explode with mirth.

'Spartacus,' Penny butted in. 'His name is Spartacus. Carry on, Eileen.'

'As you may or may not know, I gave him a photo of Colin and he ran it through a facial recognition thingy. He phoned earlier to say he has a match. Colin Dogood was really, drum roll please, Colin Dogwood.'

If Eileen was expecting a big hurrah, she didn't get it. Instead, there were shrugs, blinks, a few frowns and almost a full house of confused faces. That is, all except for one face, which looked both surprised and excited.

'You're joking!' Muriel exclaimed.

'This is no laughing matter,' Eileen assured her.

'Crypto Col? I can't believe you found Crypto Col. Has anyone told you you're a genius?'

'Once or twice,' said Eileen nonchalantly.

Penny smiled. She pictured her friend sitting in bed, a bag of frozen peas on her leg, playing it cool on the outside, while on the inside she'd be doing a Highland fling.

Everyone else looked quite curious now, their faces

betraying a desire to be let in on what, after all, did appear to be exciting news.

'Crypto Col,' Muriel explained, 'was the creator of ColCoin, Australia's answer to Bitcoin. He and his partner, Brian Collindale. People invested heavily in it, some of them exchanging their life savings, and the value quickly shot up. Then, about eight years ago, Colin and Brian went sea fishing and never came back. Their yacht was found wrecked miles off the coast. Brian's body washed up a long time later, but it was too decomposed to be able to say how he died. Crypto Col's body was never found, and he was declared dead last year.

'Of course, there are lots of conspiracy theories out there about Crypto Col having killed Brian, fuelled by the fact that when they disappeared, died, whatever, they took the passwords with them. There are hundreds of millions of pounds sitting there and nobody can get to it. It was a huge scandal in Australia at the time, although we didn't hear much about it over here. I only know about it because my sister lives in Melbourne and she had a few thousand invested.

'So, it looks like Crypto Col faked his own death and made his way to Vik. I wonder if he killed Brian and that's why he disappeared. It's a shame we'll never be able to ask him. And now there's no chance of those people getting their savings back.'

Muriel stood up and took her coat from the back of her chair.

'Well done, Eileen. Now, if you'll excuse me, I've got a killer to find and a Frenchwoman to invite down to the station for a wee word.'

'Au naturel, Murielle, it was nice to meet you.'

Muriel smiled. 'Au revoir, Eileen.'

After Muriel had departed, the group gradually broke up and drifted off to do their own thing, satisfied that they had taken the investigation as far as they could. The proper authorities were in charge now. Mrs Hubbard and Elsie went off in the library van to visit Mr Hubbard in hospital, taking Johnny with them. Fiona and a somewhat shamefaced Gordon left for home.

Tying her coat belt neatly around her waist, Sandra Next Door, who had been surprisingly quiet throughout the evening, told Penny, 'She was right, you know. Mrs Hubbard. What she said about friends. I know I'm not very good at friends, probably because I never had many, but I do appreciate you all. In my own way. Now, I'm off to have words with your mother. Geoff just texted to say that damn cat has shit in my begonias again.'

And then it was just Jim and Penny.

'This would make a good meeting spot for Losers Club,' Jim suggested as he helped stack the chairs.

'Yes, it would be great,' said Penny. 'Mrs Hubbard could drink her own weight in cocktails, and we'd all eat chips from a giant basket.'

'Chips are vegetables. Cocktails are fruit,' protested Jim.

'And tomato ketchup counts as one of your five a day. Yes, yes, we've been through all this before. We're sticking to the church hall where there are no temptations. You're forbidden from having temptations on church premises,' said Penny.

'That's Otis Williams fucked then.'

'Is it just my imagination, or was that a Temptations joke?'

'Ha! Good one, my girl.'

Penny acknowledged this with a grin and said, 'I'm glad you're in a good mood because I have a tiny favour to ask of you. And I ain't too proud to beg.'

'I'm a ball of confusion,' said Jim, grinning.

'Well…nope. You win. The only other one I know is Papa Was a Rolling Stone, and I can't think how to fit it into a sentence. I was going to ask if you'd help me break into Hélène's Drawers again. She'll be at the police station so it's risk-free.'

'No, no, no, no, no!' exclaimed Jim. 'You know how I feel about breaking into places. For a start, it always involves me shoving your fat arse over a wall. Secondly, it means we'll get caught. And thirdly, it means we'll go to jail.'

'But you already broke in there once. I don't see the harm in going back.'

'What are you talking about? I haven't broken in anywhere. Breaking and entering is your hobby, not mine.'

'But I thought…bugger. When Eileen and I broke into Hélène's Drawers the first time, we had to hide in a wardrobe from someone else who was also sneaking around in there. I thought it was you.'

'Why on earth would you think it was me?'

'I thought maybe you were being chivalrous and doing the breaking in for me. Then, when you saw the diary was missing, you must have broken back out again.'

'Thank you,' said Jim.

'For what?' asked Penny.

'For calling me chivalrous.'

'I didn't call you chivalrous.'

'You mostly did and no takesy backsies. That's the Space rule.'

'I didn't and if it wasn't you in Hélène's Drawers, who the heck was it?'

'You did and how should I know?'

'I didn't and that's kind of creepy, breaking into places and sneaking up on strange women.'

'You're right,' said Jim.

'Thank you,' said Penny.

'You *are* a strange woman.'

'Oh, sod off. Anyway, are you going to help me break into Hélène's Drawers or do I have to ask Alex?'

Jim scowled at the mention of Alex's name. The little minx had brought him up on purpose.

'Why do you want to break into Hélène's Drawers?'

'To put the diary back. I told Muriel Johnny had spotted stuff in it, so she'll probably go looking for it, and she's never going to think to look under Eileen's bed, where it's currently residing. She'll probably look somewhere logical like, I dunno, maybe Hélène's Drawers?'

'Why would you ask Alex? What about Fiona or Gordon or Johnny? In fact, I think you're being very ageist not giving Elsie and Mrs Hubbard the opportunity.'

'Everyone else has been through the mill tonight! There'd be a massive scandal if Johnny got caught, and can you really imagine Mrs Hubbard and Elsie getting up on Hélène's extension roof and squeezing in her bedroom window?' Penny smiled at the thought. 'The only other option is Sandra Next Door, and I really don't want to spend an hour with her banging on about her shitty begonias. So, it's you or Alex. I know for a fact he'd help me out.'

'You really trust Alex?' asked Jim, slightly miffed that Penny would put her ex-husband on the same chivalrous pedestal as himself.

'One hundred per cent. He wouldn't let me get caught because he'd have to look after the twins while I'm in jail. Parenting was never his strong suit. He'd rather say it was all his idea and do the time. Only, don't tell Hector that. He still thinks his dad walks on water.'

Jim sighed a very deep sigh. If sighs could talk, this one would have said, 'Oh FFS, okay, if I really must, because I'd rather amputate my own nut sack with a pair of pinking shears than see you spend time with Alex Moon.'

Penny couldn't fully interpret the sigh, but she knew she'd won.

'Righty-ho, let's go to Eileen's and get that diary.'

Ricky and Gervais were so excited to see their Auntie Penny and the weird vet man who was always hanging around, that it took some time for Kenny to persuade them to go and watch a video, quietly, no fighting, no they couldn't have chocolate biscuits, no they couldn't watch a fifteen rated film, for crying out loud could they please just agree for once and put something on the damn telly?!

Kenny was still in his mechanic's overalls and looked a touch frazzled. Normally, Penny would have offered to look after the boys so he could at least have a shower and get something to eat but, as she explained to him, she and Jim were on an important secret mission.

'Aye,' said Kenny. 'You'll be taking the diary back, then. Wait 'til you see what her ladyship upstairs has in store for you.'

Eileen was sitting up in bed, dressed in Mickey Mouse pyjamas and a cycling helmet. When Penny and Jim entered, she switched the television off and shuffled over to make room for them to sit next to her.

'I have a treat for us,' she said gleefully. 'As soon as you phoned and told me what you were up to, I started getting it ready.'

'What is it?' Penny asked.

Eileen pointed to her own head and said, 'Helmet cam. You can live stream yourself breaking into Hélène's Drawers and I can watch from here. It's Kenny's. He livestreams his cycle rides around the island to YouTube, but I didn't think you'd want to go viral, so I've downloaded the app to the telly. Bates family viewing only.'

'I'm not wearing that thing,' said Penny.

Eileen turned to Jim.

'It's a very firm no from me,' he told her.

'But I sent Kenny to the shop for popcorn, and the boys were looking forward to it. Look,' Eileen handed Penny a pair of wireless earbuds, 'I got these. If you put them in, I can give you instructions from here.'

'We're not raiding Osama Bin Liner's compound, you know. We're just going to nip in there and put the diary back. In, out, gone.'

Eileen looked hurt. 'I went to a lot of trouble, best friend for life who I love and adore and whose mother still doesn't know how the heel on her Louboutins got broken.'

'You swore you'd never tell,' Penny hissed.

'Just wear the damn camera,' said Jim.

'Alright!' said Penny, exasperated yet knowing when she was beaten.

She plucked the helmet from Eileen's head and plonked it on her own, shoving the earbuds in place. Then she had to take the whole lot off again so that Eileen could sync them to her phone.

'When did you get so good at technology?' she asked.

'My dark web contact has been teaching me,' said Eileen.

'Who's been teaching you? Do you have to pay?' asked Jim, his eyes dancing with barely contained mirth.

Eileen shook her head. 'Ivan Kimov and his friends, for free.'

Jim's laughter began as a splutter, quickly progressed to a roar and ended with him lying on the bed next to Eileen wheezing, 'Oh God. I can't breathe. Make it stop. No, don't.'

His laughter was infectious and when Kenny came to enquire what all the noise was about, he found three adults lying in bed, clutching each other as tears flowed freely down their cheeks.'

'What's so funny?' he asked.

'I don't know!' Eileen cried. 'It just is.'

Once they'd gathered their wits about them, Penny donned the helmet and earbuds, and they made their way downstairs. She was just passing through the kitchen on her way to the back door, when a voice sounded in her ear.

'Winnie the Pooh to Rubber Duck. Tell him to put an extra sugar in. Over.'

Penny nudged Kenny, who was standing by the kettle and two mugs. 'She says not to put sugar in hers.'

'Ooh, you sneaky cow. Chris de Burgh, if I knew any French swear words, I would use them on you right now,' said the voice in her ear.'

'You forgot to say over,' said Penny. 'Over and out.'

The house behind Hélène's drawers was in darkness and the bedroom window was locked. Penny and Jim sat atop the extension debating…scratch that…whisper-shouting about what would happen next.

'I didn't want to do this in the first place,' hissed Jim.

'We're not going home. There must be a way in,' said Penny.

'We're at the other side of a locked window. What do you suggest we do?' Jim grumbled.

'Whip your bra off,' said the voice in Penny's ear.

'Break the window?' said Penny.

'Bra off! Bra off! Bra off!' said Eileen.

Penny could hear Kenny in the background saying that it was just as well Jim wasn't wearing the camera. He'd already had one argument with the boys about watching a fifteen tonight and he wasn't having another.

'I am not taking my bra off,' said Penny.

'Unexpected yet disappointing news,' said Jim, unaware of the third wheel in their argument.

'Go on. It's multi-tasking. You can use the underwire to pick the lock and give Jim a sexy treat at the same time,' said Eileen.

'For goodness' sake, we're sitting on top of someone's house in the middle of the night and all you can think about is sexy treats!' Penny exclaimed.

'Sorry,' said Jim.

'We've tried the upstairs windows, but we haven't tried downstairs,' Penny told him.

She swung herself around so that her legs were dangling over the edge of the roof, above Hélène's back garden. There were some pots and a small patio by the door, yet if she pushed off hard, she would land on the lawn. She sincerely hoped that the cat had a litter tray cat and there would be no brown surprises in the grass. Grasping the roof, she prepared for lift off.

'Just dangle yourself down and I'll catch you,' said a voice below her.

'Jeeze. How did you get down there?'

'When you're not a short-arse, it's easy,' said Jim. 'Come on, short-arse. Dangle down and I'll lift you off.'

Penny did as instructed and, with some huffing, puffing and muttering about her being a lard arse as well as a short arse, Jim deposited her safely by the back door.

For his part, Jim tried very hard not to think about sexy treats as he held her by the waist. If she felt something unusual as he slid her to the ground, she didn't say anything. But he was quite prepared to remonstrate that it was a torch in his pocket. God's teeth, get a grip on yourself, he thought as he moved a flowerpot so he could check a downstairs window. She's been straight with you all along about being friends, so there's no point in thinking about it. You're in the friend zone. He put the flowerpot back and tried another window. No luck.

So focused was he on shifting pots and trying windows, that he didn't hear the tapping at first. Tap, tap, tap. Tap, tap, tap. Eventually, the noise seeped into his consciousness, and he looked around for the source.

The source was a gruesome figure in the kitchen window, its features twisted into a ghoulish rictus, glowing eerily in the darkness.

Jim would later deny squealing 'Mum!' but would admit that his scampi in a basket almost made an involuntary early exit into his boxers.

'See,' said Eileen. 'I told you we could make him shit himself.'

Giggling quietly, Penny switched off the torch, returned her face to its default setting and stuck her head out the back door.

'Are you nae coming in?' she asked.

'How the…what the…?' spluttered Jim.

'The back door was unlocked.'

'You nearly made me shit myself!'

'It was funny, though.'

Jim had no idea what he ever saw in the woman. She took Being A Nuisance to a whole new level.

'Revenge is a dish best served cold,' he retorted before tiptoeing as quickly as possible out the kitchen door.

Penny was about to go after him when she remembered the cat. Dreamies, she thought, opening the cupboard under the sink.

In her ear, Eileen said, 'Did he just flounce?'

'Can you flounce on tiptoe?' Penny asked, popping a bag of Dreamies in her pocket and making her way after Jim. She heard a muffled thump and concluded that he'd probably reached the shop and was now walking into the furniture in the dark, like a giant, sweaty pin ball.

'That was surely a flounce,' declared Eileen.

Penny could hear Ricky and Gervais agreeing in the background, followed by a loud rustling.

'Are you really eating popcorn?' she asked.

'Mmmmfff gno,' said Eileen. There came the sound of liquid hitting glass, a few gulps, then she came back on. 'Crisps. Kenny said the shop didn't have any popcorn, so he got crisps instead. And wine. It helps with the pain.'

Penny couldn't see Jim in the gloomy interior of the house, so went through a curtain which led to the shop. As before, the shop was faintly lit by the streetlights outside, the large furniture dark sentinels around the edges of the cluttered room. Penny peered vainly into the dark corners, straining her eyes to see if Jim was hiding somewhere, preparing his revenge.

She took the diary out from the waistband of her trousers, feeling the residual warmth from her belly on the stiff, cardboard cover. She picked her way around tables and drawers, trying not to knock over any of the hundreds of vases, plates and glassware that festooned their surfaces, until she reached the desk. Now, where to put the diary? She couldn't just leave it on the desk. It had to be somewhere that it could have fallen or been misplaced by Hélène herself.

Penny tried the drawer from which Hélène had taken the folder yesterday and was relieved to find it unlocked. Anyone could have a brain fart and put something away in the wrong place, she reasoned. Why, she'd once hunted everywhere and found the remote control for the telly in the fridge. Right next to the giant bar of period chocolate she'd persuaded herself not to eat in one sitting. Well, maybe not a bar. Six pieces. Okay, four. But it still counted as not eating a whole bar in one sitting.

Penny leaned down, lifted a couple of folders and slid the diary underneath. Voilà. Hélène would assume she was having un moment senior.

Quietly, Penny closed the drawer. She was just about to straighten up when there was a faint rustle behind her, and a hand clamped around her arm.

'Very funny. You'll have to do better than that to frighten me,' she whispered, a mischievous grin forming at the corners of her mouth.

The grin went no further as she felt her arm being twisted behind her back. The need for stealth was instantly forgotten.

'Ow! You're hurting me. Stop it!' she cried, trying to pull away.

'I'll hurt you some more if you don't stay still, you nosy bitch,' a voice hissed in her hear. A voice that definitely didn't belong to Eileen. Or Jim.

The man gave a sharp tug on her arm, pulling it further up her back. A burning pain shot through her shoulder, causing her to swallow her retort in favour of a loud yelp.

He didn't relent. Keeping the pressure on her twisted arm, the man steered Penny across the shop, heedless of the trail of shattered glass he left in their wake, then through the curtain and into a small living room. He switched on the light before giving Penny a hard shove, sending her sprawling face down onto a rug by the fireplace.

Her shoulder aching, Penny used her good hand to lever herself onto her knees so that she could turn to face her assailant. It took a few seconds for her brain to catch up with her eyes. Then.

'Holy shit!'

'Sacre shit!' said Eileen. 'I'm calling Muriel.'

'You just couldn't fucking leave it alone, could you?' said Crypto Col.

CHAPTER 16

'But you're…what the…how did…your face!' said Penny, scrambling backwards on the rug, sore shoulder forgotten.

'You're in no position to ask questions. But *I* want some answers from *you*. Take the helmet off,' said Crypto Col.

Penny ignored him and looked away. Her mind was buzzing, yet her mouth appeared to have disconnected from her brain. Her first question was WTF. Her second question was - can you actually say WTF out loud or is it the sort of thing you only write down? Her third question was - are you Colin's twin and if not, who's the dead guy? She had other questions, but one had to prioritise these things.

A voice in her ear snapped her back to the moment.

'Penny!'

She looked up, just in time to see a fist heading straight for her face. It connected with the side of her mouth, and she felt pain explode across her jaw and cheek as she was propelled into the hearth behind her. As her head bounced off the stone fire surround, the tiny part of her brain that wasn't rattling around like a set of keys in a tumble drier sent a silent thank you to Eileen for making her wear the helmet.

Suddenly, a pair of hands were at her throat. She tried to

cry out, to beg him not to kill her, but she had bitten her tongue, the inside of her mouth mangled and raw, the blood and spit dashing uncontrollably for any exit until she felt she would choke herself to death, long before Crypto Col could squeeze the life out of her. All that emerged was a primal howl, a wail wrenched from her very being, that told of pain and terror.

'Jiiiiiiiiiiiiiiim!'

Or more accurately, given the state of her mouth, 'Giiiiiiiii-iiiiiiin!'

Shit, her battered brain said, the next word out of your mouth better be tonic and you could definitely do with the ice.

'Shut uk,' Penny told her brain. 'I'n actually dyin' here, so t'ould gee nice if you could gee sensigle for once.'

You're not dying, her brain retorted, you've been punched in the mouth and he's taking the helmet off, you big drama queen. Muriel's on her way. Try to keep him talking, Rubber Duck.

It took her a moment to realise that her brain sounded remarkably like Eileen. Despite the bashing she'd taken, the earbuds were still firmly in place.

'You're not dying, and I don't think we need Crypto Col The Movie,' said Colin, fiddling with the strap beneath her chin and wrenching the cycling helmet from her head.

He tossed the helmet and camera through the open door behind him and looked down at Penny, his smile so smug that her first instinct was to wipe it off with a hefty kick in the balls.

Colin saw her tense and anticipated the move. He delivered a hefty kick of his own, straight to her ribs. She felt something give, followed by a sharp pain which left her squealing and gasping for breath.

'Stay down,' he told her. 'Tell me what you know.'

'Hare's Gin?' asked Penny. Jeeze, it hurt to talk. Her mouth refused to move properly and her tongue felt like a big, hurty marshmallow. She saw the look of confusion on Colin's face and tried again.

'Hare is Gin? Guy I hoz 'ith?'

'Oh, him. You don't need to worry about Gin. He's no longer with us. Fireplace pokers are very handy things. Your friend is currently residing in the cupboard under the stairs.' Colin withdrew a phone and a wallet from his pocket and waggled them gleefully at her. 'And he appears to be missing a phone, a wallet and a pulse. These will start me off nicely in my next life. Not the pulse, of course. I already have one of those. Now, tell me what you know. You obviously figured out I was alive. Who else knows?'

Penny had stopped listening. Assailed by a hot, swooping sensation in her stomach, she sagged back, resting her head on the cool stone behind her. Jim, dead?

In her ear she could hear Eileen's trembling voice assuring her that Muriel would be there any minute. Urging her to hold it together for just a little while longer. She took a breath, wincing at the pain in her ribs, and glared at Colin defiantly.

'I not answer kestions. You cunched ne in the hucking nouth. I tink you droke ny jaw!'

'Unless you want your face to end up like the cleaner's, you better answer my questions,' Colin snarled.

He saw Penny's eyes widen in shock.

'Oh, you didn't know he was the cleaner. Wrong place, wrong time, poor bastard.'

Penny was in shock, but not so much at the revelation that the murdered man was the cleaner, as at the revelation that the cleaner was a man. The answer had been staring her in the face all the time, if only she'd thought a little outside the box. That wasn't strictly true. If only she'd been a little less sexist in assuming that the cleaner was a woman. Sandra Next Door had even mentioned a man cleaning the church. Oh Penny, you let the side down.

'Is cleaner? Dead nan is cleaner?' she asked, more to give

herself time to get her head around her whopping mistake than because she needed it spelling out.

Colin nodded. 'Couldn't have anyone recognising him before Hélène could find a boat to get me off the island. It worked then? Everyone thinks he's me?'

Penny nodded. Carefully. It was becoming oddly difficult to breathe. Any movement set off a chain reaction and the nerves in her face seemed to have temporarily connected themselves to the nerves in her ribs. Both ends were sending urgent messages to her brain that this would be a good time for a nap. Forget about the pain for a while. Penny consciously willed away the blackness she could feel fluttering at the edges of her vision.

'Laird's Ladle?' she asked.

'That was the fun part. It was handy, so I shoved it down his throat. Reckon it kept you all distracted, though, trying to figure out the clue.'

'Why you kill hin?' Penny asked, trying to keep Colin's attention on her. Behind him, the door of the cupboard under the stairs had moved. Heart racing, she kept her eyes fixed on Colin, lest he follow her gaze and spot the faint movement. Please, please let it be Jim and not a breeze.

'I don't suppose it'll make much difference if I tell you. You'll soon be joining your friend in the cupboard anyway, now that I know everyone still thinks I'm dead. I didn't kill him, just made his face unrecognisable. I found him with his skull bashed in, already dead, when I got into work. I didn't want the coppers figuring out who I am, so I turned him into me, called the cops pretending to be the cleaner and hid out at Hélène's, waiting for the fuss to die down.'

'Sho, who killed cleaner?' Penny rasped. She was lightheaded now, the darkness pressing closer. In her ear, Eileen was sobbing, unaware of the slim possibility that Jim was slowly pushing on that door.

'How the fuck should I know?' Colin giggled. 'For once, it wasn't me. Ironic, isn't it? You kill your business partner, fake your own death, end up on an island where the biggest news is Mrs Hay's bunions, burn a woman alive, fake your own death again and, somehow, the one murder you didn't do is the one they'll all blame you for. Once they figure out he's the cleaner, that is. And now it's time for my second murder of the night.'

'Hold on. Gurn a...' Penny didn't have a clue how to say "woman alive" without moving her jaw. She tried again. 'Who you gurn?'

'Granny Cairns, of course. Stupid old biddy, hinting that she knew where the treasure was. My treasure. Said she was the last direct descendent of Mhairi Cairns. That's Duguid as was, in case you didn't know. Maybe so, but she never thought about the other rellies, did she? Bruce Duguid was the guy who originally hid the treasure. His great nephew was convicted of robbery and sentenced to transportation for seven years. He stayed in Oz and became the respectable Mr Arthur Dogood. A mistake by a clerk in the nineteenth century, and the name became Dogwood. Ah! I can see you recognise that name.'

Colin bowed, doffing an imaginary hat.

'Colin Dogwood otherwise known as Crypto Col. Pleased to kill you. Anyway, Granny Cairns wasn't going to tell me anything, so I got rid of her. Spared the dog, though. Cute mutt. Shame I never found the treasure, but you can't have everything.' Colin shrugged. 'Now, I reckon it's time you and me parted ways before the cops come back with Hélène.'

'Say something!' shouted Eileen.

Penny's strength was fading fast, and her eyes kept closing, as though she was no longer the one in charge of eyelids. This was very inconvenient, she told herself, forcing them open with great effort of will. Her breath was coming in short gasps now and her hands had a bluish tinge to them. Punctured lung, she supposed. As if through a fog, she recalled that there was something she ought to do. What was it again?

Colin. Yes, she had to think of what to say, anything to distract Colin.

'You rich. Not need treasure.'

'Nah, mate,' said Colin, reaching behind the armchair. 'Brian changed the passwords before he died. He must have known I was coming for him.'

Colin lifted the poker from behind the chair and smiled at her, his eyes glittering with excitement.

'Now, you be a good girl and stay nice and still for your Uncle Colin while he caves your skull in.'

Penny could barely hold on to consciousness. So far, only the pain had kept her awake, but it had begun to consume her, filling her mind and body until all was torment. Just before her eyes closed for the last time, she saw the cupboard door in the hall swing open and a very large, red man come stumbling out. Then she succumbed to the blessed darkness.

Jim stirred, groggy, in the darkness. Where was he? And why did his face feel funny?

He was somewhere small and very uncomfortable. Things were poking into him. He wasn't a fan of poking. Unless he was the one doing the poking, of course. He almost snickered at that but, having deduced that someone appeared to have stuck him in a cupboard, he figured he better be quiet.

Who had put him in a cupboard? He forced his mind back. He'd been with Penny, aye, and she'd done her ghostie thing, aye, then he'd stropped off. Hélène's Drawers. Aye, they were in Hélène's Drawers, and someone had hit him over the head.

He flexed his hands experimentally. All fingers appeared to be intact and working. He moved, intending to test his feet as well, but the movement brought with it an agonising throb in his head. Staying very still, he scrunched his toes and stretched his feet. Feet working, check. With great care, he levered himself into a sitting position and brought his hands to his face. It was slippery and sticky, like one of those tea tree face masks that Penny made him try when he got stung on the nose by a wasp. Had somebody put a face mask on him while he was unconscious? Very strange behaviour indeed.

He shook his head, trying to clear the fuzziness but merely causing a fresh wave of agony, this time accompanied by a stinging sensation on the top of his scalp.

He remembered now. He'd been tiptoeing down the dark hall when he'd bumped into the open cupboard door. Someone had whacked him over the head a couple of times with something hard. The last thing he recalled was someone shoving him into the cupboard as he fell.

Jim raised a hand to his scalp and felt a dip. Something moved beneath the skin. Oh, this wasn't good. His hand came away, wet and slick with what he presumed was blood. At least that answered the face mask question, he thought, looking around him. He could see a sliver of light around the cupboard door and, as his eyes adjusted to his surroundings, he made out an impressive collection of plastic bags and a pile of shoes. Ah, that explained the smell. Wasn't it weird that French women's feet stank of camembert? Did your feet take after your national cheese? Were there Swiss ladies limping around on feet with big holes in them? Once more, he had to stop himself chuckling at his own nonsense.

Slowly, Jim became aware of voices. At first, he'd assumed, in his addled state, that someone had left a television on. It was only after a couple of minutes that he recognised Penny's voice. It was faint and she didn't sound like herself. She sounded muffled, like she was slurring her words. The other voice was louder and belonged to a man.

Ignoring his throbbing head, Jim struggled to his knees and edged closer to the cupboard door. Gently, he pushed, trying to open it a little so that he could hear what Penny and the man were saying. The door didn't budge. There was no handle. Of course there was no handle. Who puts a handle on the inside of a cupboard? Maybe people who live in cupboards, his brain replied. Like perverts and stalkers. He put an end to this internal conversation before he could start wondering how stalkers and perverts managed to fit internal cupboard door handles without the cupboard owners noticing.

He lowered his head to the point in the door where there would be a handle, if he were a pervert or a stalker, and peered through the gap. He could see that the door was held closed by an old-fashioned gate latch on the outside. If he could slip something through the gap, he could lift the lever from its cradle and open the door.

Scrabbling around the floor, looking for something long and thin, Jim's hand fell on one of Hélène's shoes. Across the front of the shoe was a small metal oblong held in place by a thin chain. I'm probably destroying seven hundred quid's worth of shoe here, he thought, but needs must. He tore the metal shape off the shoe and slotted it under the lever. Very gently and very quietly, he pushed up. With a tiny click, the lever came free, and the door opened a fraction.

Jim could hear the man clearly as he boasted, 'That was the fun part. It was handy, so I shoved it down his throat. Reckon it kept you all distracted, though, trying to figure out the clue.'

He pushed the door open a little more and could see the cycling helmet on the hall floor, the broken camera dangling from it. Fuck. The killer was confessing, and it wasn't even being recorded. Jim had a vague memory from his university days of something about corroboration being needed in Scots law. Penny didn't sound right, though. Should he listen or should he pounce? Torn, he decided to listen then pounce. Whatever happened, there would be pouncing.

The man was saying that he hadn't killed the cleaner but had beaten his face to a pulp to make him unrecognisable, so that everyone would assume that the cleaner was the man. Hang on. *His* face. Fuck. Jim had assumed the cleaner was a woman. Well, everyone else had too, so he wasn't the only sexist bugger in town. Jim filed the thought away under "What's Done Is Done" and continued to listen as the man talked about faking his own death, killing his partner and murdering Granny Cairns. Chris de Burgh, as Eileen would say, what sort of man burns an old woman to death? By the time the man got to the Colin Dogwood part, Jim had already figured out his identity. After all, not many people went around killing their partners and faking their own death.

It was only when the man said "Pleased to kill you" that Jim realised the time for listening was over. It was pouncing time. He levered himself off his knees and attempted to crouch while the blood returned to his extremities. Crouching was very uncomfortable, so he straightened his legs and bent over. This was perhaps not his best decision of the night because he promptly banged his head on the door, causing it to swing open just as he roared in pain. Pins and needles hampering his progress, Jim stumbled out of the cupboard towards Colin.

The man was standing in front of an unresisting Penny, his arm raised, ready to bring a poker down on her skull. At the sound of the roar, he turned to see a red-faced six-foot demon bearing down on him, wild-eyed and snarling. He stepped backwards, preparing to defend himself with the poker, but his foot caught on the hearth rug, and he found himself toppling backwards.

Jim's momentum carried him forwards and he tried to reach out for Colin, to catch him before he fell, to possibly throttle him and make him pay for what he'd done to Penny, who Jim could see lying bloody and lifeless against the stone mantle. His heart took no time to grieve, filled as it was with anger and hatred for this arrogant bastard who had destroyed the woman he loved. His hands snatched at Colin but met only air as the man slipped beneath him, his head smacking into the corner of the hearth.

The pool of blood pouring onto the rug and carpet was sufficient sign that the injury was fatal, but Jim wanted to be sure. Panting, he got on hands and knees and felt for a pulse. It was just as well that nobody ever asked him afterwards what he would have done if he'd found a pulse, because Jim honestly didn't know.

He crawled to the other side of the hearth and slumped down next to Penny. The same hand that had checked for Colin's pulse now checked for hers.

'Fuck,' he said. 'It's a bugger you're alive because now I'm going to have to tell you I love you.'

Then he gently laid his head next to hers and passed out.

CHAPTER 17

Penny reached out a hand to switch off the damn alarm clock. The constant beeping was getting on her nerves. Her hand patted the air, trying to reach her bedside table, but it wasn't there.

'Can someone switch the alarm off?' she croaked.

Oh. This was interesting. Her voice was all funny. Her face was all funny. Like somebody had put a hat on her, only upside down.

'Can someone take the hat off my chin?' she croaked.

She opened her eyes and looked up at the wall, expecting to see Chesney and Sharleen gazing down at her impassively, like they did every morning. Except they weren't there, and someone had clearly sneaked in during the night to paint her bedroom wall a horrible shade of mustard. Only her mother would do such a thing.

She tried to open her mouth to call for her mother, but it hurt, and the darned chin hat was in the way.

There was a sound of scurrying feet and Penny looked over to see Mary and Len rushing through the door. Not her door. Just the door.

'Why did you paint not my bedroom?' she mumbled.

She didn't hear the reply because suddenly she was very

sleepy. Far too sleepy to be interested in mustard walls and chin hats.

The next time she awoke, it was to see Len by her bedside. He was staring at a laptop and hadn't noticed her stir. She took a moment to get a fix on her surroundings and realised that she was in a hospital bed. At least the beeping had stopped, thank heaven for small mercies. The walls were still a horrible colour and the chin hat remained.

She moved her hand up to her face, wincing as a canula moved beneath her skin. What were all these tubes and wires? She must be really ill. She didn't remember getting this ill. She felt the bandage on her chin, her cheeks, her forehead, bloody hell, it went all the way round her head. What sort of illness made them bandage up your head? Oh no, had they sawn off her skull and done something to her brain? She hoped they hadn't shaved off her hair. It had taken her ages to grow it and it was the only thing that kept…

The only thing that kept Colin from noticing that she was wearing Eileen's earbuds.

Penny remembered. She remembered the punch and the kick, Eileen crying and telling her to keep Colin talking, Muriel was on her way and Colin wasn't dead. Colin wasn't dead! He'd bashed in the cleaner's face and pretended the cleaner was him so he wouldn't be caught for killing his partner. And Granny Cairns. Oh God, poor Granny Cairns.

'Colin's not dead,' she croaked.

'Yes, he is,' said Mary from the door. 'Nice to see you awake, Chunky. We were awful worried about you.'

Len reached out and put his hand on hers. He looked old and tired. Never a very tall man, he seemed to have shrunk in height and in girth, his favourite burgundy tanktop loose where once a small paunch had filled it. Even his neck looked a little scrawny, the collar of his shirt too large.

'Awful worried,' he told her. 'How are you feeling?'

'Very sore. What happened?'

'To Colin or to you?' asked Mary.

'Both.'

'Well,' said Mary, settling herself into the faux-leather chair beside Penny's bed, 'you had a dislocated jaw and a punctured lung. They shoved the jaw back in place, but you have to wear that stupid looking bandage for six weeks. Honestly, you should see yourself. You look even more ridiculous than when you were six, put turmeric in the bath and dyed yourself yellow. Three weeks it was before you stopped looking like Homer Simpson's love child.'

'The lung, Mum?'

'Oh, yes. Sorry. Collapsed lung. Quite a bad tear, apparently. They had to put in a chest drain to reinflate it, so you'll be in hospital for at least a few days. Never mind, you're in good company. Jim's just down the corridor.'

'Jim? What's wrong with Jim?'

'Cracked skull. Apparently, Colin bashed him over the head with a poker. You should see his chart. It's a wonder he made it out of that cupboard alive. How that woman had room for a full-grown man in her cupboard, I'll never know. I mean, where did she even keep her ironing board?'

As her mother wittered on about cupboards, Penny closed her eyes and thought back to that moment when the red man had staggered out of the cupboard. The red man had been Jim, with his face covered in blood. She'd been too weak to make sense of it at the time. She vaguely remembered him roaring, but it was drowned out by a hysterical Eileen screaming at her to be brave, help would be there any minute, I love you Rubber Duck! Then nothing. No, not quite nothing. Jim's voice saying…saying what? Saying that he loved her. Oh. He loved her and he'd tried to save her. They'd come so close to losing each other and she'd wasted all this time thinking she wasn't ready for another relationship.

'Why are you crying, Chunky?' Mary had abandoned the subject of cupboards and there was a note of concern in her voice.

'Am I?' whispered Penny, opening her eyes.

'You are, dearie,' said Mary, taking a tissue from her cavernous handbag and gently wiping Penny's cheeks.

'I nearly lost him, Mum. I don't think I could bear to lose him. I have to tell him.'

'You see, I said you wanted to shag him. Jim and Penny up a tree, S-H-A-GG-I-N-G,' said a voice.

'Eileen?' said Penny, starting and holding a hand up to her bandaged ear.

'I forgot to tell you,' said Mary, 'One of the earbuds got lodged in there. They're taking you down to ENT later to pull it out.'

'Can you not just disconnect the call?'

'Rude,' said Eileen.

'She wouldn't let us. Insisted on staying with you until she knows you're okay,' said Mary.

Penny attempted a smile and sucked in her breath as pain radiated through her jaw.

'I'm okay, Winnie the Pooh. Thanks for sending help and staying with me. Are you okay?'

'I'm fine, Rubber Duck. Things got a bit hairy back there, but it's all good now. I'll let you be with your mum and dad. Au gratin.'

'Au revoir.'

'That as well.'

Eileen disconnected the call and Penny looked at her mother.

'How long have I been here?'

'Only a few hours. The police arrived and got an ambulance to you straight away. Fortunately, the worst of the food poisoning has passed, so they were able to find you a bed. It's not much, only a glorified store cupboard, but the police wanted you in a room so they could speak to you privately. That Muriel's a very forceful woman. I like her.'

'What about Colin? You said he's dead?'

'Tripped over a rug and smacked his head off the hearth,

I'm told. Len, get your head out of that computer and come and talk to your daughter.'

'Sorry, Penny-farthing. I'm letting Mum do all the talking, although it is usually safer that way.' Len turned the laptop towards her and pointed to a graph. 'It's all this inflation. I've been tracking my stocks and shares, and they've gone right down. I don't know how we're going to keep your mother in panty girdles.'

'It's not 1953, dad.'

Len looked flummoxed.

'Your mother looks very sexy in a panty girdle,' he protested.

'A panty girdle is like a giant pair of knickers that hold your tummy in,' Penny told him.

'What's that thing you've been wearing to sex night then, Mary?' he asked.

'Basque and stockings, dear.'

'Ah. Your mother looks very sexy in a basque,' said Len, gazing off into the middle distance as his mind wandered in a direction that Penny didn't want to contemplate.

'Up hands who's glad that Eileen's not here for this conversation,' she declared.

Fortunately, further discussion of her parents' extra-curricular activities was prevented by a tap on the door. Muriel's face appeared in the glass porthole and Mary beckoned her in.

'I hope you don't mind,' said Muriel, 'but I wanted to have a chat as soon as you were awake. Get some of the basics down.'

'We don't mind, do we Chunky?' said Mary.

Muriel smiled sweetly at her and said, 'This might be an opportunity for you two to take a break. Grab a coffee?'

'I'm fine here,' said Mary. 'Anyway, I'm mostly drinking Gatorade at the moment. It's American, you know.'

Len sighed and closed his laptop.

'She means we should go away so she can have some time on her own with Penny.'

'Aha! *Soooo* Muriel. I'm telling you, force of nature, that one.'

After her parents had gone, Penny smiled weakly at Muriel and commented, 'Mum likes you.'

'Is it bad that I find that a wee bit scary?' Muriel asked, returning her smile.

'And you work with Sergeant Wilson. Now, there's a scary one,' said Penny.

'She's feeling better. She was on the phone earlier telling my DC she's coming back to work. I think her exact words were "pucker up for a good rimming, son, because my arse will be the one you'll have to kiss to get anything done around here." You can probably guess why she was posted to Vik.'

'Ew,' said Penny. 'That's just…unhygienic. Especially after the food poisoning. Although, you'll be glad to get back to the mainland, I expect. You must be shattered. What time is it?'

'Three in the morning. We'll stay on and finish up here, though. Colin murdered two people that we know of and what with the international angle, it's a major case. Then there's the digital currency fraud. The Australian police are tracking down Brian's wife to see if she can help with the passwords, only she's being suspiciously hard to get hold of.'

'You think she's made off with the money?'

'I think Colin intended to make off with the money and Brian thwarted him. I suspect she's gone to ground with the passwords, although there's nothing to say she's benefitted in any way. I'm leaning towards Colin or a third party threatening her, so she disappeared.

'After he faked his death, the Australian police linked Colin to a particularly nasty organised crime group. We think he needed money to pay them off, which is why he intended to steal the cryptocurrency. Brian wouldn't tell him the passwords, so he killed Brian, intending to go after the softer target – the wife. She was Brian's secret keeper. Neat twist, eh? Except Colin realised he could solve his problems by disappearing altogether. When he disappeared, the OCG came looking for him and either he or someone he knew pointed them in the direction of Brian's wife. It's just a theory for now.'

'Wow, you've done loads while I was out of it,' said Penny.

'As soon as she realised you were in that house with Crypto Col, Eileen hit the record button. We have the whole conversation. Unfortunately, she didn't record any video.'

'About that…erm,' Penny hesitated, her exhausted brain struggling to come up with a plausible excuse for she and Jim being in the house in the first place.

'It's okay,' said Muriel. 'Eileen has explained everything. You and Jim were taking a walk to test the night vision on Kenny's new camera when you spotted Hélène's cat stuck on her extension roof. You went up to rescue it and, aware that Hélène was at the police station, you checked to see if the back door was unlocked, so you could return the animal safely home. Like a good citizen, you even went in to feed it. We found the Dreamies in your pocket. The two of you were then attacked by Colin.'

'Well, that's not exactly what–'

'As I said, you were rescuing Hélène's cat and there is no video recording that says otherwise,' said Muriel firmly.

'Thanks. What about Hélène?' asked Penny, curious to know how the Frenchwoman explained the presence of Colin in her house.

'Oui, oui. We haven't interviewed her yet about Colin. That's a treat for later. She's admitted that he stole things from the museum and that she gave him the contacts to sell them, so she's been arrested and charged for that. By the way, the brooch that you said came from Laird Hamish. Colin bought it from him and gave it to Hélène as a gift. Seems the two of them were in love.'

Muriel grinned and winked. 'She's obviously devastated that Colin was murdered in the museum. I imagine she'll be delighted to discover that he was alive and well and sharing her bed all this time.'

'So, she and Laird Hamish?'

'Fizzled out long before he met Cara. Nothing doing between Colin and Cara either. Laird Hamish is in the clear.'

'Which leaves us with the cleaner. Who killed the cleaner?'

'Not a fucking scoobie,' said Muriel. 'Fifty quid says it's Elsie in the library. Seriously, it's a sad story. The victim's prints were in the immigration system, and we checked his visa records.

'His name is Aleks Antoniv and he came to Scotland a few months ago as a refugee from Ukraine. He had a heart condition, which meant he couldn't fight, so a charity found him a host family in Aberchirder. That's as much as we know. Somehow, he turned up on Vik then was murdered.

'We don't know why he was murdered, but we have a couple of theories; either he was targeted, or the real target was Colin and somebody mistook Aleks for Colin. Given what we know about Colin, we think the last one is more likely. Colin probably came to the same conclusion. Which means he wasn't just worried about the police finding him. He was shitting himself because the organised crime group had found him. I guess Colin thought it was manna from heaven that they'd accidentally killed someone the same height and build as him, the wee sod.'

'That really is sad,' said Penny. 'To go through hell, end up somewhere safe, then get murdered because you look like someone else.'

Muriel grimaced. 'Unless forensics comes up with something, we might never know. We'll pass it on to the National Crime Agency to do some work with the Australians, but justice will likely be a long time coming for Aleks. I feel like we're letting him down.'

'You've done your best,' Penny assured the detective. 'Do you need me to give a statement?'

'We'll get one later. I just heard you were awake and thought you'd appreciate the update, considering everything you've been through.'

'Have you updated Jim?'

'Did Mary not tell you? The doctors are keeping him in an induced coma so they can treat the brain injury. They don't have the facilities to deal with serious trauma here, so they're just waiting for an air ambulance to take him to Aberdeen.'

'She probably didn't want to worry me.'

Penny could feel more tears making their way up what felt like a direct pipeline from her heart to her eyes. She might never get the chance to tell Jim she loved him too.

Seeing her distress, Muriel squeezed her hand and said, 'You must be very tired. I'll leave you to get some rest. You know where I am if you need me.'

'Thanks,' said Penny hoarsely.

After Muriel left, she lay fretting about Jim. The tears flowed freely now, along her cheeks and into her hair, as she tried to think of ways to be with him. Maybe they'd let her go in the air ambulance? She could smuggle herself out of the hospital in a laundry basket…actually, no, yucky hospital sheets…it would have to be a laundry basket where they were bringing clean laundry back in, sort of the opposite of what she intended.

She'd never felt this overwhelming ache in her heart before. Yet the thought of him alone in a hospital far away. She didn't have the words.

Her parents popped in to say they were going home now and that the twins would visit later in the morning. She vaguely waved them off and returned to her all-consuming thoughts of Jim.

She shouldn't have let herself be distracted, that day when she was going to tell him. Scary as it may feel, she knew in her very bones that he was her forever person. She couldn't lose her forever person. She quite simply wouldn't.

Unable to keep her eyes open any longer, Penny closed them and imagined a life with Jim. Their house, the twins, walking Timmy, going to the church sale together and telling him off for eating too many peppermint slices, having his dad and Eileen's mum over for Sunday lunch, the sun always shining on each happy scene. Somewhere along the way, she drifted off into a long, healing sleep.

Since the moment she was released from hospital, Penny had been pestering her family to take her to see Jim. Mary and Len had refused, saying she wasn't strong enough to make the journey. Hector grunted that he had rehearsals for the school play. It was absolutely vital that, as director, he role model the desired behaviours. Pompous twat. Edith simply couldn't be bothered, although if Penny was going anyway, she wouldn't mind a pair of trainers, and some leggings, ooh and maybe a–. Penny had stopped her there.

The other Losers Club members were all busy. Mrs Hubbard had stopped by to visit her in hospital a few times. She told Penny that she'd been doing a deep clean of the shop to "improve customer continence, dearie, and rebuild trust in the community", before admitting that her Douglas had made her do an online small business management course and she hadn't quite nailed the lingo yet.

Elsie was raising money to restore some of the old books and documents that she and Mrs Hubbard had found in the library. The restoration fund was coming along nicely, mainly due to her adding a few pounds to the price of a bag of weed. She blamed inflation and fuel prices, telling her customers that it wasn't cheap to run a library van, never mind that the local council funded it.

Fiona and Gordon had made up and appeared at Penny's bedside a few times with fruit from their smallholding.

Gordon fervently promised that he grew them himself and Fiona gave her personal guarantee that she'd washed them three times. They'd abandoned Project Pubes and, as Fiona kept referring to Gordon as her hairy tiger, Penny assumed that all was fluffy in the gentleman's department. She really didn't want to give it much more thought than that. She was pleased, however, to hear that they'd had a weekly order from The Greengrocer in Inverurie. Fiona's future visits to the pub were assured.

This left Eileen, her partner in crime since they were little, a true friend easily blackmailed by the four decades of dirt Penny had on her. Which is how she now found herself being pushed through Aberdeen Royal Infirmary's myriad of corridors, in a borrowed wheelchair, by a grown woman making vroom vroom noises.

At last, Eileen hung a sharp left and they arrived at Jim's room. The story of Crypto Col had been all over the news, with Jim dubbed "The Hero of Hélène's Drawers" and, having caught a photographer sneaking a snap of him on the ward, the hospital had moved Jim to a private room. Which was rather lovely, Penny decided. Much better than her broom cupboard on Vik.

He lay on the bed, the covers tight across his still, pale form. His head was wrapped in a bandage, and he was surrounded by a multitude of tubes and monitors.

Penny gazed at him, assailed by feelings of love and worry and, yes, that ever-present terror that she might yet lose him. Her eyes misted over at the sight of him there, alone and vulnerable.

Eileen went to the bottom of the bed and picked up the clipboard there. She flicked through the pages and frowned.

'They said there had been some complications. What does it say he has?' asked Penny.

Eileen regarded her solemnly. 'Garlic chicken and pineapple jelly with ice cream.'

'That's tomorrow's lunch order,' said a voice from the bed.

'Jim!' Penny exclaimed, rising from her wheelchair.

Eileen pressed her back down.

'We're only here because you promised to stay in the chair, remember? Jim!'

'Bugger me with a soufflé, you look like something out of The Mummy. But, by God, it's refreshing to see you,' he said.

'Why?' asked Penny.

'Well, I'm in enough pain as it is and I'm not sure my bum could take anything pointy right now.'

'No, why is it refreshing to see us?'

'Ah, right, aye. My dad's been in, and the police came round, but I haven't had any other visitors. Muriel brought me up to speed, by the way. I have no memory of anything that happened after I got hit on the head.'

Penny nodded. 'It's good to see you too. I've missed you. Listen, I wanted to talk to you about something.'

'Aye. I've a few things I wanted to talk to you about as well.'

'I'm so glad you're not dead,' Eileen burst out, throwing herself on the bed and hugging his legs.

'I'm so glad you're both not dead,' she mumbled into the blanket. You both nearly died, but you nearly died the most, Jim.'

Jim shifted uncomfortably and looked at Penny with a pained expression. He was thinking about something important; she could tell. She leaned forward expectantly, holding her breath. This must be the moment. The moment when he officially said he loved her, and she could say me too. The moment when neither of them had lost the other and they could be each other's forever people. A moment they would have for the rest of their lives.

'Eh, could you shift over a bit, Eileen? You're lying on my catheter.'

CHAPTER 18

Penny and Eileen took the Buckaroo Boat back to Vik. As ever, it was crowded with shoppers, metal detectorists and tourists, although slightly fewer looky-loos now that the film set had wound down. Tonight, Mary was throwing a party to say goodbye to Johnny and Alex. She'd invited the cast and crew, all the Warrior Islanders and Penny's Losers Club friends. Even Sandra Next Door. But only because Penny had told her that she couldn't invite Geoff without asking Sandra too. And, no, she wasn't allowed to write "Geoff Next Door + 1" on the invitation.

Eileen vroomed Penny down the gangway to Kenny's waiting car and he whisked them off to Valhalla, gamely pretending to be their chauffeur.

When they arrived, he hopped out and held Penny's door open.

'We're here, madam,' he said, helping Penny out of the car.

He then ran round to the other side of the car and opened Eileen's door, doffing an imaginary cap and extending a hand to her.

'À votre service, madame?'

'Décolletage, monsieur. Ooh, you're sexy when you speak French.'

Penny rolled her eyes and walked stiffly into her parents' bungalow, where the party was already in full swing. Her mother glided over on a cloud of champagne bubbles and whisked her towards the buffet table.

'No booze for you according to the instructions on the antibiotics, but I know how much you like your food. Get stuck in, Chunky.'

'Do you think you could lay off on the weight jokes, Mum? It's been a long day.'

'Sorry, my wee darlin'. How's Jim?'

'Much better. Definitely on the mend. They're talking about moving him back to Vik hospital next week provided he doesn't get another infection.'

'Good. Your dad's missing someone to do the crossword with. He's been under my feet ever since he got over the food poisoning. Although, if I want to get rid of him, all I need to do is take a tub of ice cream out of the freezer. I think it'll be a while before he can face ice cream again. Anyway, where is he?'

'I'll go and look for him,' Penny offered.

She knew exactly where her dad was. Where he always hid from Mary.

She tapped on the shed door.

'Dad, are you in there?'

'Is that you, Penny-farthing?'

'Unless you have another person who calls you Dad.'

'Oh, I have secret children stashed all over the island. Come in.'

Len was sitting in an old armchair, smoking the pipe that Mary had banned twenty years ago. Penny wondered how her mother had never caught him. She supposed the revolting smell of the cannabis plants behind him masked the smell of pipe smoke. Dad had his farming jumper and his house jumper, but he still stank sometimes.

'Mum's on the warpath. Are you coming into the party?'

'In a minute. I was thinking about the future. Your mum and I are getting on a bit, and I was wondering if I should cash in my stocks and shares. Buy you and the twins a house. Something for the next generation.'

'Wow, Dad. That's very generous of you, but I can afford my own house. I suppose you're right. It's time we moved out.'

'Oh, I'm not trying to get rid of you, angel. I love having you and the twins here. It's more about giving the three of you something while we're still here to enjoy it. I've a broad portfolio, but it's no use to me and Mum once we're gone.'

Len reached over to a small table and opened his laptop. He turned the screen towards her to show her what he'd been looking at.

'It says here that I can make an online appointment to discuss it with an adviser. You could have the money within a couple of weeks. I'm never sure about these online thingies, though. Why can't they meet you in person like they used to? Explain things properly.'

Len grumbled on, but Penny wasn't listening. She was staring intently at the screen. Something had just clicked into place in her mind, and it was a very big something indeed.

'Can I borrow your laptop for a minute?'

'Alright. Be careful because they're very expensive,' warned Len, handing the laptop over.

Penny moved her finger over the pad, quickly typed in some search terms and scrolled through a number of pages before handing the laptop back.

'What do you think of my plan?' asked Len.

'I think you should discuss it with Mum first, Dad. I don't want to seem rude or anything, but I've just realised that there's something I have to do. A very urgent something.'

· · ·

The Losers Club members sat, shoeless, in Sandra Next Door's living room, or "front parlour" as she preferred to call it. There was a loud squeak as Mrs Hubbard's bottom shifted on the clear, plastic sofa covers. She had taken her cocktail with her to this extraordinary meeting and was leaning over to place it on the coffee table. A second squeak heralded the lightning quick response of Sandra, who managed to slip a coaster under the glass before it hit the table. Later, Elsie would swear she never even saw the woman move.

'Sorry to drag you away from the party,' said Penny. 'I need to run something past you. I'm well aware that I'm not at my best right now, and I'm relying on you to tell me if you think I've lost the plot. By the way, welcome to our guest member tonight, Sergeant Wilson. Also, nice to still have you on board, Johnny. You don't have to be here if you don't want to. I know you're leaving on the early ferry tomorrow.'

'It's okay,' Johnny told her. 'I'll stick with Elsie. We're going to her place after this. She's giving me a bag of wool for the plane.'

'Can we please stop all this pussyfooting around?' groaned Sergeant Wilson. 'I've finally got my appetite back and there a big plate of sandwiches in there with my name on it.'

'Polygraph sandwiches?' asked Johnny.

'Martisha sandwiches, you cheeky bastard,' said Sergeant Wilson.

'I'm getting to the point, Sergeant Wilson. Or can we call you Martisha since you're off-duty?' asked Penny.

Sergeant Wilson glared at her. 'I am never off-duty. Ever fucking vigilant, that's me.'

'Okay, Sergeant Wilson and everyone else,' said Penny. 'My dad was showing me the website for his stocks and shares tonight, and I had an idea. Muriel thought that the most likely reason for the murder was that someone mistook the cleaner for Colin. Now, she was thinking of an organised crime group, but I'm thinking it was a bit closer to home.

'The broker my dad uses for his investments is Burdocks in Edinburgh. I checked their website, and they do trade in cryptocurrencies. None of us knew about Crypto Col because it wasn't on our news much. However, I wondered if someone who trades in cryptocurrencies might recognise Crypto Col. Someone who may have invested in ColCoin and lost a lot of money. Someone who might want revenge if they happened to bump into Crypto Col.'

Penny sat back in her armchair and smiled, pleased to have set out her theory so succinctly.

'And?' asked Fiona.

'Ooh. Sorry. And there's someone on the island who used to work for Burdocks. That person is...'

Penny paused, savouring the suspense. Now she knew how Mrs Hubbard felt when she did a big reveal.

'Conclusion and next steps please!' commanded Mrs Hubbard. 'Goodness, now I know how you all felt when I did it to you.'

'That person is, drum roll please, Chris Spencer!' Penny announced, with what she hoped was aplomb. 'You probably don't know him. He's Laird Hamish's new factor and I remember Hamish telling Jim and I that it was his factor's idea to sell the Laird's Ladle. Colin was selling stuff off discreetly for Hamish. What if Chris went with Hamish when he took the ladle to Colin at the museum?'

'It would certainly be ironic. Colin stuffed the cleaner's throat with the very thing that led you to Chris,' said Gordon.

'That's a very good theory. I'm impressed,' said Sergeant Wilson, before ruining it by adding, 'You're not such a useless trollop after all.'

'Aye, you're a clever girl,' came Jim's voice from the phone in the middle of the coffee table. 'I always knew there was a reason why I love you. Aw, bugger me, I meant like. I like you.'

'No takesy backsies. That's the Space rule, remember?' said Penny, her heart doing happy little backflips.

'I think we need to talk,' said Jim. 'Somewhere a bit more private.'

'Awwwww,' said everyone else.

'Yes, I think it's about time,' said Penny.

'No, it's not. It's about shagging,' whispered Eileen.

Johnny winked at Penny.

'Badabing.'

Vik Herald

30th April

MUSEUM MURDER ARREST

A man was detained yesterday for the murder of Aleks Antoniv, the Ukrainian refugee cleaner at Vik Museum.

Chris Spencer, an employee of Laird Hamish Deer, is expected to appear in court today, charged with the brutal murder of Aleks, who was found with the famous Laird's Ladle in his throat.

Police Scotland has released a statement saying that the murder is linked to the death of Crypto Col, the Australian cryptocurrency king whose fake death led to investors across the world losing their savings. The Chief Constable made special mention of Sergeant Martisha Wilson, who she said conducted an exemplary investigation, yet another example of the initiative and quick-thinking of one of her finest officers.

    The Vik Gazette spoke to islanders to get their views on the recent events on Vik.

. . .

Mrs MH, who didn't want to be identified, disagreed with the Police Scotland statement, saying that she had demanded a full investigation into a spurious complaint about her cat defecating in her neighbour's begonias, yet no action had been taken.

The Vik Gazette will bring you more on this story tomorrow. The murder, that is. Not the defecating cat.

EPILOGUE

Mrs Hubbard listened intently at her living room door. Only the creaks of an old house and the distant snores of her Douglas. Good.

Awkwardly, she got down on her hands and knees and pulled back the rug in front of the fireplace. She ran her hands over the floorboards until she felt one wobble. Taking a knife from the table beside her, she slipped the blade through the gap in the floorboards and pushed upwards. With a muffled crack, the wobbly floorboard came free, and Mrs Hubbard gently laid it to one side, taking care not to make any noise which would wake her Douglas up. This was possibly the most important mission of her life and only one other person was aware of it. Much as she loved him, that person was not Douglas.

She shone a torch inside the hole in the floor and couldn't help once more feeling awe when she saw what was down there. It got her every time. The final casket containing the Vik treasure.

Long before Granny Cairns had died, she and Mrs Hubbard had struck up a friendship. In fact, she was, she suspected, the reclusive woman's only friend. Every day, Granny Cairns would walk to Mrs Hubbard's Cupboard for her shopping. Over time, the conversation evolved from polite chit-chat about the weather to a sharing of gossip and personal stories. Knowing that she didn't have many years left, Granny Cairns turned the conversation to the Vik treasure, eventually confessing to being the secret keeper. She was worried that if something happened to her, the treasure would be lost.

'For coming on three hundred years, the secret keepers have been selling the treasure bit by bit,' said Granny Cairns. 'The money was used to help the people in the community. My time is nearly over, which is why I want you to be the secret keeper and keep up the tradition. All my people are long gone, so there's no second secret keeper just now. I suggest you find one. Someone you can trust with your life.'

When Granny Cairns died, Mrs Hubbard and the second secret keeper moved the treasure from its hillside cave to the more convenient confines of her living room floor. She was hardly a spring chicken and it had taken multiple trips, but slowly they had brought what remained of the treasure down to the village. If only she hadn't left that button behind, nobody could have even been sure the treasure still existed.

With Colin and Hélène gone, Mrs Hubbard had worried that she would no longer be able to sell off the odd item. In fact, she was surprised they never noticed, given how intent they were on finding the treasure for themselves. Ah well, greed made you blind. Things came alright in the end, when she found a new dealer. That list Penny discovered had turned out to be very handy.

'Right, Elsie dearie,' whispered Mrs Hubbard to herself.

She pulled a glittering jewelled necklace from the casket, taking a moment to wonder at the beauty of it.

'Let's give your book restoration fund a wee boost.'

AFTERWORD

I hope you enjoyed this book. If so, I would be grateful if you could take a moment to pop a review or a few stars on Amazon.

You can hear more about my books and get access to exclusive material by subscribing to my newsletter via my website, https://theweehairyboys.co.uk . You also can drop me a line using the contact information on the website or treat yourself to a signed copy of one of my books.

Did you know that there's a [Losers Club](#) on Facebook for fans of the Losers Club series? Yes, you really can join Losers Club, although our fellow Losers are far more interested in cake and chocolate biscuits than diet sheets. I think it is best described as a warm, friendly and creatively bonkers place. Please do join us.

Other than this you can find me at:

Facebook [Growing Old Disgracefully](#) (blog)

[Yvonne Vincent - Author](#)

Instagram @yvonnevincentauthor

Threads @yvonnevincentauthor

X (Twitter) @yvonnevauthor

Tik Tok @yvonnevincentauthor

Amazon Yvonne Vincent Author Page

Until the next adventure.

Yvonne

ALSO BY YVONNE VINCENT

Losers Club

The Laird's Ladle

The Angels' Share

Sleighed

The Juniper Key

Beacon Brodie

The Losers Club Collection: Books 1 - 3

The Losers Club Collection: Books 4 - 6

The Big Blue Jobbie

The Big Blue Jobbie #2

Frock In Hell

You can find all of these via my website at https://theweehairyboys.co.uk or on Amazon.

Printed in Great Britain
by Amazon